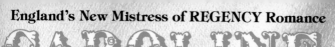

CAROLINE COURTNEY

LOVE OF MY LIFE

Because she loved him
she must help him win
his heart's desire—
another woman.

PQG950476

15

As soon as the Prince Regent was seated,
the whole stage was illuminated as a shell
carrying Venus-Aphrodite, drawn by two
white ponies, came into view.

Lady Olivia's appearance brought a storm of
applause, for indeed she looked superb. She leaned back
languourously against silken cushions and commanded
her hand-maidens to usher in her suitors. These were
noblemen, representing minor gods of Olympus. The
goddess feigned boredom until a beautiful youth in
green tights, short boots and a leopardskin over one
shoulder came to serenade her on a golden lyre.

It was Lord Desmond as Adonis, the half-mortal
with whom the goddess fell briefly in love. In a clear
tenor voice, he sang of his undying love, phrasing the
words with growing passion until Jessica clenched her
hands on her lap, and tears came to her eyes. Oh, he
must not, *could not,* be denied!

The goddess stepped down from her couch and
gave him her hand. Then, just as he had cast away
his lyre and was about to embrace her, Jupiter, the hero,
heralded by a clap of thunder, sprang onto the stage.
With a flick of disdain, he struck Adonis, forcing him
to one knee, while he himself took an adoring goddess
by both hands, and they sang a duet of love. Jessica
felt the tears spilling over at the naked adoration and
pleading on Lord Desmond's face as he knelt rejected.

"I know we are both suffering, my dear,"
Lady Shayne whispered, taking Jessica's
small hand in hers, "but we must not
show it for Desmond's sake."

Novels By Caroline Courtney

Duchess in Disguise
A Wager For Love
Love Unmasked
Guardian of The Heart
Dangerous Engagement
Love's Masquerade
Love Triumphant
Heart of Honor
Libertine in Love
The Romantic Rivals
Forbidden Love
Abandoned For Love
The Tempestuous Affair
Love of My Life

Published By
WARNER BOOKS

CAROLINE COURTNEY

Love of My Life

WARNER BOOKS

A Warner Communications Company

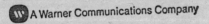

Love of My Life

One

itting beside Aunt Lucy in the stage coach travelling
rom London to Brighton, Jessica Court leaned forward
eagerly, gazing out of the window. Her heart sang. Soon
he coachman would stop and set them down in the village
of Shore Vale, where Jessica had been born and had spent
all her seventeen years before her widowed father had
married again. Then his new wife had insisted on moving
the entire household to London. Jessica found it wretched.
She hated the fuss and bustle of the city and much preferred to walk in the Park rather than spend hours with
milliners and dressmakers.

But now, for a whole month, she was to stay with
her father's sister, Miss Lucy Court, and she intended to
find a job as a governess or unpaid companion—anything
so that she might remain in the countryside that she loved.

Now, as Jessica watched with delight for familiar
landmarks to come into view, her aunt studied her. How
like her dear late mother she was! An enchanting girl,
small and slender with enormous velvet-dark eyes framed
by tendrils of dark, curly hair. But, whereas her mother

had been gentle and delicate, Jessica had an independent spirit that feared nothing, and, as she looked out on the woods and green fields, Jessica vowed that never, never would she return to London.

Suddenly, disaster struck. The coach reined in sharply as the horses reared and whinnied with fright. The coachman swore, and a small man sitting beside Aunt Lucy clutched the pouch of gold sovereigns at his belt as he said in a high-spirited voice:

"Highwaymen! Oh, may the Good Lord save us."

A moment later the door of the coach beside Jessica was wrenched open, and a masked man with narrow, greedy eyes thrust a musket at the passengers. Mounted on a raw-boned horse, he wore shabby and stained clothing, and a dirty bandanna was knotted round his throat.

"Out—all o' you. Then stand and deliver!" he cried.

They scrambled out, one woman declaring she would swoon while another went into hysterics. Jessica took Aunt Lucy's arm firmly and said in a low, steady voice:

"Pray do not be afraid—we have nothing worth stealing."

Three other vagabonds were flinging the valises and packages off the back and roof of the coach while the hysterical women shrieked, losing all control.

Through the screaming and cursing a thundering of hooves was heard, causing even the highwaymen to pause. Down the hillside a magnificent horseman appeared, galloping on a black stallion, his drawn sword flashing in the sunlight.

The four highwaymen cowered as, without slackening speed, the rider went straight at them, laying about him with the flat of his sword, his blade catching one on the side of the head, another on the shoulder as his voice rang out loud and clear:

"Be off, you cowardly scoundrels! Frightening helpless citizens. If I have to come at you again you shall feel cold steel between your ribs, so ride for your lives!"

The two men, already staggering from his blows, reeled awkwardly around and scrambled onto their horses. The other two were going like the wind. The gallant rescuer rode after them, brandishing his sword and laughing. Soon all the riders were lost to view and gradually calm was restored among the travellers. Only the woman in hysterics could not stop screaming and crying.

The coachman, still swearing, reloaded the baggage and, having settled Aunt Lucy back in her seat, Jessica returned to the poor, hysterical creature, now prone on the ground. Gently but firmly Jessica slapped her cheeks. Then, opening her reticule, she brought out a bottle of smelling salts which soon brought ease. She had just supported the sufferer to her feet when their rescuer galloped back, still laughing:

"You are safe now, ladies and gentlemen, and Brighton lies but six miles further." Then, seeing Jessica so self-possessed and helpful, he doffed his tall beaver hat, revealing shining, chestnut-brown hair above a lean, powerful face with gray eyes still filled with amusement.

"Ha! A brave sprite, I see. Well, your courage shall be rewarded for you will be troubled no more. You have my word on it."

Wheeling the stallion away, he vanished up the hillside as swiftly as he had come.

"Who was he—do you know?" Jessica demanded of her aunt as she took her own seat and the coach began rumbling on. "I declare, I never saw such a handsome man in my life!" Indeed, her dark eyes were glowing as she remembered his tall, elegant figure.

"I swear it was Lord Desmond Shayne," replied her aunt, smiling. "He is a great beau at the Court of the Prince Regent. Shayne Park lies some five miles West of our village so we rarely see him. But his mother, Lady Shayne, is most diligent and kind about all the villages. Whenever there is sickness—real sickness, you understand—she visits with broth and potions and, if needs be, insists that Dr. Pettigrew visits with her. He much prefers wealthy patients, but her ladyship will have none of it."

"Has—has Lord Desmond a wife?" Jessica knew she was blushing but she didn't care. She knew she would dream of the noble earl for many nights to come, yet such folly must be held in check if he was a married man. It would be highly improper, even in the privacy of her own room.

Aunt Lucy shook her head. "No, more's the pity. They say he is bedazzled by that baggage, Lady Olivia Lufton, who has every young blade for miles around under her thumb. Oh, see Jessica! Our church spire— we are arriving."

The other passengers had been too busy discussing their unpleasant adventure to hear a word that passed between aunt and niece but, as the coach slowed to a halt in a pleasant village street, they broke off to shake hands cordially and two of the women thanked Jessica warmly for her assistance. The coachman helped them to alight and brought down Jessica's valise.

"Ye're a mettlesome lass." He grinned and touched his hat respectfully. "Hope you enjoy your stay in these parts."

"Oh, I shall—thank you." Jessica was deeply touched by all the praise and gratitude, yet she hadn't felt in the least brave at the time. She had simply done what seemed helpful.

As they walked the ten yards to Aunt Lucy's pretty, gabled house, she longed to ask more about Lord Desmond and Lady Olivia, but her aunt was preoccupied with planning the thrilling tale she would tell her cronies over a dish of tea tomorrow. Why, she would be quite the heroine!

Lord Desmond Shayne rode home, still amused by the afternoon's events. If only coach travellers were not so old and showed defiance instead of fear, they would soon find what craven cowards most robbers are. That child now, in her prim gray duster coat and bonnet, *she* could have fought off the villain single-handedly if the others hadn't flown into such a panic. Remarkable eyes she had, too—she might grow up to be quite a beauty. Like most people, he had been deceived by Jessica's small stature and had thought her just a child, but he then promptly forgot all about her.

Tonight he was dining with the Duchess of Almesbury and the delicious, infuriating Olivia would be there; win her he would before this season was out, and he licked his great horse into a gallop.

Lady Shayne was cutting roses—a pleasure she reserved entirely for herself although gardeners brought in great baskets of other exquisite flowers every day for the house. She was a tall, graceful woman in her fifties with a beautiful, tranquil face shaded now by a wide-brimmed straw hat tied loosely under her chin with lavender ribbon. She glanced up as her son strode across the terrace of Shayne Park on his way in from the stables, and a small sigh escaped her. That wretched Lufton girl! How could such a fine young man as Desmond be so blind? Or, for that matter, how could all the other men of high birth whom the blond witch played off against each other like pawns in a game of chess be so misled?

Lady Shayne, however, had a gentle, philosophical nature, and she cut such anger short. Of what use was it when she could do nothing in the matter? Widowed for many years, she loved her only son deeply, but, now that he was twenty-five, God, Fate, and Desmond himself must decide his future. She went indoors to arrange the bowls of roses.

Five miles away Jessica, washed and changed into a fresh print gown, was dreaming idly by the open lattice window in her bedroom. It would be half an hour before she was summoned to dinner, and Aunt Lucy was resting after their ordeal. Yet, instead of impatience to roam her beloved meadows, her mind was filled by Lord Desmond. How brave he was, how gallant and, above all, how handsome. Was there any way in which she could contrive to meet him again?

But Lord Desmond had no further thoughts of the courageous little sprite of the afternoon; he was donning a new silver-gray skirted coat of satin and a matching waistcoat embroidered with silver thread and small pearls, his thoughts entirely on the much-desired Lady Olivia. Would her mood be kind or cruel?

A month at Shore Vale with her aunt had seemed like a blessed eternity to Jessica when she had first arrived; filled once again with her rambles and cherishing every hour, her days soon slipped by.

Aunt Lucy was troubled. She found Jessica a charming guest, but felt unable to give her a permanent home. She had ample means but considered herself too old to offer the girl the young companionship that was her due. Now, just eighteen, Jessica was a beauty and should be launched into society at Brighton where she would soon gain a worthy husband. But, although all Aunt Lucy's friends gladly joined in the search, no likely post of governess or companion in a good family offered itself.

A few days before she must return to London, Jessica felt desperate. Surely somebody, somewhere, would offer her a home since she needed no salary; indeed, Papa was most generous.

She seldom indulged in tears for they solved nothing and only caused wretchedly sore eyes and a throbbing head. But, as she took her favorite walk they would not be stemmed. She sat on a lonely stile and wept most bitterly—*she would not go back to London.*

Through her misery she became aware of a rider approaching. Hastily, still blinded by tears, she stood up, attempted to jump the stile and hide behind the hedge but she missed her footing and fell heavily. Her right ankle twisted under her.

And so Lord Desmond found her. He, too, was in a black mood that morning; after favoring him for more than two weeks, Olivia Lufton had dismissed him with her light laugh and turned her attentions to Sir Walter Cheston, a dark, ruthless man whom Desmond disliked intensely. To find a maiden in distress was at least a distraction. He dismounted and climbed the stile.

Jessica recognized him and tried to hide her face, sure that her tears must have disfigured it. But she was one of those fortunate girls whose beauty crying actually enhanced. As Desmond turned her head to face him he saw huge, dew-wet eyes and a pretty, trembling mouth. At first he did not recognize her—indeed, in a crisp blue muslin gown that delicately outlined her small breast and

12

with a straw bonnet swinging from her wrist so that her shining, dark curls were revealed, she bore little resemblance to the modest traveler on the coach. Then she spoke.

"I am all right, my lord, pray do not trouble yourself over me."

He let out a shout of laughter. "By my troth—it is the sprite!" He looked her over in amazement but quite without offense. "And I thought you a mere child! Come, let me see your ankle for I fear you have injured it. I saw your leap and it was most unwise."

"I—I seldom cry so I wanted to hide," she confessed. But he was already feeling the ankle with gentle hands.

"No broken bones," he said, for he was well used to mishaps on the hunting field. "A nasty sprain, I think, and you cannot walk on it."

Her small chin went up. "I shall manage, Lord Desmond; my aunt lives scarce three miles from here."

"But my mother is only two miles distant, and she is famous for her doctoring. No," he said firmly as she was about to protest again, "I insist. I shall lift you over the stile and onto my saddle and you will have expert care within ten minutes."

Without waiting for further protest, he lifted her onto the stallion and then mounted behind her. Jessica felt grateful but more miserable than ever. She had longed to meet Lord Desmond again, but not like this, not as a tear-stained cripple.

Yet he was charming and kept the great horse to a quiet pace, careful of her painful ankle.

"Why were you so ashamed of your tears?" he asked. "I declare most women indulge in them as a device sure to cause attention."

"I despise that." Jessica was vehement, but she smiled in spite of herself for he was so very kind. "But then I know little of the ways of ladies of fashion."

"How old are you, sprite? Forgive me if I may be too bold."

Jessica laughed. "Indeed you do not, my lord. I am eighteen, and it is no secret."

13

"I confess, you puzzle me," he admitted. "You appear to be a child, traveling by the stage yet able to calm old women; now I find you weeping in a meadow, a full-grown young lady and well-born, I swear, from your speech and manner. Where *have* you sprung from if not from Elfland?" he chuckled.

"Nothing so romantic, I fear—I come from .... oh!" she paused as they came in sight of Shayne Park, lying mellow and beautiful in the sunlight, surrounded by lovely flower gardens. Wisteria, the clusters of blooms hanging like pale lilac grapes, covered one wall, while, in front, sweet-scented early roses climbed up to the first story and over the wide front porch.

"Oh," repeated Jessica softly. "I have never seen a house so beautiful—it is too perfect to be true!"

Lord Desmond was pleased. "I assure you it is quite true—I have lived here all my life. It was built by my great-grandfather when he tired of London, and I trust my heirs will inherit it." At this, Jessica sensed a shadow of melancholy over his mood and said no more until he reined in at the open front door.

There, he lifted her down and carried her up the steps into a wide, cool panelled hall, fragrant with bowls of flowers. Lady Shayne heard them arrive and came out of the morning room where she had been writting letters.

"I have brought you a patient, Mother," Lord Desmond said. "But I warn you—she is more than half-sprite." His eyes were laughing. "She must have lost her wings, for I found her fallen from a stile and her ankle injured."

With a soft rustle of silk, Lady Shayne came forward and with long, expert fingers, felt Jessica's ankle for a moment.

"Fortunately it is not broken," she said with a reassuring smile. "A nasty sprain, I think. Carry her into my room, Desmond, and set her comfortably on the sofa. I must fetch my things."

The morning room was charming and not at all formal, in spite of some pieces of antique furniture. The deep armchairs and the sofa were covered in pale gold brocade, and there were roses everywhere; an open work-box with an unfinished piece of petit point embroidery and skeins of bright silk stood near the fireplace, and quill pens and notepaper lay on the escritoire.

"You have been so very kind, my lord," Jessica smiled up at Desmond when he had laid her on the sofa. "And it is all so beautiful I still think I must be dreaming!"

"I promise that you are not."

When Lady Shayne returned she told Desmond, "You must introduce me to your young friend—you have not mentioned her name."

Looking astonished he said, "Egad! I declare I have never inquired." He looked quizzically at Jessica. "Do sprites have a mortal name?"

"Of course we do," Her eyes were merry. "Mine is Jessica Court."

"You must leave us now, Desmond," interrupted his mother. "I fear I must hurt Miss Court a little at first." She had set down a small basin of cold water and was busy drawing out pieces of linen and bandages from a box beside it. Her son went to the door. "Then if I can be of no further assistance I shall continue my ride up to the Spinney. I want to see how the young pheasants are progressing." He was gone before Jessica could thank him again.

"Now, my dear, we must remove your shoe and stocking." The shoe was simple, but when her ladyship rolled down the fine silk stocking, Jessica winced as it was drawn over her ankle.

"There," said Lady Shayne soothingly, "now I shall apply a cold compress and you will be surprised how swiftly the pain eases. It will help the swelling, too."

It was true. After the first shock of the ice-cold cloths, Jessica began to feel little pain. Yet, to her inner fury, she was afraid that she might cry again. It was as if her earlier tears had finally broken through her iron self-control to the deep unhappiness so firmly held in check. She fought them back valiantly, but to be surrounded by so much care and beauty brought home more poignantly than ever the fact that, within days, she must return to the gray life in London.

The tears welled up silently, and she prayed that Lady Shayne would not notice. A quick glance told her ladyship the truth, but, thinking that Jessica wept only from shock and pain, she went on steadily with her bandaging. But the tears did not stop, indeed, they increased. Her ladyship possessed the great gift of patient understanding and realized that the poor child was obviously suffering some deep sorrow. She sensed that the girl had staunch courage and that the events of the morning were not what made her weep. At last she placed a kind, supporting arm around the slender, trembling shoulders. As soon as she could trust her voice Jessica spoke.

"Forgive my weakness, my lady. I am not in the habit of tears, I vow, yet this morning I could hold them in check no longer." She looked up at Lady Shayne's concerned face and added honestly, "It was only because they blinded me that I stumbled so foolishly over the stile; I have always lived in these parts and could vault a five-barred gate before I was forced to wear long skirts."

Her sympathetic listener smiled. What glorious eyes the girl had. With skilled dressmaking and coiffeur she could be a beauty. "Do you wish to speak of what troubles you, my dear. It can be a help sometimes."

Jessica paused, yet the longing to unburden herself was compelling.

"It sounds stupid, I fear," she began tentatively, "but—our lives were so happy at the Old Manor before dear Mamma died when I was fifteen. After that, poor Papa began to ail. A broken heart my Aunt Lucy declared, but she sent for Dr. Pettigrew. He listened carefully to Papa's heart and tut-tutted several times, then he looked at me: 'H'm, you are a sight too young to care for a heart case,' he said. 'I know a kindly soul, however, who is the very person. A Mrs. Constance Browne, but recently bereaved herself and left in straitened circumstances. She lives in Wellerby, five miles from here—but I am sure you will send a gig for her each morning?' Poor Papa was so shocked about his heart, I think, that he could only nod his agreement."

16

Jessica stopped. Then she went on with a trace of bitterness that sat ill on her fresh young voice, "And so Constance Browne came the very next day. Oh, she was very kind to Papa, and he liked her for she could never remind him of Mama. No, Constance is tall, fair and a little stout, but she disliked me on sight and I her, I fear! She treated me like a tiresome, awkward child and has made me feel so ever since; I took to walking out all day, for the only time I enjoyed was the evenings when she had gone home and I would sit by Papa and read aloud to him. I was well past sixteen when the blow fell. Jessica's voice trembled for a moment. "One evening Papa said he wished to talk with me instead of our reading. I should have been prepared for what he would say, but I had refused to expect it. He had asked Constance to be his wife! He explained that it was all he could do now that he was an invalid and she would never accept any money for her care, although she had two newly grown-up daughters and must be in some need. To my shame I said nothing. I *could* not. To replace darling little Mamma with *her!*" Jessica paused to steady herself.

"They were married very quietly soon after, and she moved in with her two daughters, Ophelia and Juliet. She said her dear, late husband had been devoted to the works of Mr. Shakespeare! At first I tried to look forward to their coming but they were tall and fair, like her, with empty blue eyes and they despised me.

"Constance must have discovered that Papa is extremely wealthy, for I believe she had planned everything beforehand. She set about changing the house and interfered in the whole household—especially the kitchen. So our faithful servants left, one by one, and at last our dear old Cook, Annie, went away in a storm of tears saying there was no way of pleasing Her Ladyship. Her gravy was too thin, her lovely crême caramel all wrong and, the final insult came when Constance told her she could not prepare a pheasant properly."

This time the pause was longer until at last Lady Shayne interrupted it gently,

"What a terrible experience, my dear. Did your father not understand what was going on?"

"Oh, no." A cynical little smile curled Jessica's lips. "Constance was far too clever. She replaced our own servants with a hateful group of women, greedy for high wages. Then after six months as Mrs. Court she launched her final blow—she persuaded Papa that we must move to London! 'My dear girls are more than ready to be launched into Society,' she told him, I think—I can well imagine her crafty arguments. Why, she had even heard of an ideal house on the very edge of fashionable Mayfair, she said.

"Poor Papa was quite ill with shock, but he is such a loyal man he would not confide in me any more. I think he dared not, for he knew how violently I should protest. We had always been so happy at the Old Manor—loved the quiet country life—and now we seemed powerless, although all the changes were funded by his money.

Jessica managed a short laugh. "The house is *horrible!* It is tall and draughty, and situated in Pimlico—although Constance has 'Mayfair' printed on the notepaper! She stored most of our precious furniture, preferring to choose her own which she considered 'modern.' Oh, it is so vulgar and ugly! That is all, really—except that Aunt Lucy invited me to stay with her for a month, back in dear Shore Vale, and I resolved to find an unpaid post in this area so that I need never, *never* return there!" Suddenly appalled at herself, Jessica turned and clasped Lady Shayne's hand.

"Pray forgive me, my lady. My outpouring is *unforgivable,* but I have so far failed to obtain such a position, and today I could scarce bear the thought." Her small head went up, "But never think I am not proud to be the daughter of Arthur Court. His decision to marry Constance was so honorable."

"Arthur Court," Lady Shayne repeated thoughtfully, then her face lit up. "Of *course!* I knew that you reminded me of someone, but that was so long ago. I am ashamed to say I had forgotten. You are very like your beautiful Mamma, my dear."

"You *knew* Mamma?" cried Jessica.

"Indeed, yes. I called whenever I could, for I found her charming; and now that you have mentioned the relationship, I can see you have inherited that charm. Oh, I never met you." She gave a little laugh. "I was told that you spent all your daylight hours out of doors. I fully understand how unhappy you must be in London."

"Thank you—but perhaps it will be better now that I have been away," Jessica's smile was brave, even hopeful. "Now, I feel sure I should return or Aunt Lucy will be concerned. It must be past mid-day. You have been so very kind, Lady Shayne, and I fear I have wasted all your morning!"

"Not at all, my dear, and I have a much better idea. If you will give me your aunt's address, I shall send a message to her immediately, for I should like you to stay and take luncheon with me; then you shall rest for a little and I shall take you home myself later in my carriage."

It proved to be a day of revelations for Jessica. Her ankle improved steadily after Lady Shayne's care, and, although she was forced to limp a little, the pain was not severe.

They talked easily and with growing pleasure; indeed, the age barrier between them ceased to exist. Because her father had always been a scholar, and Jessica had read widely and well under his guidance for as long as she could remember, Lady Shayne thought she would enjoy seeing the library. Jessica handled books with care and reverence, exclaiming with delight over beautiful editions of many of her favorite classics.

From there it seemed natural that they should go into the famous Shayne Gallery where rare works of the old masters hung as well as family portraits and one or two more modern paintings.

"*That* is what makes our London house seem so lonely," Jessica exclaimed suddenly. "At the Old Manor Papa had a splendid library in which he and Mamma studied much of the day, then encouraged a love of literature in me in the evenings. But my stepmother allowed him to take only fifty or so of his favorites to London. She said there wouldn't be room in the new house, and besides he could not bury himself in studies

19

there but must go out and about to escort her. So our books have all been stored."

Lady Shayne was sympathetic. "Well, my dear, whenever you are in Sussex you are welcome to use this library at any time."

Jessica's face lit up with gratitude, then fell again as she remembered. "I should love that, I declare, but I only have five more days."

Her ladyship smiled. "A great deal can happen in five days, you know."

Aunt Lucy was quite put about by the message from Shayne Park. Jessica being brought home at tea-time by no less a personage than Lady Shayne herself! In a fine fluster she hurried about getting the best silver tea service from its baize wrappings and setting her maid, Mary, to polishing it. She herself sorted through the best table-cloths, finally choosing a delicate swiss lawn exquisitely embroidered around the edge with small flowers to cover the gate-legged tea table.

Then she went to the kitchen to check on her justly famous soda bread and a fruit cake which had been baked that very morning. Miss Court had always scorned having a cook. "I do it a deal better myself," she declared. "Besides, I enjoy it."

When everything was arranged on the finest *Sevres* plates, suitably covered by lace doileys, all was ready.

At last, by four o'clock, when, a little flushed and shy, Miss Court was changed into a charming gray silk afternoon gown with a lace fichu, the carriage, emblazoned with the Shayne coat of arms, drew up at her gate.

Jessica noticed with amusement that every lace curtain shifted a little as they drove through the village.

"My aunt will be besieged by callers tomorrow," she said.

"But how nice," replied Lady Shayne. "I had forgotten how delightful Shore Vale is. I should call here more often."

Aunt Lucy hurried to the gate to welcome the august visitor and embrace her niece.

"I fear Jessica must have given you much trouble, my lady," she said.

"Not in the least. In fact it was I who detained her. I am delighted to meet you, Miss Court."

After that, all went smoothly. Lady Shayne excelled in putting people at their ease; she praised the soda bread and the cake, admired the needlework around the cloth, and declared that the pattern on Miss Court's *Sevres* was prettier than her own set at Shayne Park.

Within half an hour Aunt Lucy was her natural, chatty self. Then Lady Shayne turned to Jessica.

"I think you should rest that ankle, my dear. Besides, I should like a few words alone with your aunt."

Puzzled, Jessica went to her room. What was so private that she must not hear? With a tremor of fear she wondered if, in some way, she had given offense? But no, surely she could not have done that. All the same, she had to wait on tenterhooks for nearly an hour before Aunt Lucy called up the stairs, her voice oddly excited.

"Pray come and join us, Jessica."

Nervously, looking from one to the other, Jessica returned to the drawing room. Both ladies were smiling.

Lady Shayne held out her left hand and Jessica took it.

"I trust you will approve our agreement, my dear. I should like you to come to Shayne Park as my unpaid companion when your visit with your aunt ends on Saturday." Jessica blushed, speechless with disbelief at this amazing good fortune. "If you agree, I shall write to your father this evening, asking his permission to keep you—at any rate through the summer months. You are a very pretty girl, Jessica. I declare I intend to call you that from now on for I am almost old enough to be your grandmother! And it would give me both pleasure and an interest to introduce you into Brighton Society," she laughed lightly. "Oh, I assure you, there will be much excitement when the Prince Regent comes to the Royal Pavilion—balls, firework displays and so on—and I think it is time *you* had a little pleasure as a charming girl should. Your duties for me will be extremely light. Do you accept the idea?"

"Accept?" Jessica's face was acceptance enough and Lady Shayne said,

"I told you that much could happen in five days. Now it has only taken one. My carriage will call for you at noon on Saturday."

The rest was leave-taking, with Jessica vainly trying to express her overwhelmed gratitude. Actually to *live* at Shayne Park—not only amid such beauty and kindness but actually in the home of the handsome, gallant Lord Desmond whom she might see every day! This shameful thought she swiftly forced back into her most secret heart. He was passionately in love with another, Aunt Lucy had told her. Besides, why should he notice his mother's young companion whom he already treated as a joke—a sprite? However, first love—even though it was probably just hero-worship—could not be stilled by reason, Jessica discovered. It must remain under iron control in her innermost being.

Lord Desmond himself did not favor the idea. Returning home to dine with his mother—a rare event since he had been squiring the Lady Olivia—he was in a bad humor. Restless. So, when Lady Shayne outlined her plan he seized on it as an outlet for his general disquiet.

"My dear Mother—you must have run mad!" He raised a quizzical, critical eyebrow. "By my troth, you are still a young woman with countless friends, and, above all, you know how often you prize solitude! What in heavens name will you do with that—that *child* yapping around your heels all day long?"

His mother continued eating her delicious, jellied consommé with complete composure.

"Jessica Court is neither a child nor, as you so unkindly put it, a 'yapper at heels.' She is a beautiful and highly intelligent young woman. I warrant she will be as glad to spend hours alone in the library as I do in my rose garden. Besides, I have a mind to enjoy the coming season in Brighton by bringing her out as my protegée."

Desmond stared at her, pushing his consommé away untasted.

"Well—keep her out of my way, I pray," he said moodily. "I refuse to act as an escort in public to such

22

an unknown little creature. I should be a laughing stock, I declare!"

Lady Shayne smiled, signalling to a footman that he might remove the plates and serve the fish course. "Several of my friends have young sons who, I am sure, will be delighted to oblige. I know how—*occupied* you are, my dear."

"It is sheer folly," retorted her handsome son, and her heart ached for his unhappiness—and the cause of it.

Two

When Jessica had been at Shayne Park for a week she felt completely at home. And she had changed. With the burden of unhappiness lifted from her slim shoulders, her eyes glowed, and Lady Shayne often heard her singing softly in a sweet, melodious voice. To complete her joy, Papa sent a letter full of love and gladness at her good fortune. To Lady Shayne he wrote his thanks and included a most generous check "for all my dear Daughter's expenses—I wish her to lack nothing during her debut in Brighton."

"Poor Papa," exclaimed Jessica. "To think he will have to escort Ophelia and Juliet in hot, dusty London!"

"Yes—but you must remember that his wife looks after him with great care," Lady Shane reproved her gently.

Jessica nodded: "I know." Then she looked up with a new impishness in her smile. "But it is hard to credit someone with virtues when you dislike her. Surely you, too, find that, my lady?"

Her ladyship sighed. "Indeed, Jessica, I fear that that

25

is true." She paused, then added absently as though it had no connection with this confession, "Lord Desmond tells me he may bring a guest to tea sometime this week, but I hope he will not choose my At Home day; for once I think I shall take a little rest in my room on that afternoon. If I cut some roses before luncheon I shall be grateful if you will arrange them in the silver rose bowl for the tea table."

Jessica blushed. "It will be a great pleasure," she said, overwhelmed with pride at such a trust, although she guessed that the guest would be Lady Olivia. If only she had the power to lift the sadness clouding Lady Shayne's normally serene eyes, but her own heart was heavy, too, at such a prospect.

After the first day, Lord Desmond had accepted her presence in the house with good grace. He teased her, called her "sprite" and, when he found her in the library, humming *Greensleeves* as she dusted some books, he joined in in a charming baritone descant.

"You are a surprising girl," he said at the end. "My mother tells me you are a scholarly reader, an amusing companion and now, it seems, music thrives in you as well!"

"Do you enjoy music, too, Lord Desmond?" she questioned. "I declare I can play simple tunes on the pianoforte to which you might sing—your voice is very fine."

Hastily, he beat a retreat. "Some other time—I must mount my steed within five minutes." He paused, "Can you ride, Sprite?" he chuckled. "Or do you favor only Pegasus, the magic flying horse, on midsummer eve?"

"I swear I have never seen Pegasus—and why is he connected with midsummer eve?"

"Because, like you, he is a mythical creature of legend. Surely you go dancing on the hilltops on that great occasion?"

Jessica smiled and shook her head. "I fear I am too mortal. But I have always longed to ride."

"Then I shall teach you—when I can find the time," he swiftly qualified his generous offer.

"That would be a pleasure—and an honor, my lord."

He paused at the door, looking at her curiously. "Most girls would accept such an offer as their right, with a touch of hauteur, in fact, demanding that the lessons should not disturb appointments with a dressmaker or coiffeuse, yet you treat the invitation as an *honor*. Why? Are you never proud?"

Jessica flushed a little but she drew herself up very straight, her eyes flashing. "I am extremely proud, Lord Desmond, but you happen to be the finest horseman I have ever seen. Therefore, I repeat, to be taught riding by you *will* be an honor."

He sketched a small, mock bow. "Forgive me, Sprite. I have judged you mistakenly. Your feminine wiles are a deal more subtle than I am used to, I swear; and after such a handsome compliment, I see I must keep my word."

Jessica relaxed and smiled. "In return you have my word that a riding lesson will always be more important to me than any dressmaker. If you only knew how I long to be able to ride out over the countryside, to explore so much farther than is ever possible when walking."

As if for the first time Lord Desmond saw her clearly—the fine set of her perfectly shaped head, the slender, taut body and sensitive hands. "Why, I warrant I could make a splendid horsewoman of you. My offer was made idly, but now I repeat it in earnest."

"And I accept with gratitude," she replied formally.

When he had gone she stood very still, clasping the book she had been dusting close against her breast as if to steady her rapid heartbeats. Oh, how splendid he was —yet, so remote, only teasing her as if she were really a fey child, a changeling. But, perhaps, if she proved an apt pupil on horseback, she might break through this brittle shell and come to know him as a friend. Beyond this her imagination dared not go. The very thought of riding out beside him over the hills, free as the air, made her quite dizzy.

Soberly she returned to her pleasant duty at the book shelves.

That evening as they were dining alone she asked Lady Shayne, "Do you think, my lady, that even before

27

we begin ordering ball gowns next week, I might be fitted for a riding habit?"

Her ladyship looked up in surprise. "Why, Jessica, I had no idea that you enjoyed riding."

"I—I am not sure that I do, yet; but Lord Desmond has kindly promised to teach me, and I *know* I shall do well. It has long been one of my great wishes, but he will not take me seriously if I have neither boots nor habit," she said, blushing.

Lady Shayne looked at her thoughtfully. "You like my son, don't you? Yet I declare he does nothing but tease you."

"I—I admire him immensely, yes."

"Then a habit shall be ordered immediately. A message shall be sent asking the tailor to call here tomorrow."

"Oh, *thank you*," cried Jessica, her eyes like stars. Once she had the habit she would find courage to remind Lord Desmond of his promise . . . it mattered to her so much, so very much.

And so the habit was ordered, her measurements taken, and, guided by Lady Shayne, Jessica chose a rich, chestnut brown velvet.

"Nothing could set off your coloring better," her ladyship assured her. Furthermore, the habit was promised within three days. It seemed that all her dreams were within reach.

The habit was delivered on Friday. Studying the effect in a long, cheval mirror, Jessica was astonished at how different she looked. The warm, golden tints in the chestnut velvet highlighted her fair skin and dark eyes, while the small, velvet hat with a green osprey feather at one side, curled just over her left cheek emphasizing her dark, shining curls.

"Oh, how clever you are, my lady," she cried, turning to Lady Shayne who was smiling with approval. "I pray you will choose all my ball gowns, for I declare I should never have chosen this velvet without your advice."

"It becomes you perfectly."

Jessica twirled once more in front of the mirror. "I hope Lord Desmond may take me riding tomorrow. I swear he will be surprised!"

But it was the very next day that she learned Lady Olivia Lufton was probably expected to take tea. Lord Desmond had breakfasted in his dressing room and had left the house early.

Sadly, Jessica hung the habit back in her wardrobe. She strove very hard not to resent Lady Olivia's treatment of men. Somehow, she must keep an open mind until they had met, and, with shame, she knew her resentment was only jealousy. And a jealousy without reason, since Lord Desmond had never treated her as a young woman, much less a desirable one. She had fallen into the ready trap for the young—dreaming dreams and half-believing they might become reality.

Because of this shame, she took extra trouble to arrange the rose bowl for the tea table to perfection. When Lady Shayne came down after a brief rest in her room, her smiled glowed although her lovely eyes were still shadowed and tired.

"You are full of unexpected gifts, Jessica, and flower-arranging is obviously one. I shall call on your help often in the future."

Jessica was delighted, but it was still scarce more than three thirty and by no means certain that Lady Olivia would come at all. Her whim might be to visit somewhere else altogether, and, deep in love as he was, Desmond would follow her.

There was nothing to do now, but wait.

Then, on the stroke of four, Desmond and Olivia came riding up through the park, a splendidly matched couple. Watching from a window, Jessica sadly relinquished all her dreams. Lady Olivia possessed not only matchless beauty but style and elegance. She wore a black riding habit, tall, silk hat, and her blond hair was controlled by fine veiling tied back on the nape of her neck. Riding a gleaming, chestnut mare, she smiled up at Lord Desmond who rode close at her side. When they reached the front steps Lord Desmond, laughing, lifted her lightly to the ground.

Jessica turned away. No matter how becoming her habit, how fine her Ball gowns, she had no chance at all against such statuesque, fair beauty.

Resolutely, with her usual charm, Lady Shayne rose to greet them in the drawing room, signalling to the footman at the door to bring tea. In high, clipped tones, Lady Olivia said,

"How delightful, Lady Shayne—tea! I am parched, I declare. Desmond is a terror and forces one to ride so *many* miles!"

He looked at her with such warm, quizzical intimacy that it seemed,as if they were alone together. "You hypocrite, Olivia! *You* insisted that we go an extra ten miles!" She laughed.

Two footmen brought tea, one setting the silver tray in front of Lady Shayne, the other carrying a tall cakestand. As Lady Shayne poured, she tried not to convey the frostiness she was feeling.

"Desmond will tire anyone out if she lets him," Lady Shayne said pleasantly.

Olivia tossed her head and replied lightly, "Oh, I swear I have yet to meet the man who can tire me!" Then she turned to Jessica, eyeing her with amusement. "So *you* are Desmond's *Sprite!* How small you are. Are you child or changeling? I declare the name suits you very well. Tell me, do you fly when you aren't stumbling over stiles?" She accepted a cucumber sandwich and bit into it with sharp, white teeth.

Jessica clenched her hands together, her very soul curling with anger. How dared Lord Desmond make sport of her to this haughty girl! With great dignity she raised limpid eyes to meet Olivia's cold, blue ones.

"Not as a rule, Lady Olivia," she said evenly. "Although on that occasion wings would have been most welcome."

"Well, whenever you do I hope you will let us all watch—a winged fairy would be a charming diversion, I declare."

Lady Shayne interpolated smoothly: "I fear I did not introduce you properly. Lady Olivia. This is Miss Jessica Court, a daughter of old friends of mine. She is to make her debut shortly at the start of the season."

Olivia cast only a cursory glance at Jessica this time.

"How pleasant that will be for all the undersized

young men! I declare, most members of the *ton* are tall, like myself, so they are hard put to find suitable partners."

Jessica's spirit rose, as did her dislike. "Oh, I daresay, a few tall men will partner me as well—I am scarce a dwarf!"

Lady Shayne backed her up, "I expect Miss Court to be a splendid success," she announced firmly.

But Lady Olivia was bored. She did not care for feminine company knowing that, on the whole, her own sex did not care for her. She much preferred the company, and generous adoration, of men. She glanced at the small enamel and diamond fob watch pinned to the breast pocket of her jacket and stood up.

"This has been delightful, Lady Shayne." Her smile was brilliant, artificial. "Pray forgive me if I leave now; I had no idea it was so late, and I must make my toilette. Sir Walter is fetching me for dinner at seven o'clock, so shall we go, Desmond?"

He rose without smiling. Indeed, he was stricken, so sure had he felt that he was in high favor with his love. His mother sensed his hurt and Jessica briefly wished that she were a street girl and could slap that beautiful, bland face.

The pair left.

The room was silent for a few minutes after they had gone, both women occupied by their own thoughts. Then Lady Shayne said,

"Ring the bell, my dear. I think we could both do with some fresh tea."

When Jessica had pulled the tasselled bell-rope she spoke with a venom strange to her. "She is a *hateful* young woman," she said fiercely. "I am not sure whether to be glad or sorry that I have met her."

"Glad, I think," said her ladyship. "You will inevitably encounter her at balls. Besides, I am pleased that we share the same opinion of her; and I cling to my great hope—indeed, I pray—that Desmond cannot remain blind to her character forever. He is by nature a kindly man, and I fancy Lady Olivia must show her true colors one day."

"I shall join your prayers, my lady, but . . ." Jessica

hesitated, then went on with brave honesty, "but she is so very beautiful and—and Lord Desmond *is* an earl, a splendid catch even for a noblewoman. It may please her, enlarge her sense of power, to torment him, but I fear she cannot mean to relinquish such a fine match. She must be very clever with men," she added wistfully.

"Do not envy her, my dear—for *you* have the true qualities a man looks for in a wife. Now," Lady Shayne went on briskly, "I must revise the menu for dinner since Desmond may well return."

On Monday the carriage came to bear Lady Shayne and Jessica to the most fashionable dressmakers and milliners in Brighton. Lady Shayne had decided that little needed doing to Jessica's pretty hair.

"Short curls are all the rage now; I shall just suggest that Monsieur René trim it a little and encourage those charming tendrils. Come, you must not be nervous, Jessica," Lady Shayne patted her hand for Jessica was tense. It was all so new, a different world she was about to enter. "Forget all about Lady Olivia. Hold your head high and feel *proud* that you are such a complete contrast, small and dark with a charming figure and eyes that will dazzle many young men, I warrant!"

"It—it feels so strange; I have never had a lot of money spent on me before."

"And that needn't trouble you now, I swear. Your father is being extremely generous, and he wants you to have only the best."

The morning had a dream-like quality as smiling dressmakers bustled around, praising Jessica's tiny waist, small, firm breasts, and beautiful neck.

"Ah, but you will be a pleasure to dress, Mademoiselle Court!"

She watched as exquisite bolts of materials were brought out: silks, brocades, satins, muslins. Lady Shayne chose unerringly: a great deal of white, pale gold, some soft emerald green and a cream brocade to be embroidered with gold thread. Morning dresses and afternoon gowns were more practical but equally exciting.

Then they went to the milliner, and Jessica was delighted to discover that bonnets were no longer *de rigeuer*. Instead, small jaunty hats were perched on her curls, tilting slightly down over the forehead and decorated with ospreys, feathers from the Bird of Paradise or, on occasion, a simple diamanté buckle.

As they drove back to Shayne Park for a late luncheon she breathed, "I can scarce believe it! So *much* finery; I declare I am quite overwhelmed."

Lady Shayne was happy and smiling, too. "You know, I always wanted a daughter after Desmond was born, but it was not to be. Now I am experiencing all the pleasure I should have felt! I am very proud of you, my dear, and you will do me great credit. Already invitations are arriving for balls, soirées, musical evenings and select dinners amongst the *ton*. I shall give a small ball myself, I think. Shayne will prove an ideal setting, especially on a summer evening."

After lunch she declared herself a little tired and retired to her room. But Jessica was far too excited to rest. She wandered outside and found herself drawn toward the stables which she had never seen. Lord Desmond had been slightly morose and withdrawn since the tea party on Saturday, and had not renewed his offer of riding lessons. Jessica felt sure he must be out at this hour, however, as he had not appeared for luncheon.

The stables were large and immaculately kept. One or two grooms were polishing harness, but they knew of the "young lady visiting the park," and greeted her with smiles. Slowly, a little nervous, she moved along the stalls where at least twenty horses looked out over the open top-half of the doors. She soon lost her nervousness in sheer pleasure at the shining necks, the soft velvety softness of black noses when she plucked up the courage to stroke them.

"How beautiful you are," she said when each head turned eagerly toward her as she moved from stall to stall, admiring them. So varied they were: black, bay, chestnut, and roan, all perfectly groomed and with the same gentle, liquid eyes. "Why, I could never be afraid of you, I declare!" At the far end she fondled the nose of a small, bay mare and the velvet nose pushed into her hand as if searching for something. A laugh from behind made Jessica spin around, her cheeks flaming.

"Why, Lord Desmond!"

He pushed the mare back a little, saying, "Don't be so greedy, Flame."

"Oh, should I have brought something for them?" asked Jessica.

"No, but they always hope for a lump of sugar or a carrot." He drew some sugar from his pocket and handed it to her. "Here, put these on the open palm of your hand and offer them to her. She will be your friend for life!"

Jessica did as he directed, trying not to flinch when the mare took the lumps quickly, showing her long, yellow teeth.

"She will be a good mount for you to learn on, I think," said Lord Desmond. "About the right size and quite easy to handle."

"When may I have my first lesson?" she asked quickly. "I confess, I feared you had forgotten!"

"And *I* must confess that I had, Sprite! I apologize," he gave a small sigh, his face serious. "Take my advice and never fall in love—the price is too high." He began walking slowly away and Jessica fell into step at his side.

"Why, my lord?" she asked earnestly. "I am to come out very shortly, and I have always understood that to give love and receive it in return is the very pinnacle of happiness." Although not for me, she thought sadly. The tall man beside her had already captured her heart. But she was curious to hear what he would say.

"Oh, do not allow my moody views to distress your young heart. I have come late to the emotion, perhaps."

"And Lady Olivia hurts you, I think," she said quietly.

He looked down at her sharply. "You are surprising me again, Sprite. You are too perceptive."

"I have met her, Lord Desmond. She is extremely beautiful and I envy her the power such beauty brings." They had left the stables and were walking through a leafy grove.

"It can be a cruel weapon," he mused. "But come,

I shall not depress you with my own problems. You will enjoy the season, Sprite—even though you are such a funny little thing!"

For a moment hurt caused her temper to flare. "I vow I am neither funny nor so very small!" Then she laughed lightly. "Wait until you see me in all my new finery. Your mother has been so kind and she has selected such wonderful gowns for me! I declare, the dressmakers *praised* my size!"

"Why, Sprite—I believe I ruffled your feathers! I did not intend to. I am sure you will be a great success, just . . . be gentle with your suitors."

"Of *course* I shall—if I have any. I think that to be loved must be a great honor. I swear I could never keep a poor man in suspense," she added with more feeling than she meant, but she hated Lady Olivia more than ever for her behavior.

He paused and looked at her again. "I think that any man who loves you will be fortunate indeed." Then he smiled. "How serious we have become! It is not considered the thing to be serious with a young woman. Now, if you want a riding lesson I shall expect you at the stables at half-past eight in the morning!"

Her eyes twinkled and she gave a little mock salute. "Yes, sir!"

Laughing, he turned and left her, making his way back to the stables to arrange about the little mare, Flame.

Jessica wandered on until she found a secluded seat. There she sat down and collected her thoughts. Were her feelings for Lord Desmond simply hero-worship? The reactions of a sheltered girl meeting such a handsome gallant for the first time in her life? She prayed that this might be true, otherwise much heartbreak must lie ahead when cold, cruel Olivia eventually married him as she surely would. Meantime, when she and Lord Desmond began riding together, perhaps she could just be accepted as his friend—an amusing companion who could make him laugh and forget the black moods. She ached so to help him.

35

Dinner that evening was a happy affair. Lady Shayne was at her sparkling best, describing the events of the morning to Lord Desmond and suggesting her idea that a ball might be held at the park.

"If there is still a free evening in the social diaries then yes, Mother, I think it a splendid plan," he said. "I must make sure that Olivia will be available when you choose the date."

"Of course, dear," said his mother smoothly. "Do try one of these peaches, they are the best we have ever grown."

Jessica presented herself at the stables five minutes early the following morning. She felt shy in the unfamiliar habit, hoping that she was holding the long skirt correctly and longing desperately for Lord Desmond's approval.

And he gave it willingly with his eyes, "By Jove, an elf in elfin colors! And very punctual—you are splendid, Sprite. Now we must make sure that your riding does justice to that habit."

Flame was out in the yard, already saddled and bridled, held by a groom. Lord Desmond had decided to mount a quiet roan rather than his mettlesome stallion who might grow impatient during a first lesson.

Jessica eyed the side-saddle with some misgiving. Secretly she would have loved to ride astride, to feel the horse's movements steadily under her, but it was unheard of for a young lady to do anything so unconventional. This time she had brought two sugar lumps for Flame, saved from her breakfast tray, and the mare enjoyed them.

Then Desmond lifted her lightly off the ground, explaining how she should place her legs, one knee higher than the other so that the pommel gave her a sense of security. Then, leaping into his own saddle he gathered up the leading rein and they set off.

They went at a sedate pace to a wide meadow.

"Now, Sprite, the lesson begins," he told her.

Within minutes Jessica felt at home on the mare. She knew that her instinctive longing to ride had always been right. Her hands on the reins were light but firm and she could feel the mare responding to her slightest direction. Desmond, who had been regretting his promise to teach her, felt mounting exhilaration. She was an apt pupil indeed, and, before long, he removed the leading rein.

"I swear, Sprite, you do not need a teacher—just the horse. Now trot but keep her going in a wide circle. I don't expect you to run wild and take any risks!"

Jessica was utterly happy, fulfilled in a way she had never experienced before. From a trot she urged the mare into a steady canter, their mutual trust and understanding increasing steadily.

At last Desmond cried, "Whoa!" When she drew up beside him, reining in the horse easily at his side, he looked at her accusingly. "Sprite—you have lied to me, I declare. You already know how to ride."

Face flushed, eyes shining she said, "I swear this is the first time I ever sat a horse, but I have craved to ride for so long I knew it would seem natural." She bent forward and patted Flame's neck. "May we not venture a little further, my lord? Going round and round a meadow grows tedious."

"Well, I must warn you that if we go on you will feel too stiff to move a muscle tomorrow."

"Stiff?" she retorted scornfully. "I swear I have never been stiff in my life!"

He chuckled, "There has to be a first time for everything—but do not blame me. If you wish, we could ride as far as Dyke's Farm, 'tis but a mile or so, and then I insist you obey me and return."

They settled into an easy canter, and Jessica said, "It is like nothing else in the world! Oh, please give me permission to ride Flame every day, even if you cannot accompany me. I know I shall be safe."

"You will have a groom with you at all times," he said firmly. "Imagine what my mother would say if I allowed her social protegée to be injured."

After what seemed to her a very short time, Lord Desmond insisted on turning back.

"I swear I could go on and on," she said with a trace of disappointment.

He smiled. "That is for the future. Meantime, as my

pupil, you must obey orders for your own good! You have made an excellent start."

"And I am more grateful to you than I can say," she replied warmly. "And I declare I shall *not* be stiff!"

He shrugged, "Perhaps sprites are constructed differently—but if you are a mere mortal you'll find every movement hurts at first tomorrow."

Jessica was aglow with her new achievement all day. "Oh, how spoiled I am here," she cried as she bade Lady Shayne good night after dinner. "Your arranging the season and choosing me such wonderful gowns—and now Lord Desmond's riding lessons! It is like living in a dream."

But it felt like no dream in the morning. As Lord Desmond had promised, on waking every muscle felt as if it had been stretched on the rack. "Yet I will *not* be defeated!" Jessica vowed through clenched teeth as she gingerly moved one leg then the other to climb slowly out of bed. The time was seven o'clock, and the maid had just drawn back the curtains and placed a generous brass can of hot water in the basin, wrapped around in a clean towel to keep in the heat.

Jessica stood still, considering what best to do. Her shoulders were more than a trifle stiff, too. Then, stripping off her nightgown she filled the basin with hot water, placed a thick towel on the floor and began to sponge down her whole body with the welcome warmth as vigorously as she could manage. To her relief, it grew easier. When the water was cooling she had to desist, and her legs, though better, still ached. So she began to walk up and down the room, each step at first an agony but slowly improving, although she could not have broken into a run to save her life.

It was half-past seven.

"I will be there at eight-thirty—I *will*," she kept repeating. Yet Lord Desmond had made no mention of a second lesson so soon. Indeed, he would probably not be there, expecting her to lie late abed.

"But there will be grooms," she thought, "and I am determined to prove . . . ." Her fierce determination wavered—prove what? That she was different from other girls? That Lord Desmond had been wrong in her case?

Slowly she sat down, trying to imagine what Lady Olivia might have done, for she must hold some secret to her power over men. And Jessica suddenly knew. The statuesque blond would have spurned stiffness as she had done, but she would have languished, most fetchingly, on a chaise longue in the drawing room, reproving her present suitor gently for causing so much pain and accepting flowers, a bonbonniere, or simply a humble apology for lack of consideration. It was Jessica's first insight into the strength of true femininity and it made her impatient. She could never dissemble with a man she cared for to make him a sycophant to feed her egoism.

Yet she must not go to the stables that morning. Lord Desmond might treat her as a child, a half-fairy for his own amusement, but he would never see her as a young woman if she proved herself stronger than his advice. Superior to men—indeed, he might admire her spirit but never forgive such arrogance.

Three

Jessica, feeling something of a fraud, limped dutifully about that day, and Lord Desmond was delighted.

"What did I tell you, Sprite? I warrant you will take the word of your riding master now! But the stiffness will not last long. Tomorrow we shall ride up to the forest if you wish."

She looked up, smiling, "I declare, I can hardly wait to be on Flame now! Will—will the stiffness come back?" she asked demurely.

"I doubt it—your muscles will soon become used to the exercise." To his surprise, Lord Desmond missed her that day—Olivia was still spurning him in favor of Sir Walter, and the Sprite made a lively, amusing companion. Later in the day, Lady Shayne watched Jessica moving about with her usual, light step and gave a silvery laugh:

"I swear you are learning feminine wiles fast, my dear! Were you stiff at all?"

Jessica blushed. "Dreadfully—when I first woke. But I overcame it because I longed so much to ride again . . . then I thought Lord Desmond might be angry if I disregarded his warning so—I limped." She gave a radiant smile, "And he was pleased, I know, for he has promised quite a long ride tomorrow."

To her delight, when she presented herself at the Stables at eight-thirty the following morning, there was no sign of a leading rein on the little mare.

"You are an obedient Sprite," teased Lord Desmond, "but if you break into a wild gallop you will be in disgrace!"

"I promise not to but . . . ." Her smile was mischievous, "If I do *very* well, perchance you will allow a short gallop on the way back? I confess, I long to go like the wind just to know how it feels."

"I make no promises," he said, lifting her into the saddle, but his eyes twinkled. It was good to have her with him—her youth and enthusiasm lifted his spirits enormously.

They rode quietly to the forest, first at a sedate trot, then a gentle canter. Although it was early, the sun soon grew hot; and, once under the green shade of oak trees centuries old, he said,

"We will dismount for a while. There is an old fallen tree just ahead which makes an ideal seat."

He has sat there with Lady Olivia, thought Jessica with a sharp pang. Instantly she was repentant; and, as she dismounted lightly without help, she looked up at him, her great eyes warm with gratitude.

"It is more than good of you to take such trouble, my lord. It must be irksome to travel with me, when, alone, I know you cover many miles."

"In truth, I am enjoying it hugely, Sprite! I have never had a pupil before and never dreamt you would show such aptitude. I promise you shall have a short gallop after all."

She sat gracefully on the old tree, and, when he had tethered the horses to a low branch, he joined her. Jessica stole a look at his face, sad to see it suddenly sombre.

"I fear you are far from happy," she ventured. "Oh pray do not think I am prying but—as your mother has taught me—it helps to talk at such times. I have never betrayed a trust I assure you. Indeed, I have been deeply unhappy myself and always keep my own counsel."

Desmond looked at her for a moment. "How strange —I swear I have never considered talking to a girl in my life—such chatterboxes, I find, and titterers, as well! But you are neither, Sprite, and—to my surprise, I confess— I do trust you. Perchance because you despise tears!"

Her heart was beating fast at such a compliment, but she sat very still and waited. At last, reluctantly, he began,

"You know, I think, that I am deeply in love with the Lady Olivia—indeed, I am determined to make her my wife before this season is out. But, I warn you, Sprite, that love can be cruel, beg you to be kind to your suitors —and I fear that she is not." Then he added hastily, with loyalty, "Oh, she does not mean it so—she is still young and loves to play games; blessed with such angelic beauty how could she resist? Indeed, I am glad that she is stretching her wings a little before settling down, for I am convinced that her heart is warm and kind—pure gold."

Jessica felt otherwise, but, when he lapsed into silence she ventured to probe a little, knowing that there was a sharp thorn in his wound—a doubt that tormented him when Olivia turned him away.

"I am absolutely certain you will succeed in your suit, my lord—how can you fail? Indeed, you make a magnificent couple. Surely you have no serious rivals?"

His riding crop hung between his knees and now he began tracing a pattern with the tip in the bare ground around the tree, his head bent.

"I fancy there is one," he said slowly. "The others are mere poppinjays, darlings of society and the court, patched and powdered, yet tall and manly enough, I suppose. No, the only threat is Sir Walter Cheston. He is two years older than I and even wealthier. I have disliked him since we were mere boys, but he has a strength, a ruthlessness like Olivia's own." He was so deep in his own thoughts that he did not realize this remark had escaped him. "He was always a bully, taller than any of us and strong, with hair black as night, and he would stop at nothing to gain his own ends—even if he wanted only an orange or a few sweetmeats. He has tired of many beauties, but Olivia has bewitched him, I think—and how could she fail? She has bewitched *me!*" He looked up with a rueful grin which made him endearingly young and perplexed. Jessica laid a small hand on his lean, brown one, her heart aching with pity.

"I do not really know Lady Olivia," she said gently. "But I feel sure she is very clever. She could not accept a bully for a husband! Not when she might have you."

Lord Desmond sprang up, his dark mood quite dismissed. "What a friend you are, Sprite! I declare, I have never opened my heart to a living soul before, but you are right—talking *does* help! And, as a reward, you shall most *certainly* have your gallop."

Jessica rose, too, her face radiant. "I have always longed to help you—and your mother—after all the goodness you have showered on me. Besides, I need a friend, too, for I swear I have never had one—not to talk to with trust, I mean. Now, when may I gallop?" Her tone matched his new light-heartedness.

"When we reach the big meadow—and not one inch before!" he said with mock sternness. "The ground there is soft if you should fall—and fall you will at some time, perhaps more than once before you become a seasoned horsewoman."

"Not from Flame, I swear," Jessica said confidently.

But half an hour later she was sitting in the meadow in a most undignified manner, her skirt in disarray, her small hat several yards away while Flame frisked around and around in ecstasies of freedom. Jessica's pride was more bruised than her body and Lord Desmond looking down at her, roared with laughter.

"I warned you, Sprite! A good gallop is a wonderful thing, but you must follow the rhythm of your mount and not pull suddenly on the reins as you did! Of course she reared and threw you."

"I—I feared she would jump the hedge," admitted Jessica, shame-faced. "I am sorry."

"No, you're not—you're angry at yourself. Now, catch her and mount again."

"Now?" She was aghast.

"Most certainly. Then you will not be nervous of next time. It is a most valuable lesson."

Jessica scrambled up and, with some trepidation, chased the mare, calling her name coaxingly; and, when they came within reach, caught the reins, saying firmly, "Whoa, Flame!" Surprisingly the mare pulled up and nuzzled her shoulder as if in apology. Jessica stroked her neck. "I'm sorry, too—I won't pull you up sharply again, I promise."

For the first time, she mounted without Lord Desmond's help. He merely watched to see how well she would cope, and, when she trotted toward him, he smiled. "You'll do, Sprite. By my troth, you'll do very well."

They went back to the stables. She did not like to ask if they might ride again tomorrow, afraid of boring him. But, as it turned out, this was to be their last ride together for many days.

A note had been delivered by hand for Lord Desmond. In a lavish, sprawling hand, Lady Olivia bade him attend her at dinner that night at Lufton Castle, her parents' home. Instantly, Jessica was quite forgotten, as gray eyes alight, he told his mother he would be out and went up the wide staircase like an eager boy, taking the steps two at a time.

The following week Jessica made her formal debut at a soirée given by Lady Shankton. She wore a simple, white dress with a wreath of small, white flowers around her dark curls. Her only jewelery was a pearl necklace that had belonged to her mother which Papa had sent just a few days before.

Lady Shayne watched with approval her coming downstairs. Yes, she could be rightly proud of her protegée. Beside her stood Lord Desmond in full evening dress, smiling. For a moment Jessica's heart soared. Was it possible that he was to accompany them? But his first words ended such a foolish hope.

45

"I congratulate you, Sprite, I declare you look quite bridal, and I'm sure we shall be plagued with eager young men seeking you out before long! I confess, I almost wish I could be there to see your first entrance among the *ton,* but I am for a ball at Lufton Castle. The Countess would have preferred to hold it after the Prince's arrival next week, but every single evening during his stay is already engaged. I fear his schedule makes your ball impossible as well, Mother, unless it takes place after the court have left again for London."

"I shall see," said Lady Shayne noncommittally.

"Oh, you need not be anxious about Sprite's success —it is certain, I assure you." He then turned to Jessica. "Now do not be nervous, I pray. Musical soirées are dull fare, but it will be a chance to meet people of your own age; besides, Lady Shankton's supper buffets are famous. Now, I must be off."

He swung a splendid opera cape lined with royal blue silk around his shoulders and went out to his own carriage.

Lady Shayne watched him go wistfully.

"He was—and still would be—the most popular young man in all Brighton with every hostess clamouring for his company, but now he refuses all invitations when Olivia Lufton crooks her little finger." Then she turned to Jessica with a smile. "But come, my dear, we shall not let *that* girl cast any shadows tonight. I want you to enjoy yourself, and soirées are *not* dull, whatever Desmond may say!"

For Jessica it was yet another new world, and her face glowed with pleasure and interest from the moment they entered the beautiful hall. Lady Shankton had exquisite taste, and great banks of pink and white flowers glowed softly in the light of three crystal chandeliers. Her own daughter, Charlotte, was also making her debut and the evening was planned for young company.

When they were announced by a flunkey, Lady Shankton welcomed Lady Shayne most warmly with a kiss on the cheek. "My dear Lydia, what a joy it is to see you." Then she looked at Jessica, and her smile was approving. "And this is your young guest, Miss Court? But I declare she is charming—quite charming. Come, my dear, and let me introduce you to my daughter and her friends. I can see that you will be her rival as the prettiest newcomer to society!"

What a change from her step-mother's acid comments, thought Jessica briefly, then dismissed Constance Court from her thoughts completely.

Charlotte proved to be very pretty with fair curls, round blue eyes, a warm smile and no trace of shyness. Already, at least half a dozen admirers clustered around her, but her welcome to Jessica was quite sincere. "Why, how lovely, Miss Court! Mamma feared we should be rivals but, by my troth, we are different as day and night! Is she not delightful?," she exclaimed to her courtiers. "Let me introduce you all."

Jessica was slightly bewildered by so many names all at once, some with titles, some without. But one of them, a James Crighton, seemed quite taken with her and drew her aside in conversation. His passion in life, it seemed, was riding and hunting; and Jessica was proud to say that yes, indeed, she did ride, and hoped to hunt in time. He had nice dark eyes in a round, tanned face and insisted on squiring her throughout the evening.

The soirée was held in a small ballroom with tables and gilt chairs scattered about, a raised dais at one end for the musicians and a long buffet table along the far end. Everywhere there were flowers, and the atmosphere was light and young, punctuated by laughter. Jessica forgot her shyness and began to enjoy herself. Besides, already she had gained one admirer.

Because she loved music, she liked the recital, too. A pianist and a violinist played many of her favorites and added a few very new valses and a polka to which she found her foot tapping in rhythm.

By the time they left, James Crighton had begged Lady Shayne to permit him to call, and Charlotte insisted that Jessica come for hot chocolate in the morning so that they could go shopping in Brighton for the reticules and fal-lals so dear to every girl's heart.

"You did very well—very well indeed, Jessica," Lady Shayne said on their way home. "I can see I am going to enjoy this season more than I have for many years. Did you realize that you have acquired two admirers, not James Crighton alone?"

"Why, no," Jessica was astonished. "He was so attentive all evening I confess we only spoke to other men in passing."

"Poor young Sir Charles Daynton is extremely shy, but his parents are old friends of mine; and he, too, has asked if he may call. He is a pleasant young man, more interested in books, than riding, but perhaps you noticed him? He is as tall as Desmond and very fair. I swear he could scarce take his eyes off you during the recital."

Jessica blushed with pleasure in the dark carriage. She *had* noticed the tall youth with fair hair and would have liked to talk to him. Now, it seemed, she would have the chance.

It was after midnight when she went to bed. Now that Jessica was launched into the season, Lady Shayne had hired a young maid, Bella, to help her dress, undress, and care for the washing and pressing of her gowns. Bella was asleep in a chair when Jessica entered her room but she sprang up, her face rosy and smiling as a child.

"Oh, Miss Court—was it a wonderful evening? You —you looked so beautiful, meaning no offense."

Jessica smiled, "How could it be offending to be told one looked beautiful, Bella? And yes, it was delightful. Why, I even had lobster for supper and I have never tasted it before."

Bella's eyes were two round Os of horror. "Lobster! Why, my Mam who cooks up Lufton Castle says they be wicked brutes with nipping claws. You weren't nipped, were you Miss?"

Jessica laughed. "No—the lobster was cooked and mixed in a delicious sauce."

It took little time for her to undress and, when Bella had hung up her gown carefully and put the gold slippers into an embroidered bag, Jessica went to bed feeling happier than at any time since her mother died. She meant to relive the whole evening, savoring it, but within two minutes she was fast asleep.

Desmond was nowhere to be seen the next morning, and Lady Shayne insisted on Jessica taking her carriage in to meet Charlotte. "It is nice for you to have girl friends as well as admirers, my dear," she said. "When you get older and marry, you will find such friendships deepen and become precious. There are many problems that women can discuss only with each other."

Indeed, Charlotte was awaiting her eagerly. She was bubbling with her own news of last night's occasion; young Lord Ware had paid her such marked attentions she even thought he might propose! "Imagine, Jessica, being betrothed before even the first grand ball!"

"How lovely, Charlotte, but might it not be wise to meet some other men first?"

Charlotte giggled, "I declare, you sound like Mamma! Surely marriage is the aim of every girl? Besides, Lord Ware is delightful and has a splendid mansion here, in Brighton, so I shall entertain vastly."

"Well . . ." Jessica sounded slightly dubious.

"Do *you* not wish to marry?" asked Charlotte in astonishment.

"Why, yes—of course I hope to in time, but only to the right man." So it will probably never happen, she thought sadly. It was unthinkable that anyone could replace Lord Desmond in her heart.

"Oh, many girls begin with romantic dreams," laughed Charlotte. "But in their second season they will accept any man sooner than be pitied, I declare. Come, drink your chocolate, for I mean to buy a pretty reticule to match my first ball dress."

The morning was very enjoyable although Jessica was forced to agree with Lord Desmond's view that most girls were "chatterers and titterers," for Charlotte, though kindness itself, was both. Gossip was her favorite theme, and she scarce drew breath between one item and the next. Charlotte was an amusing friend, yes, but not one to be trusted with confidences.

Lady Shayne had thoughtfully made luncheon at a slightly later time, but afterward Jessica found herself tired; perhaps it was because Lord Desmond had not appeared but more likely because she had yet to grow used to the thistle-down conversation of girls her own age. She took herself off to the Library.

There, after choosing one of her favorite books, she curled up in one of the big leather chairs. She read a few pages, but it was such a sleepy, summer afternoon. The French windows stood wide, and she could hear the clip-clip of Lady Shayne's secateurs in the rose garden where bees droned lazily, their pollen sacs nearly full. She dozed

Then a footman opened the door, and she started up as he announced, "Sir Charles Daynton, Miss. Her lady-ship hopes you will both take tea with her in half an hour."

The tall young man was blushing furiously and seemed totally at a loss for words when the footman left.

"I—forgive me, Miss Court...I intrude...I—scarce spoke to you last night...I—I am disturbing you..."

Jessica was genuinely delighted to see him. She shook his hand which was not, as she expected, limp and damp but firm and cool.

"You do not intrude at all, Sir Charles. In faith I succumbed to idleness! I enjoy company. Pray sit down."

His smile was shy but charming as he advanced, still nervously, to sit on the edge of the chair opposite her own. Then his eye lighted on the volume she had laid down, and suddenly his face grew animated. "You like reading?" He seemed surprised. "I, myself, spend much time among books but I have never met a young lady who did not find any mention of such things highly boring."

"I can scarce believe it!" cried Jessica. "I declare study and books have been part of my life for as long as I can remember. But then the only girl I know so far is Charlotte, the daughter of our hostess last night." She sprang up, her eyes alight. "I warrant, this library is a treasure-house; pray come and see for yourself."

He rose eagerly, and, together, they browsed along the shelves discovering, with delight, that they shared many similar tastes and were able to introduce each other to several so far unknown pleasures. Time was forgotten until Lady Shayne came through the French windows, smiling.

"I knew that you two young people would find many interests in common; but I have been pruning rose bushes all afternoon, and tea is ready on the terrace as it is such a pleasant day."

Instantly, Sir Charles blushed with embarrassment. "Lady Shayne, I am most remiss—I declare I forgot the time!" He replaced the book in his hand as if it were red hot.

"Dear Charles, I have never known you to remember time in your life! Besides, tea has only just been served."

"It is my fault, too," interjected Jessica quickly. "Sir Charles and I have been having such an interesting talk."

The young people followed her ladyship onto the Terrace, and there, over tea, cucumber sandwiches and rich fruit cake, Sir Charles relaxed once more.

"You won't have discovered it yet, Charles, but Miss Court is devoted to music, too. She has a charming voice and plays the pianoforte delightfully." Lady Shayne turned to Jessica. "Perhaps, after tea, you will favor us with a small recital? I think Sir Charles will enjoy joining in many of your favorite songs."

It was Jessica's turn to feel shy; apart from Mamma and Papa she had played only quietly for her own amusement, and it would be quite dreadful if she disappointed this nice young man whom she already regarded as a probable friend. But she need not have worried. At five o'clock Mr. James Crighton was announced and, coming onto the terrace he was obviously surprised—and not too pleased, to find Sir Charles.

"Well, Daynton, I declare you pay your formal calls early!"

Sir Charles sprang up, his shyness returning as he stammered his thanks and apologies to Lady Shayne.

"I am so sorry—I have outstayed my welcome ... I ..."

"Nonsense, Charles," she smiled. "You are welcome at any time." Not greatly reassured, he took Jessica's hand with a small bow, apologized again, and left.

James Crighton remembered his manners and a little belatedly said all the correct things to Lady Shayne and Jessica; the latter was not sure whether to be pleased, flattered, or disappointed. She had enjoyed her afternoon so much and liked Sir Charles; but James had been amusing and entertaining last night, and he did share her latest passion for riding.

Lady Shayne rang for fresh tea and set about making James feel welcome—though, to her, Charles was preferable. However, she was pleased that Jessica's success was so obvious, and the Crightons were a fine old family. With slight surprise she accepted the fact that, during the season, she would have to entertain many young men of varying tastes, and, for Jessica's sake, she hoped that one of them might win the girl's heart before Desmond broke it by marrying Lady Olivia.

James had already taken one tea elsewhere, so, after a token cup and a piece of fruit cake, he ventured his request.

"Lady Shayne, I wonder if Lord Desmond would mind if I asked Miss Court to show me his famous stables? They are so highly spoken of, and I declare I have often hoped to see them."

Lady Shayne looked at Jessica to give her answer, and Jessica smiled. "I'm sure Lord Desmond would not mind. His horses are very fine, and, if you bring some sugar, I shall introduce you to Flame, the little mare I ride."

James grinned. "I am a horse owner myself, Miss Court, and I assure you that I am never without a knob or two of sugar in my pocket during the daytime."

Lady Shayne watched them walk away together, talking animatedly, and reproached herself. She should have accompanied them as chaperone, but the hours of gardening in the sun after an unaccustomed late night—for she no longer entertained or went out except for close friends since her husband died—had left her a little weary. Besides, young Crighton was an honorable man, and the stable was full of grooms.

Indeed, nothing could have been further from James's

mind than seduction. He admired Jessica enormously; but horses were his main interest in life, and a chance to see Lord Desmond's thoroughbreds filled his mind at the moment.

At least two of the grooms saluted him as he and Jessica went through the big gates. Mr. Crighton was a well-known figure on the hunting field as his father had been before him. James had hoped for a closer look at the big black stallion, but his stall was empty.

"Lord Desmond is out on him, I'm afraid," said Jessica, seeing James's disappointment, "but do come up to the end and look at Flame."

"I'm sure she's a fine little filly," James turned merry eyes on her. "But I fear you cannot rush a horse-lover through stables like these, Miss Court! I confess I cannot pass the chestnut or the bay—or the roan, without a closer look."

Jessica looked a little crestfallen. "And I must admit that I dare not lead any of them out for you; when I told you I loved riding, I did not admit that I am still taking my first lessons and would not anger Lord Desmond for the world." Then she saw one of the older grooms nearby and exclaimed: "Oh, Beatty, will you show Mr. Crighton around properly? I declare I am a poor guide!"

The old man was pleased and soon he and James were deep in conversation about hocks, fetlocks, width of chest, and pacing. Jessica watched with amusement but her real interest was James himself. He was an extremely pleasant young man, she thought, solid and dependable with his roots deep in this countryside she loved so well. That he could be charming and amusing she already knew but—as a suitor? She thought of Sir Charles—how different the two men were! Then she chided herself, she must not allow either to become a suitor since her heart was already wholly given.

And at that moment Desmond rode in in high good humor. Beatty had just led out the chestnut, and James was admiring the gelding's strong chest; Jessica completed the charming picture, watching with one arm draped over the door of the open stall.

"Well, well," laughed Lord Desmond, dismounting, "is Miss Court offering to sell you my stables, Crighton?" he asked. Jessica blushed.

"Of *course* not, my lord—Mr. Crighton was just anxious to see your famous horses. Do you mind?"

"Lud, no—but he has seen most of them on the hunting field, eh Crighton?" Suddenly James appeared very young and slightly abashed.

"Indeed yes, my lord—but I was tempted to have a closer look."

"Well, I fear a longer inspection must be deferred. Beatty." He handed his reins to the groom. "Hercules will need a good rubdown before his blanket goes on. Oh, and send one of the lads around to the coachhouse to order my carriage for seven thirty, will you?"

With the appearance of their master grooms, the stable lads began to scurry about. James felt it prudent to take his leave.

"Dare I hope to see you at Lady Reve's cotillon tomorrow evening, Miss Court?" he asked.

"Why, yes." Jessica was pleased—especially when he requested the honor of the first dance. Then, after apologizing to Lord Desmond for his intrusion, James left quickly.

Desmond raised a quizzical eyebrow at Jessica after the young man had gone.

"A suitor already? I must congratulate you, Sprite."

Her proud little head lifted at his teasing tone. "Indeed, I have had two callers this afternoon," she said with a touch of defiance.

"Two?" Desmond gave his last instructions to Beatty then turned back to her. "Come, walk up to the house with me and tell me all about it. If you use a magic spell to lure admirers I should like to learn it myself."

Instantly she was all concern. "You, my lord? But you look so happy I—I thought the day must have gone well?"

"If you consider riding twenty-five miles *à trois* pleasant then yes, I suppose it was all right."

"You mean—Sir Walter was with you and Lady Olivia?"

"Yes." His reply held a note of bitterness. "Oh, she treated us both superbly dividing her attention equally, but she is dining with Sir Walter tonight."

"Yet I heard you order your carriage. I felt sure . . ."

He smiled down at her. "What a strange little creature you are, Sprite! I believe you really have my interests at heart. Most girls might be jealous, listening to the praises of another."

And I am, I *am*, thought Jessica guiltily, I hate her more all the time. Aloud, she said,

"Surely loyalty is part of friendship? I just pray for your happiness." And that, at least, is true she thought.

"Then I shall pray for yours. Come, tell me about your admirers, I have been selfish talking about myself when you are tasting such success. Crighton, of course, I know as a hunting crony, but who is the other?"

"Sir Charles Daynton—oh, I know he is very shy," she went on hastily, feeling that Lord Desmond might not approve of him, "but he came upon me in the library so that we began talking about books almost at once, and he quite forgot his shyness. Indeed, I like him very well—but I confess it is strange having two sides to my character! With your help I have come to love riding as much as I expected, but I doubt if Sir Charles has ever mounted a horse! On the other hand, I doubt if Mr. Crighton has ever read a book, although he was amusing company last evening."

Desmond laughed. "In fact you will need *two* husbands—one for day and another for evening! Poor Sprite, what a dilemma!"

"And yet—you appreciate both," Jessica ventured. "You sing splendidly, and I'm sure you read a great deal, too. Is that combination so unique?"

"I don't know," he said candidly, "but you have scarce begun the season so do not feel that your first admirers will be the only ones. Men are queer cattle, and every one is different, as are women. Besides, you are too young to commit your life to any one yet!"

"I am *eighteen*," she insisted. "Most girls marry before they are twenty."

He slipped a friendly arm through hers.

"But, thank God, you are not 'most girls,' Sprite, so do not rush off with a herd to the altar. Indeed, I insist on approving your final choice myself. I claim that right as your friend!".

They strolled up to the terrace where Lady Shayne was lying back in her comfortable garden chair, her feet on a footstool. As they approached, she smiled—how delightful the young people looked together—he so tall and she so small, yet, within the space of two or three weeks, Jessica seemed to have the power to relax Desmond's high-strung nerves; nerves he had never suffered from before he met Olivia. What a fine daughter-in-law Jessica might have made had she only been a little older and met him sooner.

Lord Desmond went up and kissed his mother's forehead lightly.

"Mother, I am going out this evening to do something you thoroughly disapprove of! Many of the Prince's court circle have already arrived in Brighton, including some of my oldest friends. We are planning a gaming party before His Highness comes and insists on winning every time! So be warned—I may well lose the very roof over our heads," he teased, his eyes laughing. "Hugh Franklyn is a devil of a hand at cards!"

Lady Shayne smiled. "I think I can trust you not to do that—but, if you do, pray exclude my beloved rose garden!"

"I promise."

He went into the house, and Jessica perched on the footstool, for both women felt happy. He would not be with Olivia, for once, but among his friends.

Lady Shayne said contentedly, "It's true. I once set my face against Desmond gambling—his grandfather was such a terror—but I am so happy to think he is going to pick up old friendships again."

Before Jessica could reply Lord Desmond reappeared through the French windows.

"I have now seen the program of royal engagements for the season and the very first event is to be a buffet in the Royal Pavilion followed by the mammoth firework display. I am determined to escort you both to that affair."

He turned to Jessica. "So kindly refuse any offers you may have from anyone else!"

Jessica scarce believed her ears. "But suppose *you* have an unexpected invitation on that night, my lord?"

"I shall refuse it," he said firmly. "I insist on being the first to show you the glories of the Pavilion, Sprite. Your reaction to such magnificence will be a rare experience, I warrant! Besides, I know just the things that will please you most."

He went back into the house. Both women were silent, afraid to voice the faint hope that both his announcements had raised in their hearts. At last Lady Shayne spoke.

"Well, at least he is turning back to old friends tonight."

"Suppose Lady Olivia asks him to escort *her* to the fireworks?" Jessica still dared not believe this miracle—to be at Lord Desmond's side for the very first Royal occasion.

"My son never breaks his word," said her ladyship with a firmness she was far from feeling.

But Jessica gladly believed her. The prospect was so wonderful she dared not do otherwise.

Four

Jessica never attended dancing classes but her mamma had taught her at home. Some new dances had come into fashion since then, of course, but Jessica had such a natural sense of rhythm that she found no difficulty. Besides, many young men who partnered her could do little more than walk round the ballroom, holding themselves very stiffly.

She enjoyed the Cotillon and three of her partners danced well. They sang her praises, too, and each of them asked Lady Shayne if they might call on Miss Court.

"You are collecting quite a retinue, my dear," said her ladyship. "I admit, I am bound to favor Sir Charles Daynton having known him since he was a child, but young Lord Minden is most affable and would be a splendid match."

"I—I declare I cannot view any of them as possible husbands." Jessica's voice was low. "And, while I enjoy their company, I must not raise their hopes for I could not hurt them. It is very difficult," she sighed.

Lady Shayne was silent for some time, turning over in her mind the best thing to say. At last, she ventured,

"First love is always deep and painful. Indeed, it has a freshness and a quality no woman ever forgets." She paused. "Yet it seldom ends in marriage, Jessica. Perchance it is too pure and idealistic to bear reality, but I think it is born to live forever as a cherished memory." She smiled to herself: "I loved Charles Daynton's father Edward, when I was your age—oh, he was so dashing and handsome! I would vow my heart broke when he married Catherine—only hearts don't break! A year later I met my dear husband, and our love grew and deepened until the day he died."

"Thank you," said Jessica warmly. "I shall remember, but surely I need not accept anyone just yet?"

"Of course not! Nineteen or twenty will be quite soon enough. Getting to know several men as friends will be a great help in making your final choice."

Neither of them had mentioned Lord Desmond, yet he was so strongly in both their minds, it was almost as if he were present.

The next day he took Jessica riding, teasing her about her successes.

"I hear you are capturing hearts wherever you go, Sprite! And I am not surprised—you look pretty as a picture in your demure evening gowns."

Such praise fell like pebbles on her aching heart. He did not find her in the least desirable, just "pretty," and compared to Olivia he was right. She was by far the most beautiful young woman in Brighton.

Jessica changed the subject quickly. "When are the Royal Fireworks, my lord? I declare, it will be a grand spectacle."

"Next Wednesday. The Prince arrives on Tuesday but he prefers claret and gaming on his first evening before he opens the season. I fear he may disappoint you Sprite. He is not old in years but his habits have made him extremely fat!"

"I was not expecting a romantic figure, Lord Desmond—besides he is married. Pray, how did you fare at cards last night?" She smiled mischievously. "I see you have not lost Shayne Park."

Desmond laughed gaily. "Far from it. You know, I declare you lent me a touch of magic, for I won quite handsomely while Hugh Franklyn had little luck. Yes, I think I shall buy you a present, Sprite—what takes your fancy? A small tiara, perhaps, or a diamond brooch?"

Jessica blushed. "Gracious no, my lord—nothing so valuable, I entreat you. If you insist a—a scarf would be charming, or a bonbonniere, for I have never received one."

He looked down at her with amusement. "A little Puritan at heart, are you not? No romantic dreams about a married man, and no valuable presents from a good friend? I shall use my own discretion. And, mind you, I expect you to cast many spells for my good fortune. Come, let us ride up the next rise. A stage coach will be passing soon, and I like to keep an eye on its safety."

"You mean you often drive off highwaymen?"

"It is good sport and more worthwhile than chasing a fox although old Reynard is a pest in the countryside, too."

"If—if they *do* appear may I ride down at them with you?"

"Most certainly not!" He was very serious. "I want your oath that you will wait quietly where I leave you, no matter what happens. And don't look so downcast. There is no danger I assure you."

"But they have muskets." Jessica had gone quite white.

"Muskets are useless defense against fear. Besides, Hercules goes like the wind, and we are on the rogues before they can collect their dim wits."

"So *that* is why you are riding him today! I hoped it was a compliment to my riding. Please, my lord—" she laid at small hand on his arm, "I pray you take no risks."

"Risks? Why, all life is a risk, Sprite—and you can always throw a cloak of invisibility around me if you grow anxious."

"I wish I had such magic powers," she said wistfully.

He was in a reckless mood, however, possessed by a curious inner triumph which could scarce be attributed to winning at cards. He had not mentioned Lady Olivia so far, yet possibly, in some way, she had raised his hopes. True, she had dined with Sir Walter, but suppose she and Lord Desmond met later in the evening?

He reined in in the close cover of a spinney abreast the hill. Below ran the main coaching road and Jessica was deeply afraid. *Could* she save him if, for once, his surprise tactics failed?

As if he sensed her thoughts Lord Desmond smiled indulgently. "Sprite, I believed your heart to be as stout as your determination to master things. Now, dismount and go to Flame's head. Talk to her quietly, and give her the sugar lumps you usually give her on our return. If she whinnies it could give us away. And remember, I trust you to obey."

He moved a little deeper into the spinney as the wheels of the heavy coach could be heard faintly approaching; though Jessica's heart was pounding so hard she could scarce distinguish them. How would the Lady Olivia behave in such a situation, she wondered—then knew that she would enjoy the sight, revel in any fighting and have no fear for Desmond. Should he be struck by a stray bullet he would be a loser, a failure, and dismissed from her favor.

Suddenly Jessica felt as if she were reliving a bad dream. As the coach appeared around the bend she saw three horsemen moving stealthily into position from the other side of the road. Only three! If it were the same band, had they left one higher up to watch lest Lord Desmond attack? She held Flame's soft nose close between her hands, causing the mare to toss her head in protest as she was enjoying the sugar. Then, at second glance, Jessica thought they were different men, not quite so tattered and on better mounts. Her fear mounted.

Three against one.

The coach pulled up sharply as before, only this time two men had muskets while the third drew a short, sharp blade.

Then, as the petrified passengers stumbled out, Lord Desmond rode in to attack; and for a moment she closed her eyes, praying more fervently than she had ever done before, "Save him—dear God save him, I beg."

When she summoned the courage to look again, it was all over with Lord Desmond chasing the brigands up the opposite slope, although the man with the short sword was still attacking viciously as he rode.

At last the outlaws were routed and disappeared. But this time Lord Desmond did not return to reassure the passengers with laughter. Instead, he took a circuitous route and headed back to the spinney and Jessica saw blood coming from his upper left arm. She ran to meet him.

"Lord Desmond—you are wounded. Let me see."

"A mere scratch, dam' the scoundrel. Thank heaven it's my left arm—and don't fuss, Sprite. It will do very well until we reach home."

They were in a shelter of trees and Jessica spoke with a firm authority that astonished him into obedience.

"Dismount at once, my lord, and give me your kerchief. Mine is so small it will just made a pad to staunch the wound. If only I were in petticoats we should have plenty of material, but I will do the best I can."

And her best amazed him for he had, indeed, lost some blood although it was only a flesh wound.

"They were a strange bunch," he said angrily as he sat on the ground. "I shall have to make a new plan of campaign—but this is cursed annoying."

Jessica worked swiftly. Breaking a strong twig from a tree she made a tourniquet and bound the wound tightly:

"Only you must not move yet, a tourniquet cannot stay on for very long or it is dangerous. I will retire into these bushes for a moment and see what undergarments I have that will tear." Jessica's deep concern for Lord Desmond's wound had introduced a new boldness to her character. This was no time for modesty.

Under the long, split skirt she wore breeches, but her chemise of fine linen and the lower part of her white shirt provided four adequate strips.

63

She eased the tourniquet, glad to see that the bleeding had lessened considerably, then she bound the wound with fresh linen and said, "Now I think we can ride quietly home. Your mother will have far better remedies."

"No," Lord Desmond said sharply. "My mother must never hear of this escapade. You are the only physician I need, Sprite, and a most efficient one. Where did you learn your skill?"

"From Mama. She loved herbs and studied their uses. Then, since Dr. Pettigrew seldom came save for wealthy patients, people in Shore Vale took to bringing her children who had serious cuts and bruises. Young men came, sometimes, if they had been careless with a scythe. I loved to watch her, she had such beautiful, healing hands."

"Like yours," said Lord Desmond, looking at them.

"Oh, I have not her knowledge," said Jessica, embarrassed, "but I remember much that she did."

"Well, my arm feels easier, I declare." Lord Desmond stood up. "Let us ride home—but not one word to her ladyship, remember! I shall go up to my room through the side door, and my man Chalmers will deal with the jacket and shirt. But first you must have another gallop."

"Most certainly not!" declared Jessica firmly. "That cut will not heal immediately and must not be jolted about. I will enjoy a gallop another time. Would you . . ." she hesitated. "Would you like me to dress the arm again later?"

"Heavens, no! Chalmers has dealt with my cuts and grazes since I was a boy. He hasn't your gentle touch, but he is thorough. Now, I must tell you the good news. Lady Olivia sent a note by her maid early this morning. She wants me to be her escort for at least the first two weeks of the season. Is that not splendid?" He chuckled, "Sir Walter must have annoyed her very much last evening for her to commit herself in such a way. Why, it is almost tantamount to accepting me!"

Jessica could not look at him for a moment but clung to her reins, quite dizzy with dismay, and yet did she not pray for his happiness above all things? When she felt her voice was under control she said, "No wonder you seemed so full of triumph this morning, my lord. I expect you would prefer me to make other plans for attending the fireworks now?"

"You will do no such thing!" He was quite indignant. "I never break my word. No, during dinner this evening Olivia and I will discuss making up a party for that event. She loves to have several people around her, and it will be more entertaining for you to meet some of the court circle. Many of the men are very young, and all are witty. His Highness cannot tolerate bores."

"But—I am not witty," said Jessica in a small voice.

Lord Desmond laughed, "In faith, Sprite, no one expects wit from a young girl. Indeed the men would be abashed for they enjoy showing off! No, you will be a great success since you look very charming and are a splendid listener. One glance from those huge eyes of yours will have many young beaux at your feet!"

They rode into the stables, Lord Desmond feeling well satisfied. But Jessica, after thanking him briefly, gave her reins to a young groom and slipped away. She, too, used the side entrance, hoping to meet no one before she reached her room, for her tears could not be restrained for long.

Safely alone, with the door closed, she sank down on the floor by her bed and buried her face in her arms. She wept silently, feeling utterly bereft. Lord Desmond's promise to escort her on her very first royal public occasion had been like a beacon—a promise so dazzling she had scarce dared to look forward to it in case something went wrong.

Now it had. Oh, he was keeping his word, but with Lady Olivia and a score of her admirers around them, Jessica knew she would be shy and nervous.

And yet . . . she looked up, her tears spent—it was what she *wanted*—that Lord Desmond should be happy and win his heart's desire.

"At least he is my *friend*," she whispered fiercely. "He can never be more." But, secretly, she had hoped a little . . .

Lady Shayne was right. First love *was* deep and painful. Only Jessica felt that Lord Desmond could never be folded away as a tender memory while another man won her heart; he was too vibrant, too much the ideal companion, to lie quietly in a fading scent of lavender.

Her first proposal came on the following Saturday during a ball. James Crighton had partnered her often enough to cause a few raised eyebrows among the watching mothers and chaperones. Then, after taking her to supper he said,

"I declare, it is extremely warm. Would you care for a stroll in the garden, Miss Court?" He looked very dogged and rather pink in the face, but Jessica suspected nothing. Indeed, the air *was* close indoors, and she welcomed the idea. He had called at least three times at Shayne Park, and, with a little encouragement, told her a great deal about his home and family, his future ambition to breed fine horses, and she liked him very much.

But she was quite unprepared, after he led her to a seat in the rose garden, for him to fall on one knee and seize her hand.

"Miss Court—Jessica—forgive such presumption for we have not known each other very long but—", he stammered a little, "I declare you captured my heart at our very first meeting. Have I a chance? Will you do me the great honor of becoming my wife?"

At first Jessica felt stunned with surprise, then she grew quite calm as she looked down into his tortured dark eyes, waiting so nervously, pleading silently for her acceptance.

"Pray rise, Mr. Crighton, and sit beside me here." She made no effort to release her hand as he obeyed. Slowly she went on: "I confess, it is *you* who have done me a great honor. I like you very well and already value you as a friend, only . . . I—"

"You do not return my feelings," he said sadly. "I was foolish to imagine you could but—"

"No, no, it is not that. You see, I am scarcely eighteen and until these past few weeks, I have had little chance to meet people—even to grow up properly as many girls do much earlier. It is all a little bewildering, still; and until I feel more secure, how can I know my

66

heart? It would be cruel indeed to pledge myself to you in this uncertain state, for I would not hurt you for the world. I beg you not to withdraw your friendship nor think that I will betray your confidence to anyone—not even Lady Shayne."

"Then—I may hold a ray of hope?" he asked eagerly.

She smiled. "May we not simply leave it as it is? After all, you are young, too, and who knows whom you may meet as the season goes on?"

"I could never meet anyone as pure and noble as you, Miss Court," he declared ardently. "But you will soon be moving in court circles and will be besieged, I warrant, by finer men than I."

"I find *you* very fine, Mr. Crighton, and titles or grand speeches will never influence me! Come, shall we return to the ballroom, or our absence will be noticed." She rose, and so did he.

"I have never proposed to anyone before," he said, "and your gentleness will help me not to be so nervous with young ladies. They laugh so much, then whisper together, that I have been afraid to be thought a fool."

They were strolling back to the French windows, and Jessica thought how strange it was that this man, little more than a boy, already shared Lord Desmond's opinion of girls. Were they really so silly? If so, it would be hard to make friends among them.

As they returned, one glance told Lady Shayne what must have taken place; but Jessica was far too composed to have accepted James Crighton, and she was glad.

"May I have one more dance?" he asked with a touch of humility.

"Of course!" Jessica prepared to face another "walk" around the floor. "But I think it must be the last for this evening. We have been much together." Her smile removed any sting.

James was more in love than ever. He *would* win her.

Lady Shayne asked no questions on the way home, sensing that Jessica would never betray the poor young man.

Besides, she seemed to have thoroughly enjoyed the final half of the ball, having had some good dancing partners, including Lord Minden, whose gaze was already adoring.

He will be the next to offer, thought Lady Shayne without any feeling of satisfaction. Jessica was still far too enamored of Desmond even to consider any proposal, however desirable, and it would be a great pity if she lost any chance of future contentment simply because it was offered too soon.

That night Jessica prayed most fervently that Sir Charles Daynton would not propose. He was so desperately shy and reserved that she knew what such a declaration would cost him. If she refused him—as refuse she must—it would drive him back into an impregnable reserve, and this she dreaded. For if, as seemed almost certain now, Lord Desmond became betrothed to Lady Olivia and, later, married, it might well be, in a year or two when the pain had dulled, that she would turn to Sir Charles. In many ways he was like papa: gentle, scholarly, and would always be happier at home with a few close friends than seeking the social whirl. With Lord Desmond at her side Jessica knew she would have enjoyed every moment of a wild, gay life; but, once he had gone, that spark would be extinguished. She would revert to the quiet girl she had always been, and Charles was the only companion she could imagine in that setting. His love would never be passionate or demanding, jealous of the past, or asking more than she wished to give. They would be loving friends, their mutual understanding growing ever deeper.

Her prayer was answered. On the afternoon before the now-dreaded firework party, it was not Sir Charles but Lord Minden who sought her hand in marriage.

Correct and formal, he called at Shayne Park and asked a short private talk with Lady Shayne in the morning, when Jessica was out riding, before approaching Jessica that afternoon after tea.

"It is good of you to see me, Lady Shayne. It may seem a little precipitate but my mind is made up. I wish to ask Miss Court to be my wife—with your permission of course. I swear I have never found a girl so charming on so short an acquaintance." Then he added with a slightly self-satisfied air, "I hardly think I need to produce my credentials? She will become Lady Minden of Minden Chase and never lack for anything her heart desires."

Lady Shayne did not answer immediately; indeed, she was sorry that he planned to propose so soon while Jessica was still obsessed with Lord Desmond. After Sir Charles, she could think of no more suitable match for Jessica than this. George Minden was kind, generous, and enormously wealthy; he would make a faithful husband, too. But at the moment he stood little chance. He was puzzled at her silence—surely she did not find him lacking in some way? But, at last, she spoke:

"Of course you have my permission, but would you not think it wise to wait for a time? Jessica Court is still very young and only just coming out into society. Her life has been very sheltered, and, I declare, meeting so many people must be a trifle bewildering. I do not think she can feel ready to give her heart just yet."

Then he looked young, eager and, for the first time, as if he were in love.

"Lady Shayne, I dread losing her! I *know* she is young—but so am I; and she is so pretty she may easily be swept off her feet by one of the young beaux at court if she has no one to turn to, to be at her side constantly."

Lady Shayne smiled with a trace of sadness that Lord Minden did not notice. How impetuous the young are, she thought, but her voice was warm.

"I would not deter you for the world, my dear young man. You are an excellent match for any girl. I only hoped to spare you disappointment at this early stage."

"She has great sense, Miss Court," he said confidently. "When I have talked to her this afternoon, I am sure she will appreciate a loving guide at her elbow through the coming weeks."

He made his courtly farewells, picked up his hat, gloves, and cane and went out to his chaise.

Lady Shayne sighed. Such a worthy young man and doomed to disappointment. When Jessica came in for luncheon, flushed and happy after a brisk ride, she wondered whether to warn the girl. But no, it was dangerous to interfere, and young Minden must do the best he could.

Jessica looked particularly pretty that afternoon in

a primrose muslin embroidered with tiny leaves and a wide straw hat tied under her chin with green ribbon, for the sun was hot. Lord Desmond had been very merry that morning, telling her who would be in their fireworks party tomorrow and adding amusing anecdotes about each one.

"I know I shall be very nervous," she admitted. "They all sound so splendid!"

"And so are you, Sprite! You will look enchanting, and I shall take care of you. After all, I invited you and Mother first of all before any party was suggested!"

Jessica wondered whether Lady Shayne had told him her decision not to accompany them yet. She had never really wanted to go, except to chaperone Jessica on her first royal occasion. But when she heard of the party, organized by Lady Olivia, she said,

"I declare I have changed my mind. I have long outgrown the excitement of fireworks and, in such a young gathering, an old woman would be out of place."

"But you will be my only friend, my lady!" cried Jessica, aghast. "Oh pray, *pray* come. Or might it tire you?"

"I would prefer not to, Jessica. As to friends, I think many young men will seek your company since it is well-known that Olivia Lufton has no patience with any man under twenty-five. And Desmond will let no harm come to you. Indeed, how can it in the midst of a big gathering on the Royal Lawns?"

"Perhaps I can run a fever and not be able to go myself," said Jessica hopefully. "Yet that is cowardly; I must accustom myself to seeing Lady Olivia at his side on many occasions."

"Yes, my dear, I am afraid you must."

Now, when Jessica joined her ladyship for tea on the terrace, looking fresh and charming as a spring flower, she said,

"I am trying so hard to overcome my nervousness about tomorrow, but—oh, it is delightful to be quietly alone with you this afternoon, I hope no callers come."

Hardly had she spoken when they heard wheels on the carriage driveway. A few moments later Lord Minden was announced, bearing a handsome bouquet for Lady

Shayne and a pretty bonbonniere for Jessica. In his waist-coat pocket lay a small leather case holding an exquisite diamond ring, so certain of success was he. Early tomorrow morning Jessica should receive a roomful of flowers, for his ideas on courtship were highly romantic.

All the same, in spite of his generous gestures, Lady Shayne felt that he was a trifle nervous so she launched easily into talk of topics of the day: the arrival of His Highness, the new lavish decorations added to the pavilion, for the Prince was an avid collector of Eastern art. And Lord Minden had more news to add.

"I have seen the Program of Events," he said with a touch of importance. "Not only are there to be Grand Balls and picnics by day, but next week we are to have a masque on the lawns with a champagne buffet, and the subject will be 'Love.' Later still a totally new item simply announces 'Revels.' I declare, it will be a gay season with many innovations." He turned to Jessica, "A most suitable year for you to come out, Miss Court, and you will be the prettiest girl there."

Suddenly Jessica knew what was coming and dreaded it. Oh, not another so soon, surely? How could these young men offer their hearts and hands so quickly, after scarce two weeks' acquaintance? And Lady Shayne must have been warned for, when tea was over she said,

"I fear I am a little tired; perhaps you would care to take Miss Court around the gardens? They are very fine at present." Then she glanced at her bouquet and added, "But flowers from a friend mean far more than those one has nurtured oneself."

Lord Minden rose with alacrity and offered his arm which Jessica felt bound to take. This young man was vastly different from James Crighton; she knew him only as a pleasant dancing partner and quite handsome, if one admired neat, well-oiled fair hair and the new Dundreary whiskers. She did not. Also they had established no friendship apart from social gossip, so she did not know how to deal with the situation.

They strolled for a time below the terrace during which he complimented her on her gown and compared her eyes favorably with the deep purple violets edging the herbaceous border. Then, guiding her by the elbow, he veered toward the grove. Oh no, not there, thought Jessica rebelliously, not the place where Lord Desmond very first talked with me a little! But what did it really matter? Lord Minden danced well, turned a pretty compliment, but she could never care for him, much less marry him.

He fell silent as they entered the grassy walk between the trees, then he began in very formal tones:

"Miss Court, I am sure Lady Shayne has prepared you for what I wish to say?"

"No," answered Jessica truthfully. "She has said nothing."

This seemed to disconcert him a little.

"Well, it is not every day that I make a proposal of marriage," he sounded ruffled. "Indeed, I have only done so once before, two years ago."

Jessica stifled a cruel desire to laugh; he grew more pompous by the minute and obviously had no thought of going down on one knee. He was about to offer her a great honor and had no idea of pleading love. But that made her task easier.

She turned wide, solemn eyes to him. "My lord, are you trying to propose to *me?*" she asked innocently.

"Of course I am, but, damn, it is all gone wrong! I thought mothers and guardians always prepared a young lady for such a great moment!"

"Pray, do not continue, Lord Minden." She stopped walking and faced him. "I am sure Lady Shayne didn't mention it to me because she knows full well that I am not yet ready to receive such an offer—honored though I am. It will be at least two years before I think seriously of marriage. I have so much still to learn—so many new people to meet. Only—I hope you will continue to partner me at balls sometimes." She smiled disarmingly, and he went quite red. "For I declare you are a fine dancer and—and I trust we may come to know each other better?"

"I swear you have quite broken my heart, Miss Court," he said gruffly, showing the first signs of humanity so far. "I had felt so sure—wanted so much to claim you and be at your side during the season. Why, young men seem to have eyes for no one but you lately and—forgive me, I must leave."

He turned on his heel and hastily left the grove. Jessica stood still, watching him go—*had* she been unkind? At which moment Lord Desmond came strolling toward her from the same direction, still in riding clothes. His face was stern but his eyes amused.

"What have you done to young Minden, Sprite? I declare he just dashed past me gobbling like a young turkey cock! Now I told you to treat your suitors gently!"

Jessica began to laugh, she couldn't help it. "I feel sure I was kind, my lord—but oh, he was so pompous! Why, he did not even stop walking much less mention love—until the end when he vowed his heart was broken, but I can't believe it is. At first he seemed to expect *me* to go down on my knees in gratitude while he placed a coronet on my head!" She became serious. "But I was truly kind to James Crighton on Saturday evening—I like him very much and he was so sincere only . . . I cannot commit myself yet!" She did not meet his eyes for her heart reproached her for this lie. If Lord Desmond loved her, how gladly she would surrender herself to his arms!

"H'm! Two proposals before the season," he said thoughtfully. "I see I must keep an eye on you, Sprite. I can't have my elfin playmate flying away just yet." She sensed that he was studying her face and blushed slightly. "Yes, you have a charm all your own and will make quite a stir, I believe."

She looked up shyly then. "Do you really think so, my lord. I confess I wish I were taller and not so nervous!"

"Nervous? No young woman worth her salt is ever that—no you must sail into a crowded room like a little queen, defying people not to like and admire you." He sketched a low, mocking bow. "*That* is what you must expect from your admirers."

He took her arm lightly. "Come, that lesson must do for today. I have to change, and I feel sure Mother is curious to know what passed out here." They walked back to the terrace. "I think you should not ride tomorrow, we shall be leaving quite early in the evening for Lufton Castle where Olivia seems to be assembling most of the *beau monde* for champagne followed by dinner before we go to the Pavilion."

"I—I thought there was to be a royal buffet there."

Desmond chuckled. "Olivia swears the food does not live up to the gold and silver plates! The Lufton's chef is superb."

Jessica's heart sank; she had a small appetite, and the prospect of eating a large dinner in such distinguished company was very daunting. Then Desmond said, "I have insisted that you sit by me so that I can serve you when the dishes are handed round. I shall not overload your plate, I promise."

"How kind you are—how very kind, my lord!" she exclaimed with more emotion in her voice than she realized. He glanced down at her quickly in surprise. Surely she did not—*could* not have silly romantic notions about him? But Jessica swiftly realized her error and smiled.

"That will be delightful. I shall rely on you to hide the bits I cannot manage," and, leaving him, she ran lightly up the terrace steps to Lady Shayne.

Desmond's face cleared, how stupid of him to imagine for one moment that his Sprite felt anything more than friendship for him. After all, she was just a child!

Five

Jessica wanted to wear her gold-embroidered brocade at her first royal occasion, but Lady Shayne poo-poohed the idea.

"Nonsense, my dear—that must be for your first Grand Ball when I shall present you to His Highness. No, this evening is an informal celebration, so let us reconsider." She went to Jessica's wardrobe and looked through her new gowns.

"This, I think, will be most suitable, and I will tell Jordan to cut some of my pale green butterfly orchids for your hair." She brought out a soft, jade green silk, simply but perfectly cut in the high-waisted Empire line with a low square neck and short sleeves. "Your pearls will be just right. I'm sure Bella will weave a pretty garland for your hair, won't you child?" She smiled at the little maid, who blushed with pride at such a trust. "You have a delicate hand with flowers, I have noticed."

Overcome, Bella bobbed a little curtsey: "I love them, my lady."

When that important decision was settled the time

was still scarce eleven o'clock. "Oh, if only Lord Desmond had not forbidden me to ride today lest I be injured," mourned Jessica. "Idleness only makes me more nervous!"

"I have no intention that you shall be idle," said Lady Shayne briskly. "I am visiting several of our tenants this morning, and I shall enjoy your company; besides, I think they will interest you. The grooms and stable lads as well as several gardener's boys speak well of you, I'm told, so you may be sure of a warm welcome."

Jessica's eyes lighted up. "I declare, I shall enjoy that vastly," she said with enthusiasm. "I used to visit in Shore Vale with Mama sometimes when she called on the cottagers to see how her patients were progressing." She laughed, "We returned home so full of homemade gingerbread and cups of tea that we never could eat luncheon!"

Lady Shayne laughed too. "Oh, times have advanced a little; we shall be pressed with spiced rock cakes and deliciously warm, homemade bread spread with apricot or plum preserves. I have ordered a very light luncheon indeed!"

It was a delightful morning, and totally absorbing since the Shayne family was so generous that each cottage was in perfect condition.

"They are like something in a painting," exclaimed Jessica at one point. "So freshly painted—and how the brass and copper things shine indoors!"

"For two generations we have given any tenant who has served the estate for ten years or more, pride of ownership." Her ladyship had a pardonable note of pride in her own voice.

But it wasn't all fresh paint and pretty gardens. There were sicknesses and new injuries to be tended, and Lady Shayne carried a bag of ointments, bandages, and lotions in the carriage. After a while, Jessica ventured, "May I see to that little boy? I declare I know how to treat severe cuts and you have more serious complaints to attend to."

By the end of the morning Lady Shayne was impressed at how deft and skillful such a young girl could be. "My dear, when you *do* consider marriage you are

76

most suited to be chatelaine of an estate such as ours!" And she just managed to stop short of saying that her dearest wish was for Jessica to hold that very position at Shayne Park. Olivia Lufton would care nothing for the tenants or faithful old retainers.

To Jessica's surprise it was after two o'clock when they returned and she begged, "Pray excuse me, my lady, if I eat no luncheon, but I seem to have been eating all morning! I should like to take a glass of iced mineral water to the library and relax among the books for I declare I could not lie quietly in my room. It has been a wonderful morning!"

"I am glad for I shall ask for your assistance often on my 'rounds' in future." Lady Shayne chuckled: "I can eat no luncheon either due to Mrs. Shottley's homemade hot bread! I must ask for her recipe for it is better than ours."

At half-past-five precisely, Jessica was ready for the evening, as Lord Desmond had insisted, for it was a half-hour drive to Lufton. Bella fussed around her until the last moment, adjusting a wayward curl, making sure that the lace kerchief in her evening reticule was scented. "You will be far the loveliest young lady there," the girl declared adoringly.

"No, Bella, but not for lack of your efforts." Jessica smiled. The garland of tiny orchids was, indeed, a loving work of art, but her face was a little pale for all her nervousness had returned.

Lord Desmond was waiting in the hall, and he watched her slightly hesitant descent with growing pleasure.

"By my faith, you *are* a Water Sprite! The mythical Ondine who rose from her lake and lured mere mortals to love her—I shall be very proud of you. Oh, I have just one finishing touch to add." He brought something out of rustling tissue paper on a chair behind him. Jessica gasped with pleasure as he carefully draped an evening shawl around her shoulders. It was light as gossamer and exactly matched her gown, with tiny emeralds stitched here and there that glinted when she moved.

77

"Oh, my lord!" She was speechless with delight, but her shining eyes, raised to his face, said it all.

Lady Shayne joined them and asked the question Jessica was dying to ask herself: "Desmond, it is perfect! Now, how *did* you know what gown Jessica would wear tonight?"

He grinned. "I have my spies—and my allies," he said mysteriously and would add no more. "I promised you a gift, Sprite and, since you spurned a tiara—quite rightly now that I see your enchanting garland—I did the best I could. Besides, the evening will grow chilly later on. We must be going now."

Lady Shayne kissed Jessica warmly on the cheek. "You look lovely, my dear. I know you will enjoy the evening."

As they bowled along through the glorious countryside, the deep greens made even more beautiful by the full glow of the setting sun, Lord Desmond said,

"You are a perfect companion, Sprite, for you understand the value of silence between friends. As the season goes on and you make many friends, I beg you never to become a chatterer."

"I swear, my lord—nor will I ever titter! If I do, I rely on you to berate me at once."

"I shall indeed. . . ." He looked out of the carriage window. "How can people choose to live in cities when there is all this! Oh, I daresay, Olivia will demand a townhouse in London for the season there, but I shall rarely accompany her for long . . . I declare I feel trapped."

"And so do I," said Jessica eagerly. "That was one thing my stepmother could never understand; she loves the noise and bustle everywhere."

"How wise you were to escape," Lord Desmond turned to look at her. "You must have shrivelled in such an environment."

"I did indeed. It took two weeks with Aunt Lucy in Shore Vale before I recovered my looks at all—such as they are."

"Listen, Sprite," he said almost severely, "so much modesty can grow almost as tedious as chattering! You have forgot my last lesson. I expect you to sail among the company like a small, proud queen tonight, for you are very, very pretty with, yes, a translucent quality of magic about you. Do you really like the shawl?"

Jessica looked down and touched the thistle-down folds with reverence. "It is the most wonderful gift I have ever received." Then, to break the seriousness, she looked up with laughing eyes. "I am most grateful that you did not give me a Bonbonniere. I declare, I had heard them so much praised by girls, I expected a Pandora's box! But the one Lord Minden brought was extremely dull. Oh, the box is charming and the little gilt trays lift out sideways like a curved staircase, but the chocolates, so finely wrapped, held all the soft cream fillings I like least and the fondants were *scented!*" She chuckled, "Bella has eaten them voraciously."

Desmond laughed too. "But the donor can choose the contents—indeed, I think they are a good measure of character and, when I choose one for you—as I shall, either for your birthday or Christmas, I vow you will have no cause for complaint."

They lapsed back into silence for a while. As the scenery around them grew less familiar to Jessica she began to feel nervous again, and Desmond was looking forward to standing beside Lady Olivia as her chosen host.

"I cannot propose again during such an informal evening," he spoke his thoughts aloud, "yet her note has given me a hope I can scarce believe!"

They turned in through a very ornate gateway with stone griffons rampant on either side.

"I hope it will go well for you, my lord," Jessica's voice was quiet but he did not notice. Indeed Lord Desmond was sitting forward, his eyes shining with anticipation now they were so near.

Lufton Castle was as ornate as the main gates, fussed about with small turrets, gargoyles stationed below the roof from some long-ruined cathedral, and tall, narrow windows heavily leaded with lattice work. What had once been a moat, noble with swans, was now dense with rhododendrons. They drove over a bridge on to the wide, gravel sweep before the main doors and Jessica thought, How dark it all is—how *loveless*.

But the carriage had drawn up, and Desmond was waiting to hand her out. A footman took their names and ushered them through the long hall, lined with ancient suits of armor, to French windows set wide at the far end from which, already, sounds of laughter and merriment came toward them.

As they passed through on to a wide terrace, the first person whom Jessica saw was Sir Walter Cheston. She had not met him before but, from Lord Desmond's description, he was unmistakable. Taller than Lord Shayne by perhaps an inch, Sir Walter was very dark, with a black moustache which helped to hide his too-sensuous mouth and a slight floridness. But he was a presence to be reckoned with, conveying great physical strength and complete self-assurance.

Desmond left Jessica to go over to Lady Olivia and apologize if he were late though it was scarce six o'clock. She lifted a mock-reproving face to his, though her eyes were merry.

"No, you are *not* late, Desmond, but I fancy my other friends were a little more eager!" She looked magnificent in a most unconventional gown of fine silken tapestry, fashioned after a famous Italian painting; her fair hair was held in a loose jeweled net on her neck. Jessica sighed—silently, she believed—but Sir Walter at her side now, heard and smiled.

"Surely you are not surprised at the desertion of your Earl Errant, Miss Court? Oh, yes, I am sure that is who you are. Our riding fraternity is small and news travels fast. You must know that Lord Desmond is set on winning the Lady Olivia?"

"Of course I am aware of that, Sir Walter," she replied, stung, "and, you see, I have recognized you, also."

"Touché, ma belle Ondine." He sketched a small bow, his dark eyes amused. "You are much prettier than I expected—and wise to be a water sprite instead of competing with Olivia, for she is incomparable." His eyes strayed back to the lovely hostess.

Jessica felt angry. Why had Sir Walter echoed Desmond's valued praise of her as a water sprite? It suddenly made the treasured compliment common coinage. And the word "pretty" was anathema. Younger men had proclaimed her beautiful, and, although she knew that she was not, the word pretty, usually applied to giggling debutantes or maids, incensed her. I am *different* from Olivia—that is all, she thought fiercely and held her small head higher.

Although Olivia had now linked arms loosely with Lord Desmond, Sir Walter drifted toward them as if drawn by a magnet. But several younger guests eagerly sought Jessica's company; they, too, felt a little out of countenance, especially in Lady Olivia's company, and the young Miss Court, soon to be presented, was a subject of much curiosity.

Soon Jessica was laughing and talking easily, pushing the fact of Lord Desmond's obsession firmly out of her mind. After all, she had been honestly warned from the very beginning so she would not permit herself to be defeated by this first sight of them together on a social occasion.

Lord Desmond forgot his promise that she would sit by him at dinner and she was glad. Olivia had scarcely acknowledged her presence so far, apart from a smile across the terrace, and Jessica, remembering some of her barbed remarks during tea at Shayne Park, wanted only to escape her attention as much as possible.

Together with her new young acquaintances Jessica enjoyed dinner. After a delicious consommé and a small portion of sole, when a haunch of venison and several roast fowl were carried to the serving table to be carved, she threw up her hands and laughed gaily,

"La! You have such large appetites in society—I declare, I cannot get used to it all! Is it ill-mannered to refuse a course?"

The others joined in her laughter, and a young man with twinkling eyes drawled solemnly, "Gad, Miss Court—

you would never be forgiven!." Then he smiled most charmingly. "Take just enough not to offend my illustrious cousin." He nodded toward Olivia. "And we shall all come to your aid, never fear."

They did, and it became a game of much merriment for her neighbors to slip pieces from her plate to their own without being noticed.

"How very kind you are," Jessica cried when the plates had been removed. "I swear I have been quite nervous at meeting members of the ton in Brighton, but now I shall enjoy it."

"We are not savages, you know," said a graceful girl who had introduced herself as Grace Ashby. "I have visited London with Mama and, I declare, we are just as civilized here! I am nervous at coming out, too," she added.

This brought eager agreement from three other girls and Jessica felt deeply happy and at home. She had *friends*. Only then did she realize how foolishly dependent she had been on Lord Desmond's company. She glanced up the table to where he was deeply engrossed in amusing conversation with Olivia. She would always love him, but, perforce, she must build a very different life for herself which need not include marriage.

Her new sense of relaxed pleasure was short-lived. After dinner it was time to start for the Royal Gardens and the firework display. As they rose from the table, Olivia called imperiously,

"Sprite! You are to come in our carriage, as Lord Desmond says he is your official escort and chaperon."

Everyone in the room looked at Jessica with curiosity. The wretched nickname that had once been such a precious, private thing would now haunt her wherever she went. She blushed furiously, as much with anger as embarrassment, and avoided the inquiring eyes of her recent dinner companions. They would be wondering if she had invented her nervousness for surely she must know Lady Olivia very well already.

Once again her proud head went up and, as she moved toward Lady Olivia, she said in clear tones, "That is an honor indeed, my lady, on this, my first visit to your home."

Lord Desmond watched her, smiling, but Lady Olivia refused to be cheated of her petty triumph. This small, dark newcomer was a sight too pretty for her liking and carried herself well in company. She could never be a rival, of course, but she might well establish a court of her own and Olivia was determined to be undisputed "Queen of the Season." With a light laugh she turned to all the guests,

"We are going to see the Prince's magical fireworks now but, later, we may see yet another piece of magic—Miss Court flying high over the housetops, for Lord Shayne swears she is a fairy—a changeling come among us mortals in disguise. Pray, will you fly for us, Sprite?"

It was the challenge direct and Jessica met it squarely, summoning all her courage to still her angry heart.

"I fear I must disappoint you, Lady Olivia. It amused his lordship to dub me 'Sprite' because of my small stature, but I am as mortal as you, born and brought up here, in Sussex, at the old manor house in Shore Vale." She smiled around most disarmingly. "So pray enjoy the fireworks but expect no further wonders. My name is Jessica Court, and I trust I have now outgrown Lord Shayne's trifling joke."

She dared not meet Lord Desmond's eye for he would tolerate no insult to his chosen beloved; but, to her surprise, when he put a hand under her elbow to guide her out to the carriage, his voice was amused.

"I declare you the champion of that little bout, Sprite. Indeed, I wish I had never divulged our joke to Olivia, but," his voice grew more serious, "do not antagonize her, however, for she will be the leader of society for the next few weeks; and, once she is my wife, I want you to be a welcome guest at Shayne Park. Will you remember that?"

At last she lifted her wonderful dark eyes, sparkling, now, through his compliment. "I promise, my lord and—and I wish you every happiness." This tore at her heart, but it was the least she could do in return.

Immediately Desmond was buoyant. "Do not fear.

Blessed with Olivia as my bride, how could I be otherwise? And just wait 'til you hear some of her ambitious plans to liven up the season! It will be remembered for years to come."

The carriages were lined up, and Desmond gave his driver instructions to proceed to the Royal Pavilion and wait there. Then he and Jessica joined Olivia who was already seated in her elegant equipage with Sir Walter beside her.

"I insisted that Walter must join us so that we may continue planning the masque," she said gaily, ignoring the evident annoyance on Desmond's face. Then she turned to Jessica. "By my faith, it will be the most splendid diversion. Has Desmond told you?"

Jessica shook her head. As they bowled away toward Brighton, Olivia prattled on. "I am determined that the theme shall be love." She clapped her hands in excitement. "Yes, we shall all be gods and goddesses on Olympus, and I shall persuade Beau Brummel to plan it for us. I declare he is *such* a wicked man!"

"Perhaps you should approach the Prince first," suggested Desmond.

"By my troth I intend to—this very night! Dear old Prinny gets more extravagant every year, and he will arrange a most luxurious setting for us!" She glanced at Jessica who was a trifle shocked by such a frivolous reference to His Highness. "We must find a tiny part for you," Olivia said graciously. "Perhaps as one of my handmaidens—but no, you are too dark and small, I fear." She appeared to think. "I have it! You shall be a page, won't that be a pretty conceit?"

Jessica tried desperately not to sound stiff, but she disliked Lady Olivia more and more. How could these two handsome men not *see* her for what she was? Politely, she replied,

"Thank you, my lady, but I shall prefer to watch." She knew it sounded stilted, even rude, but she did not care. Olivia merely laughed and returned to her grandiose plans.

They were approaching the Royal Pavilion. Jessica had visited it once or twice with her parents, for there were guided tours when the Prince was not in residence so that his loyal subjects might admire the miracles of Eastern art he had collected. Some of it had seemed to a young girl overwhelming and oppressive in its opulence, but certain paintings and delicate porcelain held her spellbound.

But she had never dreamed that the exterior could look so splendid. The long facade facing the beautiful gardens was lit like something from the Arabian Nights, each turret and minaret glowed pink, gold, emerald or blue while the great Dome shone silver and palest green. The tall windows (all open) held brilliant, crystal chandeliers with at least a thousand candles in each, which sparkled and twinkled like rainbows as the light, evening breeze caused the diamond-like droplets to shift gently, turning their facets first this way then that.

There were comfortable chairs in rows to accommodate the 300 guests, facing a distant platform where the firework display was set up. Under the trees to the left stood long tables covered with priceless damask and bearing huge dishes of fresh lobster, salmon, cold ham, roast beef, cold game, and salads. The centerpiece was a model of the Pavilion itself, iced and decorated with fine, spun sugar and colored marchpane. No wonder Olivia had said that the Prince was excelling himself in extravagance!

The front row of seats was reserved for the royal party with two magnificent armchairs for His Royal Highness and Mrs. Fitzherbert, his constant companion at Brighton. Lady Olivia's party secured excellent places in the second row and Jessica found herself between Lord Desmond and the merry-eyed youth she had much liked at dinner.

"Pray excuse my ill manners, Miss Court," he said. "I should have introduced myself. I am Grace Ashby's brother, Alistair. Our family seat is in Scotland, but we always attend the Court at Brighton, and we have, I believe, taken your birthplace, the old manor in Shore Vale, for the season. It is a beautiful place indeed and you must have been sad to leave."

Jessica turned to him, her face alight, "Oh, I was! I declare, I have never felt so wretched in my life. Do tell me . . ." In her eagerness she plied him with a whole string of questions until he laughed,

"Miss Court, I have one perfect answer: you must visit us and see for yourself! Indeed, Grace will be delighted, and I know Mamma and Papa will make you most welcome."

"Oh, *could* I? I have avoided going there for fear of finding strangers, but now . . . ."

Lord Desmond attracted her attention. "We must all stand, now, Sprite—the Prince is coming out."

Jessica watched, fascinated, as an extremely portly figure, tall and very regal in gold-embroidered satin jacket and knee breeches (strained a little over the massive thighs), moved through the company, surveying them with smiles through his jewelled quizzing glasses. With him came an elderly, buxom woman with a most elaborate coiffeur above her round, pink face; her smile was warm, however, and her plump neck circled with a blaze of diamonds.

As soon as they were seated the Prince held up his hand as a signal for the display to begin. An expectant silence fell, then a blaze of colored rockets soared up into the dusk, raining down a curtain of stars to the ground. Jessica gasped, but it proved the least of the spectacles to follow. Catherine wheels whirled, whole scenes were depicted brilliantly against the sky; and, when it seemed impossible to reach greater heights, a life-sized portrait of the Prince Regent in full, royal regalia, hung shimmering in the air for at least five minutes while an unseen band played the National Anthem.

A moment's stunned silence followed, then wave upon wave of applause broke out. The prince beamed around over his shoulder, gathering all the applause to himself for his entertainment; and, indeed, even the most blasé guests were stirred to a brief fervor of loyalty and admiration. Prinny had excelled even himself.

Lady Olivia was waiting her chance, and, before anyone else could precede her, she slipped through and curtseyed most charmingly to both the Prince and Mrs. Fitzherbert, which pleased him. He knew Olivia well, of course, since her father was one of his cronies, and he had been known to visit Lufton Castle, a rare honor. He seemed delighted at the full blossoming of her beauty.

She quickly captured his attention for her daring plan for a masque to be held during the first grand ball.

"By gad, m'dear—" he slapped his knee "—you have brains as well as beauty! Come, take champagne with Mrs. Fitzherbert and me and tell us more." His small eyes twinkled. "I confess, these dam' balls bore me to death, and this sounds like a daring divertissement." His expression changed to mock severity. "I don't doubt that you intend me to lay out vast sums of money!"

"Of course, Highness," she replied demurely. "Would I dare to insult your generosity on our amusements?"

Chuckling, he heaved himself out of his chair with a little difficulty. Offering his arm to Mrs. Fitzherbert he told Olivia, "We will talk in comfort beyond this inane babel. I fancy I may have ideas of my own to add to your enchanting conceit."

"I had hoped for your assistance, Sire," Olivia said with due humility. Then, with a swift wink at her confederates, she followed the stout couple back inside the Pavilion.

"Truly, there is nothing that Olivia cannot accomplish," said Desmond admiringly. "I declare, to enlist his assistance is a stroke of genius! Come, Sprite, we shall enjoy some champagne ourselves. Olivia will tell us all that happens during the drive back."

For a moment Jessica would have preferred to go to the buffet with Alistair Ashby—to hear no more of Desmond's praise for Olivia. But after that one comment, he fixed all his attention on her, bewitching her all over again with his bantering charm.

"Well, has your first royal spectacle pleased you, Sprite? I declare, you looked about six-years old watching the fireworks!"

"I love them," she said, smiling, "and those tonight truly were royal! But," she lowered her voice, "the Prince is so *fat* I could scarce believe my eyes."

"Shhh. To keep in favor one must pretend to think he has all the charm and agility of youth, but two bottles of fine claret and one of port every day has to be placed *somewhere!* Still, the rumors from London concerning the King's health imply that Prinny will, at last, be on the Throne. Then he can work his way through the royal cellars, and, in full fig, no one will notice the paunch! Now, do you prefer dry or sweet champagne?"

"I—don't know, my lord," Jessica blushed. "I have never tasted it in my life."

"Then you shall try both," cried Lord Desmond jubilantly. "What a joy it is to introduce Ondine to mortal pleasures."

Soon they were joined by a group of Desmond's friends and also Grace and Alistair Ashby, wanting to confirm that Jessica would visit her old home. It was a happy evening under the trees with laughter everywhere.

Long before half the guests had left, Olivia returned laughing and triumphant. She had collected Sir Walter from his group and now said imperiously to Desmond, "Oh, I have such news! We must drive back to the castle while I tell you, for we have many preparations to make before the masque next week," she sparkled with excitement. "The Beau was in the Pavilion—though in his cups, of course, but still so witty. He has promised to provide our theme, and as to dear old Prinny, well just *wait* 'til you hear his magnificent plans! I swear no season will ever compare with this one."

For Jessica it seemed as though all the lights had dimmed. She had much looked forward to the quiet, starlit drive home with Desmond, and she could bear to hear no more talk of Olivia's ideas. She would *not* return to Lufton.

Olivia eyed her thoughtfully. "I declare, your Sprite is more than half asleep," she said and turned to Desmond. "I have it! Why not send the child back to Shayne in your carriage so that we may talk at ease? You shall borrow the finest horse in Father's stables to ride home yourself later."

"I fear I ought . . ." began Desmond doubtfully, with regret in his voice. But Jessica interrupted firmly,

"That is most thoughtful, my lady. I confess, I am a little tired. It will take a while to accustom myself to late nights and so much excitement."

Desmond's glowing smile was her reward. He would have been loath to leave Sir Walter alone with Olivia at this point.

"Are you sure, Sprite?" he asked. "My mother expects me to escort you . . . ."

"With the worthy squires as my driver and scarcely a few miles of peaceful countryside to travel, what ill can possibly befall me?" Jessica said warmly. "Pray, call him to the door for I have had a wonderful evening and wish to be surprised by your splendid performances at the ball."

They were all, even Desmond, so relieved at her decision and so effusive in their farewells that, alone in the carriage, Jessica was hard put not to weep a little. Had she entertained even the slightest hopes of winning Lord Desmond's heart during their closest conversations, they were completely dashed now.

For him it had to be Lady Olivia or no one.

Two days before the Grand Ball, Lady Shayne received a charming note from Lady Ashby at The Old Manor, ending: ". . . . it seems both my young people are vastly taken with your Ward, Miss Court, who, I believe, was born and reared here. So it will give us all great pleasure if you are free to bring her to take tea here tomorrow."

Jessica was delighted and Lady Shayne readily accepted. It had worried her that, since the royal fireworks, Jessica had seemed a little out of spirits.

"I hear that the Ashbys are a charming family— from Scotland, I believe. It is the first time they have taken a house in our neighborhood for the season and it will give you such pleasure to see your old home. I understand that your father never sold it, but arranged for it to be furnished most tastefully for suitable visitors."

Jessica frowned a little. "I declare, I am puzzled. I believed Papa must have sold our home for he never told me he had kept it. All his beautiful books have been stored away and much of the fine furniture. My stepmother sold the rest I think. But why did he never *tell* me? I have often been tempted to go and look at it again, but I hated to think of it belonging to another family." She smiled. "Now it will be quite wonderful to go there, knowing it is still his property."

Lady Shayne kept her far more mature, wise thoughts to herself. From all she had heard of Arthur Court's second wife, she felt that the poor man might have felt the need for a possible refuge in future.

"And who can have furnished it for visitors?" wondered Jessica. "I must write to Papa and ask him everything."

"If I were you, my dear, I should keep your counsel in this matter," advised her ladyship gently. "If your father had wished you to know, he would have confided in you."

Still looking doubtful, Jessica finally agreed, "Yes, I am sure that is true. Besides, I daresay the letters he receives are often read by my stepmother, and I am sure that *she* knows nothing of this!"

Jessica felt tears stinging her eyelids as she and Lady Shayne drove in through the old manor gates. The house lay about a mile from the village in six acres of grounds. Designed in the reign of Queen Anne, it was spacious without being opulent, the rooms laid out on two storeys with a servants wing at the back. Suddenly Jessica leant forward eagerly and cried,

"Oh, my lady, pray may we stop for a moment? That is Wade, our old gardener, standing by the rose beds!"

As the carriage stopped, the old man came up, touching his forelock, his eyes moist,

" 'Afternoon, Miss Jessica—and a right pleasure 'tis to see you. We allus knew you'd be a beauty and, with respect, so you are!"

"It's a great pleasure to see you, too, Wade. The garden looks as perfect as ever."

He grinned. " 'Twouldn't thrive without my care," he said proudly. "Calling at the Manor I take it? Real nice gentry they are—and a fine job of furnishing the place was done by some smart firm from Brighton. I trust as you'll enjoy your visit, Miss."

"Oh, I shall, I declare, Wade. And I hope to have a chance to see all around the garden later."

They drove on and Jessica turned to Lady Shayne. "I still cannot understand why Papa has not *told* me of all this," she said, perplexed. "Though I vow my stepmother knows nothing of it, Aunt Lucy *must* know."

"My dear, she would never betray her brother's confidence," replied her ladyship. "I think your father must be a wise and thoughtful man; and, if you will take my advice, you will not inform him that you have discovered his secret. I am sure he has his reasons."

"I wonder . . ." said Jessica slowly, her eyes wide as an unbelievable possibility came to her mind. Suppose, after all, that Papa tired of London altogether, where he was not at ease, and that he planned to retire here where she could join him in their old companionship? Constance would never return.

But they had arrived, and Grace and Alistair Ashby came out to bid them welcome.

It was a delightful tea party and the Ashbys went out of their way to make Jessica feel she would be welcome in her old home at any time. Then, beaming, Lady Ashby said, "I swear you two girls can scarce wait for the grand ball. Well, 'tis almost upon us now."

Jessica's spirits sank. Not only the ball was imminent but also the masque she dreaded so much.

Six

The day of the Grand Ball dawned fine and sunny. Lord Desmond tried on his costume for the masque in the privacy of his own room, wanting both his mother and Jessica to have the pleasure of surprise. The lavish entertainment was planned for 11 PM when the dancers would have finished their champagne supper.

He was rarely at home that week, and Jessica rode with a groom who, riding respectfully at least twelve paces behind her, allowed her to pretend that she was alone. Surely tonight must see Lord Desmond's betrothal to Lady Olivia, for he had hinted that his was the most romantic part. Desperately she tried to come to terms with this fact, fixing her hopes far ahead to a peaceful life with Papa at the old manor. There, she would entertain her many friends while caring for his health. The library would be restored and she almost persuaded herself that this would compensate for marriage.

Yet her heart ached—not for herself, but for Lord Desmond. Suppose, even now, Olivia disappointed him?

Meantime, Grace Ashby had become a real friend.

Since Jessica's visit to The Old Manor, the two girls had met twice at soirées and withdrawn into alcoves to talk. On the first occasion Grace tried to plead her brother's cause.

"I declare, Alistair has quite lost his wits about you, Miss Court," she vowed. Jessica, who liked and trusted the Scots girl, cried,

"Oh, pray call me Jessica. Formality between girls of our age sets up such a barrier to friendship, and I so want us to be friends, Grace."

"In faith, so do I," the other girl smiled warmly. "I must confess I—I find these Southern girls so silly! Is not that disgraceful?"

"No—for I do, too. I have not met one yet whom I would trust with any confidence." Then Jessica grew serious. "But as to your delightful brother, please, *please* do not let him set his heart on me. I would not hurt him for the world only—my heart is given for all time." She blushed as she admitted this in words. Grace's eager response astonished her.

"Why, so is mine! Yet my love is hopeless, I fear. My heart was captured by the laird who lives across the water from our lands when I was scarce fifteen, and he already twenty-five. Oh, Jessica, he is so tall and handsome and always in good humor. He taught me to row on the Loch and to stalk deer up on the heather in season. How he teased me, treating me like a young sister. He liked Alistair, too, for he was lonely I think. Then he journeyed to Edinburgh and met Mistress Jean Ogilvie of the Glens." She stopped abruptly.

"Has he married her?" prompted Jessica gently.

"Not yet—but a betrothal, at least, is expected this very summer."

Deeply moved, Jessica opened her own heart in return, ending, "So we are in the same plight, Grace, and it is forlorn indeed. I shall never marry, I swear."

"Nor shall I—and I feel very guilty, for I know that Mamma has such great hopes for me this season. Oh, we have come here every year, but this is my first official debut into society and she and Papa would like me to make a fine English marriage," she sighed. "There is still

94

much feuding between the clans at home which makes a marriage more difficult."

"Perhaps you *will* meet someone," suggested Jessica.

"*Never!* No man in the world will ever match Robert."

Jessica thought of this and subsequent conversations with Grace as she dressed for the ball; it was comforting to know that the knowledge of her own unrequited love was shared by a friend so easy to talk to frankly. Yet, it was impossible to imagine anyone else in the whole world experiencing the depth of feeling she had for Lord Desmond.

When she, with Bella's assistance, had donned the embroidered brocade gown, Lady Shayne came into the room. She looked magnificent in dark blue chiffon with a beautiful tiara and bracelets of sapphires and diamonds, and she carried two flat jewellers' cases.

"From tonight you will be a fully grown up young lady, my dear, and I want you to accept two small gifts. They were presented to me by my own dear mother on my presentation, and, as I have no daughter, I wish you to have them." From the first case she drew a jewelled coronet of pearls and small diamonds, delicately wrought into small flowers and set it on Jessica's dark curls.

"Real flowers were suitable before, but now you must sparkle a little." Jessica gasped with pleasure, unable to find words immediately. Meantime, her ladyship was clasping a matching necklace around her slender neck.

"Oh, my lady, they are glorious! I declare, I feel proud as a queen!" and she embraced the older woman tenderly.

"Now, we must find you a worthy Prince Consort," cried Lady Shayne with a conviction she was far from feeling. "Your dance card for the ball has already been filled up until supper." She went on, "All day long young men or their footmen have been calling to beg for the honor! Indeed, young Alistair Ashby has claimed *two*. I find him most charming, Jessica, and Scotland, I believe, is extremely beautiful."

Jessica's smile was wistful. "And I *feel* honored indeed, but I pray you not to fill any spaces after the masque." She hastened on, "I may be tired by midnight my lady, and would not disappoint anyone for the world."

"Certainly not. Besides you will have decided yourself whom to favor after that." Neither referred to the thought uppermost in both their minds. If Lord Desmond proclaimed his betrothal they would both wish to return to Shayne—not in unseemly haste, of course.

Lady Shayne went to the door. "I shall collect my shawl and my reticule, then the carriage will be here in ten minutes."

Jessica took a last look at herself in the Cheval mirror. For the first time, she felt beautiful—not dazzling of course, but serenely confident that she was grown-up.

Lord Desmond had left long since for Lufton, with his valet and the costume for the masque carefully packed. He might or might not appear at the ball first.

Lady Shayne and Jessica edged into the wide, ornate entrance hall to the Royal Pavilion, where the Prince received his guests. It resembled a flower garden, rivalling the muted Chinese murals lining the walls. Every debutante to be presented wore her most exquisite gowns while the mothers were bedecked with priceless jewels. The men, too, were in full fig, their brocade or satin-skirted jackets heavily embroidered, fingers beringed and often rosettes on their shoes.

"We must hope that they do not get heavy partners," whispered Jessica to Lady Shayne who smiled at the girl's revived spirits.

They saw many friends and acquaintances, but the hall was packed, and it was impossible to change positions. Besides, the girls to be presented had to be in the front row. Arriving a little late, His Royal Highness appeared rather flushed and out of temper. He was alone and it was rumored that Mrs. Fitzherbert had a grippe after eating too much lobster the day before.

However, as each girl was presented and made her curtsey he murmured, "Charming, most charming." The ceremony was over and they had all come out.

The grand ballroom was bedecked with flowers and the musicians lively. By the time supper was announced, essica was flushed and laughing. She had not sat down once, and her partners had made her fulsome compliments. Only Alistair, true Scot as he was, paid her a genuine tribute.

"You remind me of our Loch at home," he said sincerely. "So deeply beautiful and unruffled, except in Winter, that I never tire of watching it. Just seeing it gives one strength—and so do you, Mistress Court."

"You are a poet, I declare, Mr. Ashby," she said lightly, but his words moved her very much. If she were heart-free she knew it would be Alistair whom she chose. He escorted her to the supper room where they were soon joined by Grace and her partner as well as other friends. Jessica was glad there were so many of them so that her growing silence would not be noticed. She was nervous as time for the masque approached.

At ten minutes to the hour Lady Shayne came to her, saying,

"Pray escort me to our seats Jessica. I understand they have been reserved for us in a good position." Jessica sprang up, glad that they would be together. A chamberlain led them to the stands that had been erected under a silken awning facing a stage so splendid it took everyone's breath away.

It was shaped like a giant half-shell, exquisitely painted so that it shimmered like mother-of-pearl. Charming conceits of small mermaids, fish, and shells were painted along the front to conceal the footlights. As soon as the Prince was seated, the whole stage was illuminated; and, drawn into view by two white ponies, came another smaller shell, far more ornate, carrying Venus-Aphrodite, goddess of love and beauty.

Olivia's appearance brought a storm of admiring applause, for indeed she looked superb: a Grecian-style gown of finest pleated silk, gathered low across her breast, clung to her figure most daringly; her thick fair hair fell loose in shining ringlets around her shoulders while a cornet of jewelled sea anemones circled her brow. She leaned back languourously against the silken cushions and, in a slightly stilted voice, commanded her handmaidens to usher in her suitors. These, representing minor

gods of Olympus, were all noblemen; and, so ove
whelmed were they by Olivia's beauty, that they spok
their pieces with real passion, accompanied by discre
music off-stage. The goddess feigned boredom until
beautiful youth in green tights, short, buckskin boots an
a leopardskin over one shoulder came to serenade he
on a golden lyre.

It was Lord Desmond as Adonis, the half-mort
with whom the goddess fell briefly in love. In a clea
tenor voice, he sang of his undying love, phrasing th
words with growing passion until Jessica clenched he
hands on her lap, and tears came to her eyes. Oh, h
must not, *could* not be denied!

The goddess stepped down from her couch and gav
him her hand, telling him he had, indeed, found favo
with her. He cast away the lyre and was about to embrac
her when, with a clap of thunder, Jupiter, the hero, spran
onto the stage. Dressed in a cloth of gold with a crow
on his head, Sir Walter Cheston looked truly god-lik
With a flick of disdain, he struck Adonis on the shoulde
forcing him to one knee, while he himself took an adorir
goddess by both hands and they sang a duet of lov
Jessica felt the tears spilling over at the naked adoratic
and pleading on Lord Desmond's face as he knelt, r
jected, to one side.

Lady Shayne reached out a gentle hand and too
her small, clenched fists in a tender grasp.

In a whisper she said, "I know—and we are bo
suffering, my dear. But we must not show it for De
mond's sake."

The masque ended in a fine wedding procession a
led by Sir Walter and Olivia, all the actors came dov
and paraded through the cheering audience. Only Oliv
got no further than the Prince who caught her bare arm.

"I declare you Goddess of the Evening," he sai
laughing. "I would be bewitched further and insist yo
remain at my side."

There was a slow surge back to the ballroom, b
the musicians had moved out onto the greensward, tur
ing the smooth grass into a dance floor more befitting tl
romantic mood. As His Highness took Olivia's arm firm

beneath the elbow and guided her to a prepared bower with footmen in attendance to pour the wine, Desmond seized Jessica's hand.

"Come Sprite, you look like a creature from Olympus, too. We will dance." He swung her into a gay valse; although her head was still swimming with emotion her feet were nimble as ever. Desmond's eyes were sparkling with excitement, and his handsome face alight.

"Was not that a splendid spectacle? Olivia excelled even herself, and I hope you have much praise for my acting? Performers need much, in faith, while the pleasure is still on them!"

"You were—perfect, my lord." Jessica managed, knowing that she could not yet manage a joyousness to match his own, much as she wished to. At first he didn't appear to notice.

"And what of poor Walter?" He threw back his head and laughed. "Was he not comical, strutting about in his gold finery and his roll of thunder? But his voice! At least two tones flat, I swear!"

"Never mind—you sang quite beautifully," Jessica assured him with a little smile. He looked at her more closely.

"Egad, Sprite, you are pale and without spirits after your gallant efforts to entertain you."

"I—am sorry indeed, my lord, for the masque was magnificent. I think perhaps the heat ... I fear the excitement of being presented, then dancing non-stop until supper has affected me a little."

A charming, laughing girl swung past them with a most inept partner, and Desmond's eyes lingered on her, answering her laugh.

"I fear you are forlorn company for once, Sprite. Pray forgive me if I abandon you this once for more amusing fare." He danced her under the trees and released her. "Here you will be cooler. May I fetch you a drink or something?" There was obvious reluctance in his offer.

"No, no—just forgive me if I let down your hopes. I did think you were the hero of the evening."

"Splendid." He left her without a backward glance, eager to pursue the merry girl who would sustain his

mood of elation. He felt almost like the beautiful paga
he had portrayed—a being straddling the world of mer
mortals. Besides, when she took his hand after his song
Olivia had pressed it with fervent admiration, and h
anticipated many jokes between them about poor Walter'
lamentable singing.

Jessica leaned against a tree, thankful to be alon
to recover her poise. She felt sad that she had faile
Desmond in this, his moment of triumph, but there ha
never been hypocrisy in their friendship (except, a little
when she managed to praise Lady Olivia). As she grew
calmer she wondered if she should seek out Lady Shayn
for she, too, had been mightily distressed. Then sh
saw her on the Pavilion's terrace, surrounded by man
of her older friends.

The dancers swirled and spun as the musician
suited their tunes to the prevailing mood of gaiety. Des
mond passed quite close by, enjoying himself hugely wit
the pretty, laughing girl who was obviously praising hir
effusively. Indeed, the chance to dance with Lord Des
mond was rare indeed since his infatuation with Olivi
made him scorn all other feminine company.

Jessica wondered: had he not seen the significance c
Olivia choosing Sir Walter as her final hero? And, i
truth, she sang little better herself than he did, but he
beauty forbade any paltry criticism. Besides, had not th
masque been her idea? True, Beau Brummell had cor
tributed a little wit, but he had not lingered on it over
long since his sophisticated taste preferred true actors.

Jessica wished with all her heart that she could retur
home to the peace of her room. There, once Bella ha
hung her fine ball gown in swathes of clean linen an
brushed her short curls, she would be undisturbed. Bu
she must wait for Lady Shayne.

She did not hear him approach on the grass until
deep voice at her shoulder said, "Ah, Sprite—that is you
name among friends, I believe. Or do you prefer th
more formal Miss Court?" It was Sir Walter who, b
moments before, she had seen dancing and flirting with
buxom partner.

"Oh! You startled me." She did not bother to answe

s to her name. What did it matter now that Lady Olivia had debased it?

"I saw you, shimmering like a golden moonbeam alone against this tree. I saw your guardian and mentor claim you for a dance immediately after our triumph. Surely you gave him the praise he craved? He will have needed it after my choice as hero to the Goddess!"

"I did my best, Sir Walter," she answered stiffly. "But I fear I am a little out of sorts this evening."

"What? When you have just emerged as one of the beauties of the season. Come now, that cannot be allowed."

"You are very kind, but I prefer to be alone and cool."

He took her arm. "We cannot allow that—not tonight. Why I, too, am a little heated, I confess, and beg your charming company for a stroll among the trees. I am heartbroken myself that royalty has stolen my Venus with whom I hoped to dance a triumphant measure, but a command from the throne—oh yes, he will attain the crown any day now—is unassailable."

Jessica had never liked Sir Walter, now she liked him even less but she saw no escape. At least she did not have to dance with him.

They moved into deeper shadows where moonlight could scarce penetrate the leaves,

"Have you no word of praise for our efforts?" he asked in a teasing, challenging voice.

"Oh, I have indeed! It was quite splendid. Lady Olivia has never looked more beautiful, I declare, and you and Lord Desmond made most fitting final suitors." She tried to keep all trace of irony from her voice, although Sir Walter would not have been aware of it.

"I planned the clap of thunder before my entrance myself," he said. "Was it not most effective?" She realized the vanity in his words. Alas, the same failing had affected Lord Desmond, too. How they besought blind admiration! Why, they were like children play-acting. Jessica felt very mature as she said,

"It set the last scene most dramatically. I declare, we almost leapt from our seats!" It seemed amusing to

pander to this mood now that she had almost gaine
control of herself.

Sir Walter was skilled—if insensitive—in handlin
women, but he guessed that a small plea for sympath
might move the girl. She did, indeed, look very beautifu
tonight.

"Surely you understand that the evening has bee
an ordeal as well? Lady Olivia keeps both Lord Desmon
and myself on tenterhooks as to which one she wil
choose?"

Jessica paused and turned to him as they came to
glade. "But surely you must both realize that nothing wil
influence her choice? I daresay she has decided already."

Turning toward him was a grave mistake as sh
realized a moment too late.

Without warning Sir Walter held her in a vice-lik
embrace, his face exultant.

"Then, since the Prince has already deprived me o
a Goddess tonight, and you think I may be baulked of he
in the end, in truth I will sample the delights of a dark
eyed angel by moonlight." His full, red mouth came dow
on hers with such demanding force that she would hav
fallen backward but for his arms. She tried to raise he
hands to beat him off, but she was powerless as he savore
her sweet lips again and again.

At last, slightly breathless and laughing, he release
her, leaving her dazed with shock, her hands going swiftl
to her bruised mouth.

"There! At least I believe I have awakened a Vesta
Virgin. Tell me, are you glad?"

Furious, her great eyes burning with hatred sh
exclaimed, "Most certainly I am *not,* Sir Walter. You ar
a savage and I—I *hate* you!"

"Gad, how pitifully dull you virtuous creatures are!"
he chuckled scornfully, and, with a swagger, he strolle
back through the trees to the dancing.

Tears of anger blinded her for a few moments and
filled with helpless outrage, she beat her hands against
tree as if it were his loathsome face. Then, fearing to
meet any of the revellers in her present state, she turne

102

d ran, blessedly finding a side gate and running on until
he came among the carriages. Since they knew they would
ot be summoned for an hour or more, the drivers were
rouped around a long table talking and laughing as they
uaffed ale that had been brought to them.

Swift and silent as a shadow, Jessica sped until she
ound Lady Shayne's carriage and leaped in, huddling
own in the far corner where she would not be seen.

Slowly she quieted down and began to think clearly.
Vith her deep sense of honesty she was forced to admit
ow different it would have been if Desmond in his
xulted state had kissed her in that fierce, possessive way.
[ow she would have responded willingly, in spite of
ruised lips, urging him on to greater passion even know-
ag it meant nothing to him. For Sir Walter *had*
wakened her as a woman—shown her how child-like
er girlish dreams had been of passion between men and
romen. But that it should have been him, of all men on
arth, made her hate him even more. For to gratify a
elfish whim he had stolen something rare and precious
—her very first kiss—and against her will.

But from that moment on she determined to behave
ke a woman—to make herself desirable, mysterious, and
little unattainable like Olivia herself. Only not with
ruelty—never that—for, if she could not win Desmond
hen she wanted no man at all. At least not as a husband.
Iature men took pleasure in the company of a wise,
ritty woman as a companion, and this she determined
o achieve.

Exhausted by the whole eventful evening, Jessica
eant back against the luxurious upholstery and fell into a
ght, restful doze.

The jangling of bits and movement of the horses
tartled her awake, for the carriages had been summoned
o line up at the main entrance. She flew into a panic.
.ady Shayne might be searching for her; indeed, it had
een most thoughtless not to seek her out and reassure
er before seeking refuge in the carriage. But Jessica
arried no mirror in her reticule and she could not have
raved the brilliant lighting on the terrace in what she felt

sure was a dishevelled, bruised condition after Sir Walter'
onslaught. Now, she sat well forward watching for he
ladyship.

But it was Desmond who threw open the door o
the carriage and cried over his shoulder, "She is safe an
sound here, Mother. Far from flying off to fairy realms
the Sprite has played the dormouse in your carriage."
There was relief as well as teasing in his voice, for h
had, indeed, felt a certain guilt at deserting Jessica as in
different company after his triumph.

Lady Shayne came up, all concern: "My dear chil
—are you all right?"

"I am indeed, my lady, and should have told yo
my intention. But I saw you among friends on the terrac
and, I confess, so much dancing before the magnificen
masque left me exhausted after the excitement of makin
my royal debut."

Lady Shayne entered the carriage, searching Jessica'
face anxiously. It was still in shadow.

"You are not ill, are you?"

"Indeed, no, Lady Shayne; I declare your carriage i
so comfortable I fell asleep! Is it not shameful at m
age?"

Surprising both of them, Desmond climbed in afte
them.

"I have despatched my valet with my valises in m
own carriage. I declare I want the company of my famil
after such a night!" It was evident that he was stil
excited, but first he was solicitous to Jessica, too.

"I did you a grave wrong, Sprite. I now realize tha
your unusual quietness in the dance meant that you wer
still spellbound by our performance."

Jessica had retired to her dark corner where her fac
could not be seen as they drove along the lighted prome
nade.

"I was, in truth, my lord. I admired your voice onc
when you joined me, but after such a success I shall neve
dare ask you to sing a duet with me!" Her voice wa
light, flippant, in the manner in which she had decide
to continue.

Desmond laughed: "I think you are still bemused with sleep. I shall enjoy singing with you at any time."

Lady Shayne caught the girl's hand, finding it cold. "Are you sure you have not caught a chill, dear Jessica? The evening has grown a little cold."

"No, no, Lady Shayne. I was simply tired and this carriage seemed a perfect refuge."

Lord Desmond said, "If you have a rheum we shall swiftly cure it, I vow. I am so full of spirits we shall go riding as usual in the morning, Sprite."

It was difficult to maintain her new sense of womanhood in face of the invitation she had so often longed for, but Jessica managed to say coolly:

"If I may, I will send word by my maid in the morning. I confess I am still more than a little tired even now."

Lord Desmond was surprised and somewhat disconcerted. He was so used to his Sprite springing to accept all his demands that he could not understand the change in her. Lady Shayne stepped in, tactfully,

"By my faith, Desmond, even you can hardly summon a girl newly presented at a ball to be ready to ride at your early hours! Jessica has just passed one of the most memorable nights of her life."

"Oh, very well. I will await a message, but only until eight o'clock!"

"My lord, are you not tired yourself?" asked Jessica curiously. "It must be past two o'clock."

"Tired?" The excitement in his voice mounted. "How can I be weary when so much lies ahead? Oh, I declare I have the most sensational news to impart. Olivia has been named The Queen of Misrule to preside over the revels two weeks hence. It seems she had bewitched His Highness tonight and he has given her *carte blanche* to decree whatever delights she wishes."

"And what *does* she wish?" inquired Lady Shayne.

"The most brilliant plan ever brought to Court," he chuckled. "Indeed, Prinny himself seemed stunned at first, for she has ordained a fayre and a tournament to be held between all the courtiers who wish to enter the lists! Such a sight has not been seen at Court for several hundred years. There will be no lack of contestants, I swear, for Olivia herself will preside in her guise as Queen and present the prize."

"You mean—fighting on horseback?" questioned Jessica, horrified at the barbarous idea.

"Oh, not seriously. No, we are to dress as they did in Medieval times with our horses finely caparisoned, the cloths bearing the arms of our houses and decked with silver harness. Contestants will wear light, mock armour with tabards and, of course, fine, plumed helmets."

"But surely you will not use lances and battle-axes?"

Desmond laughed, "Of course not. Olivia commands that we use only poles, gaily beribboned, with which to joust and try to unseat our rivals; each man who is toppled to the ground will be eliminated until only the two champions are left to compete for the prize. I declare, it will be fine sport indeed."

"And what is the prize to be?" Lady Shayne's voice held no color for she feared the answer.

"That is what makes it so intriguing," said Desmond eagerly. "Olivia herself will award it to the winner, but she insists it shall be a secret until she does."

It will be her hand in marriage, thought both the women in the carriage; and Jessica sensed that it would only be awarded if the champion proved to be her favorite choice. Was there no end to her schemes for pitting her suitors one against the other to please her own vanity? For what a spectacle it would be, indeed—Olivia queening it over the proceedings while Knights in splendid array jousted for her favor.

"I shall ride Hercules, of course." Lord Desmond was lost in his dreams of the great day. "He responds to my every thought and how fine he will look, caparisoned in the Shayne colors of emerald, scarlet, and gold! I swear the very sight of him will daunt all my rivals," he laughed in soft contentment, picturing the scene.

"I take it you will need the services of all my sewing women?" asked Lady Shayne a trifle dryly.

"Of course, Mother—I want the full coat of arms of our house embroidered on either side of the saddle cloth and on my tabard, naturally."

"Two weeks is not long for such fine work, I had better give them orders tomorrow. Now, speak no more of it tonight, I pray, for I am tired." Lady Shayne sounded quite drained of strength, and the carriage fell silent. She had braced herself to emerge from her quiet life to guide Jessica through the season, but she had not reckoned on Lady Olivia's extravagant, ridiculous schemes to upset her whole household.

Perhaps Desmond, who was a sensitive man to mood, felt that somehow he had failed both women by his self-engrossment. In fact, he had quite forgot that Jessica had made her debut as a young woman tonight, and he felt ashamed.

So, having helped them both to alight at Shayne Park, he kept hold of Jessica's hand, and, once in the hall, he stepped back to survey her in the light.

"Sprite, I have been very selfish. Pray forgive me if you can, for, of course, tonight was highly special for you, too." He eyed her from head to foot, attributing her pallor to weariness. His smile was warm and filled with approval.

"You look absolutely lovely." She warmed to his sincerity and ultimate kindness. How could she help it when his eyes were frank in their admiration? "How does it feel to be a young lady? Will you leave fairyland in favor of the real world now?"

"In faith, my lord, I wish I knew fairyland." Her voice was wistful. "But as I do not, I think this world is delightful." She turned to Lady Shayne and held out both her slim hands. "My lady, I do not know how to thank you for all your thought and kindness—and your magnificent gifts which make me feel quite royal indeed!"

Lady Shayne drew her into her arms as she would have drawn a daughter, for had they not shared suffering together that night as well as royal recognition and lavish display?

"Dearest Jessica, you have more than justified all my faith in you. Tomorrow, of course, the masque will be the talk of Brighton; but then thoughts will turn to the debutantes who are to play such a large part in the season, and I warrant you will head the favored lists of many hostesses." She kissed her gently. "Now I intend to retire, and, for once, I shall order a light breakfast in my room." She turned to her son and smiled. "You did splendidly, Desmond, and your song was quite charming. I declare, I have every right to be extremely proud of both my children."

She swept up the stairs, although Jessica sensed a slight weariness in her usually light step. Jessica made to follow but once again Desmond caught her hand,

"Will you not stay and celebrate a while with me, Sprite? I am so filled with zest and excitement I know I cannot sleep."

Jessica was sorely tempted, but it would mean taking wine, and, after that, a stroll under the moon on the terrace while Desmond rehearsed the miracles of Lady Olivia. He might even kiss her, needing a release for his exuberance; but to her a touch of those beloved lips would mean so much more—so unforgettably much more. She released her hand.

"I fear I must disappoint you, my lord. I confess that my own nervousness at being presented, followed by a whirl of dancing before your—your *magnificent* performance—has worn me out for once." She hoped that, at least, this praise would satisfy him. He protested only a little.

"Sprite—is it really such an ordeal to emerge from the cocoon of girlhood to full woman's status? We men have no such transition so, pray understand, I cannot comprehend exactly what it means."

"It is the greatest ordeal I have ever faced," said Jessica frankly, and she managed a slight laugh. "All day long one is anxious that the curtsey to His Highness will be just so, that one's gown will please members of the ton." Then she added quickly, "Though I should have trusted your dear mother in every particular, for she chose my gown and gave me this superb necklace and coronet which proved to be in such perfect taste." She held out one hand and met his eyes. "So, you see, I have a double debt to pay the Shayne family: to you, for bringing me here, teaching me to ride and then honoring me with your friendship—and to your mother whose tender care I can *never* repay."

She released her hand and went up two stairs before she summoned the strength to turn and smile over her shoulder.

"Your performance tonight was perfection, my lord, and I know you will sleep well for tomorrow you must start practicing with Hercules for the tournament. Good night."

Seven

Jessica had a bad night tortured by nightmares—Olivia, Sir Walter, Desmond all jumbled together in chaos. Glad to wake at seven-thirty, she rose from bed although she was still exhausted; but with the nightmares hovering around her mind, she could not bear to try and sleep again. Sleep was her enemy for the time being and the beautiful, luxurious bed, a thing of dread. Suddenly she remembered—she could ride with Desmond! Although, if he had stayed up alone to drink more wine, he might well sleep late.

She took off her nightgown and sponged her face and body with cold water which proved wonderfully reviving. Careful scrutiny in the mirror assured her that Sir Walter's violent kisses had, in fact, left no physical mark—although the hate and anger still scarred her mind. Perhaps the memory of his rape of her virginal lips always would remain—it had been such a cruel awakening to womanhood.

But all her determination to become cool and distant

had vanished. She could not be anything but herself, for wiles and delicate deception were not in her nature.

She dressed in her riding habit, took up her gloves and the light, ivory-handled whip Desmond had given her, and met a round-eyed, shocked Bella at the door bringing her tray of breakfast.

"Miss Jessica!" she gasped. "Why did you not ring for me? Here, you've had no hot water, no coffee or the perfect omelette Cook prepared herself, personally. We all felt sure you would lie late abed like her ladyship."

Jessica gave her a dazzling smile of gratitude. "You are so good to me, Bella, but I declare I could not touch even a morsel at this hour. I shall ride with Lord Desmond; is he up?"

"Indeed he is, Miss. 'Ringing his bell and carrying on like a man possessed,' so Mr. Chalmers said when he came down to fetch his breakfast. Quite put about, is Mr. Chalmers, I can tell you!"

"Never mind, Bella—a long ride will set his temper to rights." Her smile took on a roguish twist. "And I have an idea! *You* sit here and consume that delicious omelette —for you will not be disturbed—then you can convey my praises to the cook."

Bella blushed—though tempted. "Oh, 'twould not be honest, Miss, and the downstairs servants are sure to report that you are gone out."

"Risk it, Bella. It looks a great deal too good to go untasted." And Jessica sped away for her small fob-watch showed one minute to eight, and Desmond would not wait one minute past the appointed time.

For Bella's sake she avoided meeting any of the servants and slipped out through the side door. But, when she reached the stables, an astonishing sight met her eyes. Far from mounting Hercules and setting forth, Desmond was in close consultation with his senior grooms. When he caught sight of her, his face lighted up. "Sprite! You have overcome your weariness and strange moods. Indeed, you look a bit fresher than I feel. I need your help."

Jessica's smile was radiant as the morning itself. Indeed the resilience of her young body, stimulated by the cold water seemed, to her, a miracle. All thought of weariness and memories of the nightmares had fled.

"My lord, this is a change, I declare—and a most welcome one. Until now it has always been you who has helped me, pray what can I do in return?"

"It is this pesky tournament," he admitted, his humor still very out of sorts. "I am determined to become the champion; and, last night, it sounded so simple from Olivia's lips—jousting with blunted, harmless poles—more like children than noblemen expert in horsemanship—but I fancy there is much more to it if one is not to be humiliated and unseated at the first thrust. You often have your nose in books, pray return to the library and seek out information on how the whole business was conducted in Medieval times."

"Gladly, my lord. I hope there may be a text book on the art—for art I know it was in those times. Forgive me if I take a little time, for the book with such information will scarce be a one recently read!"

"Take all day, if need be," Desmond's smile was grateful. "Whether we start training today or tomorrow will make little difference. There are still two weeks. Why, it took me scarce that long to break in Hercules—a raw colt at the time—to obey my wishes." The frown was rapidly disappearing from his brow. As she turned to go he said, "You are a true friend, Sprite, and I declare you and the manual shall be my trainers!"

It was a splendid tribute and Jessica prayed with all her heart that, somewhere in the vast library, she might find what was needed.

The search proved to be long and arduous, but fortunately the library had been catalogued. Jessica removed her riding jacket, set the French windows wide on the warm, sunny morning, and settled to her task. As she feared, there was no text book on jousting, but her scholarly education had taught her how to survey the numerous history books for facts, and, after nearly three hours, she was rewarded. A famous joust between two nobles had been thought worth recording in some detail since it affected valuable land and property which had been wagered.

Carrying the heavy volume to the writing table, Jessica proceeded to note down all the important information about the tournament: the correct rules, the thrust and parry, the way a long lance should be carried (and she thanked Heaven that Desmond would meet nothing more lethal than a pole), and the moment when, if both sides were unseated, it was permissible to carry on the struggle between the two contestants.

When she had finished, she found, with surprise, that it was time for luncheon, and she was famished. Desmond strolled in through the windows, and, when she showed him her work, he was delighted.

"Sprite, you may be mortal, but I swear you have provided a magical answer to my problems." Then, as he read on his furrowed brow, "Egad, though, I was right, there is a great deal more to a joust than I had realized. I will keep your notes, if I may, and learn more of the sport. Come, now, we must not keep my mother waiting for luncheon."

He opened the library door for her, and they both stood amazed at the sight of the hall. A large piece of thick, white cloth was spread out on the floor while six sewing maids crouched around the edges, carefully tracing out the Shayne coat of arms on both sides. Presiding over them was Mrs. Gieves, the head sewing woman at Shayne Park who had been with the family for half a century and still excelled at superb embroidery. When she caught sight of Desmond she came up to him.

"Ha, my lord—a fine task you've set me, I declare. I had to hire three extra maids for the fortnight to make sure your faradiddle will be done in time. As to yourself, your Lady Mother says you need a tabard to wear as well. I declare I never heard such an outlandish word." She was grumpy, and, having known Desmond since he was born and embroidered all his baby clothes, felt no need for undue deference. To her the whole affair—not to mention the amount of work—seemed like boyish foolishness, just to show off for one afternoon.

Lord Desmond put an arm around her shoulder and spoke with affection. "Dear Mrs. Gieves, you know you cannot be angry with me for long—I declare, it does seem a deal of work, but you will have it done to perfection as you always do. Besides, this tournament is far from a prank. It may well win me the bride of my heart and think what delight *that* will give you!"

Mrs. Gieves could not resist smiling up at him. "Oh, my Lord, you and your wily ways! I swear you could charm the birds off the trees!"

"No—but I promise to come to you straight after luncheon to explain the tabard; it is very simple—just a short tunic bearing our arms on the breast. You will do it yourself, won't you? Your exquisite stitches have always brought me luck."

She smiled broadly. "You and your fine tongue, my Lord," she said.

He and Jessica found Lady Shayne already seated at the table. Her eyes were still shadowed with weariness, and she received her son coolly.

"Well, Desmond, you see how you have put about my household! I declare the girls will have to work for some days in the hall since the sewing room is too small. Pray tell Lady Olivia to organize no such nonsense in the future!"

He was not used to being criticized on all sides, and his ill humor threatened to return. Jessica stepped in quickly.

"Dear Lady Shayne, pray be not too distressed. We are surely all still weary after last night, and the splendid work being done is surely for the honor of Shayne itself. Why, when Lord Desmond rides out at the tournament he will outshine all the other nobles, and you will be the proudest spectator there. Besides—though I would not presume—it occurred to me while watching all the maids at work out there, that craft need not be wasted on one day's events; surely the embroidered caparison for Hercules will make a beautiful bedcover in the future. An historic one, too, when Lord Desmond is victorious! Think how proud his eldest son will be to display this fine trophy in his room, and pass it on to his sons in turn!"

At last Lady Shayne smiled. "What a comfort you are, Jessica! I declare I had not thought ahead at all— and it will smooth down poor Mrs. Gieves who regards all the work as being done for frivolous ends. But an heir loom! That will inspire her since she is as much a part of Shayne Park now as the very house itself!"

Desmond smiled his gratitude, and luncheon passed off easily, although no one had much appetite. Jessica had felt hungry in the library, but that had passed.

"Will you not rest this afternoon, my lady?" she asked after they had eaten some of the delicious hot house peaches. "If any callers come they will only be foolish young men, and I shall turn them away. I swear I am in no mood myself to receive dancing partners who presume. They should know that we are tired."

"But some friends of mine—useful to you, my dear as hostesses, may call," said her ladyship doubtfully.

"I refuse to have your well-being disturbed today," replied Jessica firmly. "Besides, I swear they will all be taking a rest after last night themselves. Come, let me take you to your room."

Desmond grinned. "I can see, Sprite, that you will make me win this tournament and my mother overcome the disruption of her household. You are a small champion in yourself!"

"Wait until I begin drilling you in the rules of joust ing tomorrow morning," she laughed, but her heart had been deeply touched by their gratitude and, yes, curious dependence on her strength during this difficult time. Encouraging Lady Shayne to lean on her arm for once Jessica escorted her to her room and summoned her per sonal maid.

The Prince was enjoying himself hugely, laying ou plans for the fayre and tournament. It was to be held in a spacious parkland not far from the Pavilion, and his extravagant tastes were given full rein. He set an architec and a bevy of designers to copy, as closely as possible, the original scene of such an event in the sixteenth century with silken tents, flying pennants and splendid temporary sta bles. He had been warned by his chancellor that the com mon people resented his lavish spending at court—for which they were taxed when necessary—so he decided that the fayre should be thrown open for the public to enjoy. There would be stalls attended ·by pretty girls in mob caps, a *Punch and Judy* show, a small roundabout to amuse the children and free ale.

"They cannot grumble if they are encouraged to enjoy our royal amusements. They may even watch the tourney if they are cordoned off at a good distance from the royal tent." He gave a throaty laugh and coughed mightily. "By my troth, loyal citizens en masse throw up a vile stench. Do they never wash?"

"We had no choice but to put a tax on water last year, Sire," replied the chancellor drily.

"Then, damn, repeal it, man, repeal it if only for that week. Besides, surely they have the sea—and rivers," grumbled the Prince whose dyspepsia was troubling him that day. "By gad, have they no imagination?"

He promptly turned his attention to the more enjoyable features of the festival day. At least when he became King—for the old Monarch was fading fast—he would be surrounded by even higher barriers to protect from the populace who paid for his luxuries.

Meantime, the days at Shayne Park were full of activity. The splendid caparison for Hercules and the tabard were filling with glowing color as the girls plied their needles from dawn till dusk. Out of doors the training of both Hercules and Lord Desmond went apace. He had sent to court to obtain the length of the jousting course, and this had been pegged out on the broad, flat meadow beyond the stables. Jessica was there every day with her notes until the point where she said,

"Surely you now need a worthy opponent, my lord. It is too easy to thrust your pole at thin air, for I warrant it will take some severe blows from other contestants."

Desmond considered this carefully, then, with a nod he looked around the stables. He caught the eager, hopeful glance of two bright blue eyes in a young, weatherbeaten face. Brian was the son of the senior groom and had worked as a stable lad under him for several years, his passion for horses far outstripping his interest in book learning. He was a natural born rider, too, and his ambition was to become a jockey.

Desmond grinned. "All right, young Brian, I'll let

you have first try—though if you unseat me I warrant it will be your last!" He laughed, and the boy joined in,

"I swear I could never unseat you, my lord, but I have watched your practicing and believe I can put up a fair opposition."

His father clouted him playfully for pushing himself forward, but secretly he was proud of the lad.

It was arranged that Brian should mount the other stallion who came nearest to Hercules in speed and weight. It was a horse he always groomed and that knew him well. Filled with suppressed excitement, Brian mounted and followed his master to the practice ground, one of the spare poles gripped expertly in his hand for he had, indeed, watched and listened to every detail of jousting.

Jessica, her notes now no longer needed since they all knew every word by heart, gave the signal to start. Grooms clustered to watch with excitement and curiosity. On the first charge Brian was a little nervous, and the blow from Lord Desmond was so fierce it cracked his pole. Another was swiftly supplied. The contest grew exhilarating. Brian managed to break two of the poles wielded by his lordship and Lord Desmond cried,

"You were right, Sprite! Working against an opponent is vastly different from tilting at thin air; I vow none of the contestants at the tournament will have learnt the art so well and certainly none, not even Sir Walter, could find a worthier opponent!"

Brian flushed with pleasure. He had never enjoyed himself so much in his life. The morning passed in a flash and, with much regret, Lord Desmond returned to the stables; he and Jessica must not be late for luncheon and the grooms went home to good, cooked meals prepared by their wives. Besides, Hercules had put in a noble morning's effort and must not be exhausted before the great event itself.

"Right, we start again tomorrow morning at eight sharp—and if your muscles ache, Brian, as I swear they will, remember it is all good training for the fine rider you promise to be."

Lord Desmond and Jessica found the hall at Shayne Park cleared of sempstresses and all signs of their work.

Lady Shayne explained, "They are doing so well under Mrs. Gieves firm guidance that we decided the rest of the embroidery could be accommodated in a less inconvenient place. Now, my dears," she continued, leading the way to the dining room, "you must not be so caught up with this ridiculous tournament that you forget your social duties. Tonight, remember, we are all bidden to the Duchess's ball; and, I declare, 'twill be a magnificent affair with all the *Beau Monde* in attendance—if not the Prince himself." Desmond frowned, and Jessica looked taken aback. Indeed she had been so engrossed in the practicing she had almost forgotten the social side of life for a debutante. Now she felt contrite—she owed Lady Shayne so much and turned to her enthusiastically:

"Pray, my lady, will you select the gown I should wear? Your taste on each grand occasion so far has been unerring and I dare not trust to my own choice."

Lady Shayne smiled affectionately. "Dear Jessica, Bella and I have been occupied this past hour on that very matter, and all is prepared. I think the new white satin sheath overlaid with finest muslin embroidered with small posies of rhinestones will suit the occasion perfectly; it is so young and fresh and will go well with your coronet and necklace. Bella has put out your white satin shoes and your gold to see which you favor most for comfort—for, I swear, the dancing will continue 'til at least three o'clock in the morning."

Lord Desmond groaned, "Am I, too, expected to dance all night? I declare, Mother, that a token appearance on my part will satisfy Her Grace. You may call the tournament all the scornful words you can find, but, to me it is of prime concern. I will *not* dally with foolish young girls for hours at the expense of my training."

"Why, Desmond." Lady Shayne had a glint in her eye. "Did you not know that Olivia Lufton is to be one of the guests?"

Jessica's heart sank, while Desmond's eye brightened. "I am surprised she has not informed me, but I shall ride over to the castle this afternoon to claim as many dances as she will grant me."

He made no offer to put his name on Jessica's card,

but, slowly and painfully, she was coming to accept the inevitable. All her gallant efforts every morning were designed to help her one true love to win the lady of his choice.

That evening Lady Shayne surveyed her two children —for she had long accepted Jessica as a daughter—with pride and pleasure. Jessica looked quite ephemeral in her pure white gown—as though she might vanish at midnight as Cinderella had in the legendary folk tale. Lord Desmond was splendid indeed in embroidered dark green satin and knee breeches with diamond buckles on his shoes.

"I am blessed indeed," exclaimed her ladyship. "I wager that no other member of the ton will accompany such a striking young couple."

They set off for the summer home occupied by the Duchess. It had extensive grounds and, from quite a distance, they could see the brilliant lights and long parade of carriages.

"I had not thought to feel nervous again," whispered Jessica, "but—this appears even grander than the Royal Pavilion itself!"

"Oh, it is," said Desmond. "Her Grace and the Prince are locked in rivalry for splendor! They miss no chance to outdistance each other—although once he achieves the throne all honors are bound to go to him."

The ball was held in a marquee of a gigantic size to accommodate the five hundred guests. Parquet flooring had been laid over the short grass to protect the ladies' delicate slippers from green stains; light wire baskets, gilded and filled with hothouse blooms hung overhead; and there were twice the number of musicians who had played at the royal ball.

The Duchess received them graciously, dressed in magenta satin almost covered by diamonds.

As the Shayne party moved on Jessica whispered to Desmond,

"I swear, if I ever attain position and riches, I will not grow *fat!* How do all these prominent people achieve such girth?"

"Rising at noon and consuming sweetmeats and

port," he chuckled. Then he caught sight of Lady Olivia, her shining fair head crowned with a tiara, surrounded by a rainbow-clad bevy of would-be partners. He hurried to join her. She had been in a teasing mood that afternoon when he called and granted him but three dances during the evening.

"You forget, Lord Desmond, the season at Brighton attracts many new faces including foreign noblemen," Olivia had chided him. "Perchance I shall discover an Italian casanova—what a divertissement *that* might be! So I will not be trammelled by old, familiar friends."

Taking her card, Desmond noted with annoyance that Sir Walter had been before him and already claimed the supper dance.

"I see you have already bestowed the best dance of the night elsewhere. Walter must have been an early visitor. Is he not practicing for your tournament?"

As soon as he had spoken so rashly, carried away by pique, he regretted it. Lady Olivia lifted limpid blue eyes to his in astonishment.

"You mean that you are taking my revel *seriously?*" she laughed in mocking delight. "Come, Lord Desmond, it is but a splendid jape we shall all enjoy! Why, I have not even decided on the prize—some costly bauble from the castle, most likely."

Desmond looked at her seriously, "I have a different impression—that you intend the prize to be priceless—yourself."

Lady Olivia's gaze matched his own in solemnity. "You mean that I am worth jousting for?" she asked with seeming innocence.

"I would brave a hundred Crusades if you were waiting for me after hard-won victory, Lady Olivia."

Instantly she resumed her joking tone. "La, but it would be fine sport to have knights fighting for their lady's favor! Perhaps I should revise my thoughts on the prize—and I shall certainly reproach Walter for his lack of diligence."

Desmond was rarely dissatisfied with himself but, as he rode home that afternoon he was furious that he had alerted his bitter rival. Walter Cheston was as fine a horseman as he, and, if he, too, practiced for the bout it would be a bitter confrontation indeed.

He dressed for the ball with extreme care, determined to gain Lady Olivia's favor. Now, he approached the group surrounding her with a proprietary air as he announced: "Gentlemen, I must claim my first dance with the Lady Olivia." They fell back.

As he enclosed her in his arms for a valse he, in turn, teased, "Well, have you found your casanova, Olivia? Surely, if you have he should enlist in your tournament too?"

She shrugged her shapely shoulders. "All fops, Desmond. It was a girlish fantasy." Indeed, she thought, he looked very fine indeed, and Shayne Park, with a faithful husband, tempted her.

Sir Walter, meantime, watched Jessica enter the marquee. By jove, but she was enough to tempt the Devil himself! That glimmering, virginal gown surmounted by the proud set of glowing dark eyes and her dark head roused great desire—perhaps because, unlike Lady Olivia, she was totally unaware of her power to attract. Of course his interest was not serious. He needed the ruthlessness of Lady Olivia and her mature, witty cruelty, so like his own, to keep him enthralled; but he remembered the sweetness of Jessica's rebellious lips and determined to experience them again.

He approached her now, standing beside Lady Shayne and looking slightly dazed by the large crowd among whom it was difficult to see her friends at first. Seizing the opportunity, Sir Walter made a small, courteous bow to Lady Shayne and then asked Jessica to dance.

She hesitated, hating the thought of such proximity, but Lady Shayne, who knew nothing of Jessica's ordeal during the royal ball, smiled.

"You are highly honored, my dear. Sir Walter is a leader among the ton."

Reluctantly, Jessica moved into his arms, holding herself straight and taut, as far from him as was possible. He laughed down at her,

122

"Oh come, Miss Court—you are not still angry with me? I did not think to hurt you, you know. I thought it was every girl's dream to be kissed at her first ball."

"Not when she is unwilling, I assure you," she said coolly. "Besides you are betraying Lady Olivia for whom you profess such deep affection. She is watching us even now."

"Then come just outside on to the terrace. Oh, do not worry, I swear I have no ill intentions! It is brightly lit and I wish to apologize and make my peace with you in the correct manner." His eyes mocked her, but his hand under her elbow was commanding. They were close to an entrance to the marquee; and, just beyond, lay one of the terraces leading down from the house. He had not lied—it *was* brilliantly lit and edged with flowers in tubs, above all there were no pathways leading to more private places, only great stretches of lawn lay beyond. All the same, Jessica did not trust him.

"Pray say what it is you wish to say, Sir Walter. We are in full view of the dancers as they pass, and I wish to return as quickly as possible."

Highly amused, he made a melodramatic gesture, fell to one knee and clasped his hands together as if in supplication.

"I crave forgiveness, Miss Court—although I admit no sin. May we at least be friends? I warrant I now know you more—closely—than any man here."

Unfortunately, Olivia passed just then and saw them together. Jessica could see Olivia making her way toward them, and, thoroughly nervous of this display which could be so misread, declared,

"Please do not be so childish, sir; you will make me a laughing stock, and yourself also. Get up!" It was a peremptory order and he rose.

"Am I then forgiven?"

"Oh yes—anything, if only you will return into the marquee. I need a minute to collect myself after such a —a display. Pray go."

Laughing, he did, and Jessica sank on to a white, wrought iron seat trying to regain her composure. How *could* this man make mock of her in public? Had he no shame for his previous importunity? And who might not have seen this petty scene?

"Ha! So you are already dissatisfied with younger men and think to rise above your station?" Olivia answered the unspoken fear. Her eyes were cold as flint as she looked down at Jessica with distaste. "Well, I assure you, you have incurred my great dislike—no, I despise you—for the scene I witnessed just now! How *dare* you attempt to lure a man of Sir Walter's age and standing with your sly ways?" She was fanning the flames of her annoyance—jealous flames, for the whole world knew that Sir Walter was at *her* feet. "I believe your boring air of innocence and naiveté is no more than a pose! I swear you are no more than—than a common *doxy,* sprung from nowhere, determined to tempt men of great fortune with your schemes!"

Her cheeks flaming, Jessica stood up and faced this heated tirade with furious dignity,

"It is you who are common, for all your wealth and position, my *lady!*" Her young voice held withering scorn. " 'Twas but a jape you saw out here. I loathe Sir Walter and pity you for favoring him as you do; but you are right, I am young and gullible, while you are considerably older and must feel forced to snatch a suitable husband before it is too late!" She swept past Olivia into the marquee, leaving that young woman biting her lips in uncontrollable rage. No one, ever, had addressed her in such abusive fashion. She must be revenged! Suddenly, the perfect way presented itself: suppose, although he was not her final choice, she accepted Lord Desmond this very evening? She fell to pacing about and musing. Yes, it was obvious from the way she looked at him that this upstart, Jessica Court, idolized the earl. Olivia's lips curled into a vicious smile as evil plans coursed through her mind. Yet—perhaps there might be an even more perfect way to injure the wretched girl. Yes, she must talk with Sir Walter. The very traits in her character which matched his own, especially cruelty, were the magnet which drew her to him time and time again.

Desmond, who had seen the two women on the terrace, waylaid Jessica as she returned to the ball.

"I saw you with Lady Olivia. Dare I hope she was befriending you, Sprite? 'Twould be my dearest wish."

Jessica had recovered neither her composure nor her self-control after two such very unpleasant incidents.

"No, my lord, I fear we were quarrelling."

"*Quarrelling?*" He stared at her in disbelief. "But on what account? Why, Olivia's heart is pure gold—and you have the most charming nature I have ever encountered. What began such a misunderstanding?"

"Why not ask her, Lord Desmond? I am not in the habit of gossip." And she left him staring after her as she disappeared amid the throng toward the Ashbys whom she had just seen. Desmond made instantly for the terrace, much disturbed. In spite of his great courage, he was an idealist and a dreamer, too. Knowing little of woman's true nature, he had felt so positive that Olivia, when once his wife, would soon come to love his Sprite and that she would be their most welcome guest at any time.

But Sir Walter was there before him. Together, arms loosely linked, they were walking away toward the smooth lawns, their heads together as if in conspiracy.

Alistair Ashby was enchanted when Jessica appeared beside the family group and eagerly declared,

"I scarce dared to hope for a dance, Miss Court! But —may I?"

Jessica smiled and shook her head. "Not just yet. I—I am still a little confused by so many strangers, I should prefer the company of friends and, perhaps, an ice? Or is it too early to seek refreshment?"

"Of course not," said Grace, sensing that her friend had been seriously distressed by something. "We shall all go to the buffet for, I confess, I enjoy smaller gatherings myself. And there are so many older, important people here. Why, you were surely dancing with the great Sir Walter, Jessica? Pray, is he as charming as our cousin, Olivia, would have us believe?"

A small shiver passed down Jessica's spine, but she

125

replied lightly: "I do not find him so. Indeed I—I rather dislike him—is that not shocking?"

"No," said Grace with her Scottish candor. "For I do not care much for his manner, either, although I have scarce spoken to him." Chattering of other things they made their way to the buffet.

Desmond sat on the terrace alone, feeling vaguely uneasy. What had made him think that Olivia and Walter were conspiring something between them. Was it not natural that they should walk in the gardens? But no, something had definitely suggested the hateful word "conspiracy" for, had they been indulging in light banter, Olivia's head would have been high and he would have heard laughter. Was she plotting something unpleasant for Jessica? It would be very unkind to wreak revenge on a young girl over an innocent feminine tiff.

He must find Jessica and force her to tell him what the quarrel had been about. Otherwise he would not be able to help her. He dallied a moment longer, surprised how protective he felt over his Sprite, and a little shocked, too, at his disloyal suspicions of his great love. But, yes, her tendency to be unkind when roused was something he must always consider if they were to become husband and wife.

Back in the marquee, Desmond saw Jessica dancing and laughing with young Ashby; she seemed neither perturbed nor unduly put about by her scene with Olivia. All the same, he must know what had passed between them.

As the music ended Desmond went up to her.

"Sprite, I am finding this ball dull fare. Will you rescue me for a little while from boredom?"

"Why, of course, my lord." She smiled but her eyes looked at him with a hint of anxiety. He had been smiling but now his handsome face was serious, and she knew he was going to press her about the quarrel. With her whole heart she longed to tell him—disclose Sir Walter's disgraceful behavior and the horrible accusations Lady Olivia had hurled at her. But, at whatever cost—and it might be high—her lips must remain sealed. Desmond already disliked Sir Walter, and her disclosures could only

126

turn dislike to loathing, and that must not be. Besides, she thought bitterly, if Desmond accused his lady of using such abusive language, she was sophisticated enough to twist it and, finally, turn it against Jessica.

Enmity, open hatred between the two prime con-testants, might so easily turn the light jousting into something extremely ugly. Suppose they finally fought viciously to inflict injury, as knights of old had done? Sir Walter, she sensed, was not above playing foul while Desmond, whatever the fires within him at the time, would always fight fair, so he would be the victim.

As Desmond led her to a quiet spot, for he knew the place well, she fought hard to martial her thoughts into sensible order, although it was far from easy.

They came to a charming, formal rose garden, not far from the dancing. He drew her down on to an octagonal wooden seat around the sun dial.

In the clear moonlight, his eyes were unfathomable pools.

"Now, Sprite—for your sake as much as my own—I demand to know the cause of this trouble between you and Lady Olivia. I am not asking lightly, believe me."

Jessica faced him, her mind made up. Had she told him the whole truth, in his present mood, she might have won him forever but she would not stoop so low; his safety and his future happiness mattered more to her than life itself, and pride forbade her to snatch uneasy victory so easily.

She gave a light laugh, thankful he could not see the expression in her dark eyes, either.

"La, my lord! Had you not met me straight afterward, I would never have mentioned the matter! I did not dream that you would take a mere tiff so seriously; but pray do not dwell on it, for I have already put it from my mind."

He took her hands in a firm grasp.

"*What caused it,* Sprite—and do not lie."

She tried to look astonished. "Do you not yet know me well enough to be sure that I *never* lie? Nay, the whole matter was so trivial I cannot imagine, now, why I lost my temper! I fear you will despise us both, for it was such a feminine matter—a dressmaker! Her ladyship was afraid I might attempt to have her splendid Grecian creation copied for myself—as if such a noble gown could ever befit one of my stature!" She seemed to ponder. "It seemed so ridiculous an idea that I fear I *did* lose my temper for a moment—indeed it was all my fault." He knew she would say no more.

But Desmond was still not satisfied.

Eight

Much happened to assuage finally Desmond's anxiety about the tiff between the two important women in his life. He challenged Jessica on two further occasions, but she only laughed and pretended that the incident had passed from her mind. Thus by the time he rode over to Lufton Hall to see Olivia, he, too, had no choice but to regard the matter as of no importance, and he did not trouble to question his love, for she would only laugh at him.

Indeed, Olivia set herself out to charm him even more seductively, nursing to herself the devilish scheme she and Walter had devised for her revenge of the Court girl. After a delightful stroll in the garden she entertained Desmond to tea *à deux* on the terrace, raising his hopes to the skies. It was rare to find Olivia alone when he called, and he took it as a promising favor. Above all, she encouraged him over the tournament:

"You will make such a splendid champion, my dear. You must promise me that you will reach the final bout."

His eyes glowing, Lord Desmond clasped her long, aristocratic hands in his. "I swear, Lady Olivia. Indeed, I am so determined to win that I think of little else, day or night."

Her smile was warm and ingenuous. "I shall add my prayers to yours." Then her smile became mysterious. "Though I have still not determined on the prize!"

"I think, my dear love, that you will decide that when the champion comes to the throne of the exquisite Queen of the Day."

She had long decided the issue, but her blue eyes shone with admiration as she said, "By my troth, you are brilliant! I had not thought of such a simple solution!" She laughed merrily, "Suppose some country oaf should prove to have talents we have never dreamed of? Then, he shall receive that ornate, distasteful gilt vase from the hall. It will have pride of place in his farmhouse for generations to come, and they will think it a great work of Art. Oh, Desmond, how very clever you are."

She escorted him, arm in arm, to where Hercules waited patiently in the stables: "Is this the splendid stallion you mean to mount on the great occasion?" She patted the gleaming neck. Hercules, unfamiliar to her touch, moved back a little, but Desmond reproached him:

"Come, you must learn the kindness of your future Mistress's gentle hands."

As he rode home, his heart was full and his mind bedazed with happy dreams. Olivia favored him! During the whole three hours there had been no barbed quips, no teasing; she had seemed a woman in love, and he felt absolutely confident of the outcome of the tourney.

With this to spur him on, Desmond redoubled his rigorous training. Even if Sir Walter had had information of his tactics, surely he would never exert himself to such a pitch. No, for he was both conceited and lazy.

Young Brian, as his opponent, was driven to extremety by Desmond's insistence on perfection. Jessica, her notes no longer needed by either side, watched, while a strange foreboding possessed her mind. She dismissed it firmly. It was only natural nervousness, for what disaster could possibly occur during a royal revel?

Desmond had commissioned a splendid feather-weight suit of gilded armor and boots from a famous costumier in Brighton who supplied clothes for all the royal masques.

Now that the embroidered tabard and caparison were almost finished, Lady Shayne found herself caught up in excitement over the tournament. She carried a secret guilt, not even confessed to Jessica who had worked so hard on it, that her prayer was for Desmond *not* to be the victor. It seemed little short of high treason when all his heart was set on winning. To ease her conscience, however, she allowed both young people to forego all social engagements for the last few days of training.

When the final day came, Desmond, his color high, declared that training was complete by the end of the morning. He flatteringly thanked Brian for his help, then handed Hercules over for special grooming. Brian, his father and another groom had been supplied with suitable costumes to appear in the background as Lord Desmond's attendants, and they were to take the stallion over to the grounds quite early and accustom him to the new surroundings.

Jessica's face glowed, too. "You are magnificent now, my lord—quite unassailable, I declare," she said as they returned for luncheon. But that evening, before dinner, her heart swelled with admiration until she felt her breast could scarce contain it. As a surprise, Desmond paraded in all his splendor for the approval of Lady Shayne and Jessica.

He looked god-like in the candlelight, his armor glittering pure gold; the beautiful tabard gleamed with the scarlet, emerald and gold thread used by Mrs. Gieves to depict the Shayne coat of arms. And, on his head, he wore a gold visored helmet crowned by waving osprey feathers of gold, emerald, and bright scarlet.

Doffing his helmet with an elegant gesture, he bowed, then looked up, his eyes laughing.

"Well, Mother, do you approve of the Defender of the Honor of Shayne?"

"Oh, my dear son, you look . . ." her eyes misted, and she added softly, "How very proud your father would feel to see you now." It was the ultimate accolade, and Desmond, fearing that emotion might affect him, turned laughing to Jessica,

"What say you, Sprite?"

"I—I declare I am speechless, my lord. I have never seen so legendary a figure!" She, too, would have wept, for how could Lady Olivia not be won by such beauty and such prowess as he would display. "All challengers will quail, thinking an archangel has come to do battle!"

Lady Shayne sorely needed time to recover her poise.

"Desmond, I know it is not customary but pray show yourself in the Servants Hall. They are all attending the affair, and Mrs. Gieves will be quite overcome."

Desmond, forgivably a little vain for the moment, smiled.

"I will, indeed. I shall need all their support and cheering when the time comes. I think I must embrace old Mrs. Gieves for her great efforts—I have already seen the caparison for Hercules and it is quite perfect."

He swept out, and Jessica moved close to her ladyship who reached out for her hand.

"Jessica, he cannot, *must not* fail. For his sake I fear we must patiently bear the outcome." A small shiver shook her body and she glanced around her beloved room. "If—if he is right, and the prize *is* that girl, then you and I will live in the Dower House to which I shall take my special treasures." She looked up, her gentle eyes so distressed that Jessica was hard put not to take her in her arms, but Lady Shayne went on, "Or do you think that might hurt my son? That he might think I was not welcoming his—his bride?"

"Oh, no—*no,* my lady; he loves and reveres you so deeply I know that he would want you to have every comfort and pleasure that you wish," Jessica spoke vehemently. Then a vain hope occurred to her. "Besides, pray, pray remember that we are anticipating the worst. Suppose the prize is to be simply a trophy? The season is scarce in swing, and possibly Lady Olivia does not wish to express her choice yet."

Lady Shayne tightened her hold on Jessica's hand. "You are such a help, my dear. Yes, we must go to this affair with open minds."

Desmond reappeared just in time for dinner to be announced. He had changed back into his own clothing and was still in exuberant spirits.

"Egad, what a performance! Mrs. Gieves dissolved in tears, and several maids were mopping at their eyes. What it is to have such loyal support."

It was a convivial evening; Desmond ordered the butler to bring up a bottle of the finest burgundy, adding,

"I shall have but a glassful myself, for nothing must dull my wits tomorrow, but surely we must all drink to the triumph of the House of Shayne!"

Loving him so deeply, both women did so with their whole hearts. Nothing must mar his joyful hopes because of their secret fears.

Desmond retired early, soon followed by his mother who asked her maid to prepare a soothing tisane. Jessica tried to read, but the dazzling figure of her love came between her and the pages. Besides, she must look her best at the tourney, for Desmond had sworn he would dedicate the first bouts to her, which would make her the cynosure of all eyes.

However, she prepared for bed with a growing sense of foreboding, trying to dismiss it as jealousy of Olivia. Sleep was slow in coming but, at last, she fell into a sleep so heavy it was almost a coma.

In it she saw the entire scene, although she had not visited the Royal Park to watch any preparations. The noise of many voices and laughter battered at her senses —until all was still as a figure bathed in light rode out; and she knew it was Desmond, sunlight glinting on his golden armor and brave colors. A hush fell, filled only by the thunder of hooves. A dark form galloped at speed toward him and, suddenly, the air was filled by mocking laughter from all sides: Desmond was lying unhorsed on the ground, his proud colors spattered by the churned turf, his horse bolting from the scene in terror. Amid mounting jeers he lay helplessly still as the noise echoed around his unconscious chestnut-brown head. Jessica forced herself to wake, her body bathed in sweat.

It was already dawn, and, without pulling on her

dressing robe she went to the open window in her night-gown, craving only air—sweet, cool air and forgetfulness. She threw open the window wider.

Shayne Park lay bathed in a pearly mist, promising great heat and brilliant sun later. The dawn chorus was in full throat, birds calling merrily from every invisible bough; but Jessica could not relax into the utter peace, could not quite banish her dream. There was something, some detail she had seen that it was vital she should re-member, but it eluded her. Perhaps if she could sleep again—recapture the hateful scene before it dissolved in the morning air . . . . but she could not.

Bella found her, dozing on the window seat, her dark head pillowed on her bare arms. At first Bella was alarmed, then she smiled. 'Twas excitement, bless the lady —the same feeling that had kept the maids up twittering half the night, wondering what gown of their small store to wear for such a great occasion. She woke Jessica gently, handing her a robe and cup of tea, keeping up a constant chatter for which Jessica was thankful as it left her to her own thoughts. Dare she warn Desmond? But no, that was unthinkable on such a day. It might undermine his con-fidence, and dreams were rarely true. Besides, he had gone to bed so buoyantly, so sure of victory—and a blunt pole could do no harm. In faith, he had been hit often enough during practice, and she almost convinced herself that the dream had been purely selfish—a dread of her own likely loss forever of her one, great love.

The fair opened at two o'clock, but the royal tourna-ment was not due to begin until five, leaving a decent interval for the *ton* to digest heavy luncheons and set forth.

Desmond left Shayne at three; he wanted to survey the ground himself and make sure that Hercules was in fine fettle. He took the faithful Chalmers with him, carry-ing his fine armor and accoutrements. Since each com-petitor was to have a private tent, there would be no need to dress up until half-an-hour before the opening fanfare.

Lady Shayne and Jessica entered their carriage soon after four.

"There will be a crush of carriages, I fear," said her

ladyship. "Besides, I declare I am too nervous to wait longer! Once we are there, with friends to talk to, it will be better." Her smile was valiant, although her face was pale.

Jessica agreed. Anything would be better than the vacuum of watching time pass. She looked very beautiful in pale lilac muslin, a small hat festooned with violet ribbons on her dark curls and long, violet gloves.

The scene, when they arrived, quite took their breath away. It was very hot and the jousting ground was on velvet-smooth grass, marked out with pennants. Behind it stood the royal tent, the silk stripes in regal dark blue and gold, with seats arranged in front of it, sheltered from the sun by a similarly striped awning. A long red carpet stretched from there to the private entrance, through which the Prince would come, well-protected from the crowd.

Beyond this big tent ranged what appeared to be a rainbow army of smaller ones, each silken covering bearing the colors of the nobleman within. It was easy to distinguish Desmond's, close to the front, by the distinctive emerald, scarlet and gold. He was nowhere in sight. The temporary stables for all the horses were out of sight.

The noise from the fair was deafening, although the huge crowd was drifting toward the barrier from which they had a good, if rather distant, view following His Highness's commands. This made no difference to the noise, however, since loud—sometimes bawdy—comments were made freely, describing each new arrival to the royal enclosure.

"In faith, the noise and heat are almost insufferable," Lady Shayne whispered to Jessica, her face pale though this stemmed from nerves on Desmond's behalf rather than physical discomfort.

Jessica put a firm, supporting hand under her elbow although she was possibly more apprehensive than her ladyship. For try as she would, she could not banish her ominous dream. Every detail of the ground was so familiar —so terrifyingly similar to the one of which she had dreamed. And, naturally, the turf would be churned and ruined by the thunder of so many hooves.

Pages in Medieval garb ushered them to their seats

in the second row. For some reason Jessica was thankful to find they were seated at the end, beside the gangway. The seating had been most thoughtfully planned, certainly by Mrs. Fitzherbert, for their neighbors were all dear friends of Lady Shayne, and she was soon engaged in pleasant conversation. Jessica knew no one close by. Her young friends were, no doubt, placed in a stand slightly to one side; but she was glad to be left in peace, for all she could do for Desmond now was to pray—beseeching, if slightly incoherent prayers—for his protection. In between she concentrated on memories of his training, how thorough it had been, leaving nothing to chance unless there was foul play—but surely this was impossible so close to the royal scrutiny.

Suddenly there was a fanfare of silver trumpets announcing the arrival of the court. The clamorous sound hushed as all necks craned forward for a first glimpse of the Queen of Misrule. The Prince led her by the hand on to the red carpet and they walked slowly so that all could see Lady Olivia's great beauty, and she looked queenly indeed. Her gown was cloth of gold with a train carried by two small pages, while on her head she wore a charming gilt crown, glittering with jewels. Her appearance caused a storm of applause and cheering from the crowds and, in true royal manner, she gave a little bow from side to side, smiling most graciously.

Immediately behind them walked Mrs. Fitzherbert accompanied by the Lord High Chamberlain with his gold-tipped staff and, two by two with measured steps, followed all the courtiers.

It was a spectacle indeed and Jessica murmured,

"I declare, this must resemble the Field of the Cloth of Gold so long, long ago."

It was two minutes to five when they were all seated, Olivia holding pride of place on a mock golden throne. Jessica tried desperately to quell her hatred of this young woman in whose hands at the end of the next hour or two lay Desmond's fate.

The Prince gave the signal and, on to the Ground galloped two horses, finely caparisoned, their riders armored and helmeted. Desmond, being such a fine horseman, would fight later when the more amateur contestants had vanquished one another. The crowd cared nothing for the identity of the rivals. They had come to see sport and sport this certainly was; there was betting carried on as well.

It took three tilts, the poles clashing with a splendid sound, before one rider was unseated and rolled, shame-faced on the ground. Then he sprang up, doffed his helmet, and made a low bow to Olivia and the Prince, who applauded him.

The time seemed interminable before the finer horsemen came out; even then the first to appear was not Desmond but Sir Walter, looking, thought Jessica, every inch the villain she knew him to be. His stallion was chestnut and the caparison and tabard were as fine as Desmond's, but his coat of arms and plumes were dark—black, deep crimson, and silver.

But, watching him, Jessica's heart sank—he had certainly put in much practice for, at first, he merely played with his younger "enemy" then, judging it to a nicety, unseated him with one blow in front of Lady Olivia before he rode off to redoubled cheers. The battle was warming as the experts took the field.

At last Desmond rode out, ablaze in his gilt and gay colors resembling a true, heroic knight of old. His very appearance caused a burst of applause. Then he, too, showed his great skill, unseating his opponent with fine dexterity. Lady Shayne took Jessica's hand, all their nervousness returned, for it soon became quite evident that the final contest would be between the two men who hated each other in their rivalry for Lady Olivia's hand.

And so it was. The final was heralded by another fanfare, then Dark Knight and Golden Earl pitched their wits against each other. Both were expert and gave no quarters. The beribboned poles almost flashed in their hands the blows came so quickly, and were so neatly parried, as tension mounted among all the spectators. This was a match indeed, and a hush fell as they tilted again and again. Lady Olivia was leaning right forward on her throne, her color rising with excitement as first one, then the other, seemed on the point of winning.

Jessica could scarce bear to watch, yet her eyes could not look away. Then an unexpected hit caused Lord Desmond's helmet to fall to the ground and he returned to the fray bare-headed, handsome with his mouth set in anger. It was hard for the spectators to see exactly what did happen in the last tilt, for ultimate victory did not come before the royal thrones but almost at the end of a ride. A pole flashed twice—once, Jessica could have sworn, striking Desmond's bare head which was against the rules, but the following thrust was so quick no one could ever have sworn to the swift, earlier blow—not even Jessica herself.

Jeers instead of cheers echoed over Desmond's unconscious head as he lay sprawled on the ground, just as he had in her dream. Then, without a backward glance at his victim, Sir Walter, cheered to the echo, trotted back to where Lady Olivia was standing, hands outstretched to welcome him. She was smiling and she, too, gave no glance to the vanquished. Walter dismounted and doffed his helmet.

The faithful Chalmers and the three grooms, led by Brian, ran to their fallen master; Brian caught Hercules' bridle, for he had galloped off a little way, startled and frightened. Then, with gentleness, Lord Desmond was borne back to his tent.

Jessica slipped from her place like a shadow, the missing piece in her dream having come vividly to mind as she sped toward the small tent.

Meanwhile, Sir Walter, led by a glowing Olivia and a delighted Prince, was drawn back inside the royal tent to be regaled with champagne.

Jessica arrived almost as soon as Desmond had been laid on the ground, Chalmers kneeling by his head. She fell to her knees on his other side, as blood began to flow slowly from a wound which could never have been inflicted by a blunted pole. She tore off her hat and the beautiful gloves.

"Zounds," swore Chalmers under his breath, "his lordship has been fouled!"

"Hush," said Jessica urgently. "No word of this must

spread beyond ourselves." Then all her attention focused on Desmond. Knowing, at last, what she sought, her hands probed carefully, tenderly, beneath his hair.

Lady Shayne appeared in the entrance, swaying a little, her face ashen.

"He *cannot* be hurt! 'Twas not a real battle!"

Seeing that her lady's usual calm was quite shattered Jessica said to the young groom, Brian,

"Pray escort Lady Shayne to her carriage—and go with her, as swiftly as you can, to bring a flat, farm cart from Shayne to convey his lordship home in reasonable comfort. Come to a back way with it for he must not be seen."

Lady Shayne was too stunned by shock to protest as Brian led her gently away. Nearly all the Shayne household met them by the carriage, unwilling to stay and deeply anxious about their young master.

Brian, young though he was, seemed very much in charge.

"Good—pray hie you back to the park, for her ladyship needs much attention and also prepare Lord Desmond's room. His hurt is not grievous," he added, remembering Jessica's warning words. "Simply concussed, it seems, and he will be brought home anon."

They looked vastly relieved as they hurried to the big wagonette brought out specially for transporting them to and from the ground.

At last Jessica looked up, and met Chalmers' anxious old eyes.

"The wound seems quite deep—there must have been a spike or nail embedded in Sir Walter's pole, to be used at the precise moment."

"What can we do, Miss Jessica? He is bleeding more."

"Do you know a good, discreet surgeon, Chalmers. On no account must that gossip, Dr. Pettigrew, be summoned."

"I do indeed, Miss Jessica." He looked thankful to be given a mission. "The old earl once fought a mighty chancy duel and took a nasty shot in his chest. Dr. Sandler saved his life. I warrant he is the very soul of discretion, but," he hesitated, "will you be all right here, Miss? Can you manage?"

Jessica smiled wanly. "I can indeed, Chalmers. Alas, there is little to do, and I doubt his lordship will regain consciousness for some time. Pray hurry, now—and seek out the doctor wherever he may be."

"I'll bring him, never fear," said Chalmers grimly, and left.

Suddenly there was a sound of cheering and fanfares outside. Jessica looked up at the remaining groom and said:

"Pray see what all the noise is, Smithers."

He slipped out. Alone with Desmond, Jessica stroked the side of his chestnut hair on the far side from the wound, and murmured, "You will live, my dearest love, live to prove to the world that *you* are the worthy champion."

Two minutes later, the groom returned, his face set and angry.

"Not so much as a visit to inquire after my lord, and there is Sir Walter, waving and preening, while the lady has him by the hand and declares: 'I am proud to award the trophy to a most gallant knight, and the trophy is— myself. We are betrothed.' A pox on both of 'em I say, saving your presence, Miss," then village philosophy quietened his fury, and he gave a sly smile: "Not but what they don't deserve each other—high and mighty—that young ladyship, with not a civil word to say to us in the Stables."

A great orison of thanks rose in Jessica's breast. Desmond would certainly be heart-broken for a time, but at least Olivia could not ruin his whole life. Then guilt smote her and she bowed her head in shame; suppose it was her quarrel with Olivia that had lighted the spark starting this whole dastardly plot? For it had been a plot between Sir Walter and Lady Olivia, Jessica was certain— reducing Desmond to public ignominy because of his obstinate friendship with his mythical "Sprite."

Surely, she thought desperately, if not this, then Olivia, in her choice of Sir Walter, could have demeaned her rejected suitor in some other way. Jessica looked down at his handsome, still face, the blood trickling steadily from above the hairline.

"But she need not have maimed him—made him suffer physical pain." Jessica's voice was too low for the groom to catch the words. "For pain there will be when he regains consciousness. No, at least he could have sought comfort from his bitter disappointment in hard riding and other sport until his body was exhausted."

Her own anger against the fair witch grew steadily. In that moment, had Olivia appeared, Jessica would have killed her outright, small though she might be herself.

She fell to brooding tenderly over Lord Desmond's white, unconscious face.

Soon Brian arrived, closely followed by Chalmers who brought with him a tall, solemn man clad in black.

"This is Dr. Sandler," Chalmers' voice held a pardonable note of achievement, and Jessica smiled gratefully.

"Naturally, I could not let my patient travel home without my supervision," the Doctor's voice was clipped and carried authority. Jessica trusted him at once and surrendered her place to him so that he could examine the wound.

"H'm," he said grimly after a few moments. "Foul play I'd say. Now," he glanced at Brian, "you have the cart ready?"

"Ay, and well prepared, sir. We have placed a palliasse over the boards and brought cushions, too."

"Remove the cushions," was the curt reply from the man now indisputedly in charge. He scarce glanced at Jessica, assuming that she was one of the upper servants.

"Did her ladyship see this?" Dr. Sandler directed his question to Chalmers.

"I fear so," he replied. "Her poor ladyship was sadly shaken so Miss Jessica persuaded her to return to the park."

Sandler nodded. "Wise, very wise. It must have been a great shock. Now"—he became brisk—"I shall support his head while you lift Lord Desmond's body—slowly, now, and you, Miss, will you hold back the tent flap?"

It was a slow business, the men edging forward in a kind of shuffle so as to cause no shifting of their heavy

141

burden. When he was laid in the cart with Dr. Sandler by his head, Brian said,

"I shall ride Hercules home by the back lanes."

The drive to Shayne Park was equally slow for, they, too, travelled a back way. It would have been shame, indeed, to display Lord Desmond's unconscious form all along Brighton Parade, although the way would have been smoother and quicker. Jessica crouched at his side, holding his hand, her eyes never leaving his pale face. Once or twice the doctor looked up at her puzzled by this obvious devotion, yet still not able to place her. The lady could not be betrothed to him since all the *ton* knew that the young Earl's heart was set on the girl whom Sandler thought of privately as "the young Lufton vixen."

Lady Shayne was waiting for them at the front door, her eyes straining for a first sight of the small cortege. Was her beloved son dead? Had that caused a delay? Behind her the butler stood gravely, offering her respectful words of encouragement which fell on deaf ears.

When the cart drew up, Lady Shayne hurried to the side, thankful to see Dr. Sandler, who had once saved her dear husband and in whom she had great faith. But first she turned to Jessica,

"Oh, my dear, dear child," she cried. "I was craven indeed to desert you—but the shock . . . does he live?"

Jessica climbed down and took her in her young arms. "He does indeed, my lady; and Dr. Sandler has tended him all the way. Chalmers was fortunate to find him at home."

The doctor climbed down and crisply ordered that a flat tabletop or a door be brought, with two silken sheets.

"We can quickly make a stretcher and tie him firmly in place with the sheets. He has lost much blood, I think, and must travel smoothly upstairs to his room."

While everyone hurried to obey him, the man in charge turned to her ladyship, hands outstretched, and with a far from austere smile on his face spoke,

"My dear lady, 'tis always such a pleasure to see you. I am sorry only that our meetings occur on such anxious occasions. You, too, need my attentions, for shock cannot easily be overcome. But rest assured, Lord Desmond will be in little danger. He is young and exceptionally strong, like his father. As soon as he is in bed I shall cauterize, cleanse, and dress the wound, and I shall call every day. Meantime, I will send a nurse from Brighton. The wound must be recleansed and dressed every few hours, and she will stay with him during the night."

Here, Jessica stepped forward boldly, her chin lifted firmly and her eyes determined.

"I pray, Doctor, that I may assume that office. I am not entirely without nursing skill, and I—I am devoted to his lordship and dare think he would prefer to find no stranger at his bedside when he wakes."

Sandler stared at her in astonishment. Why, she was a slip of a thing and extremely young. But Lady Shayne added her entreaties.

"I beg you to agree, Doctor. Jessica has expert, healing hands and steady nerves. She escorts me regularly on all my medical visits to our tenants, and, I swear, many prefer her ministrations to mine! Deep cuts and other wounds heal excellently under her care."

Still surprised, the eminent surgeon turned and scrutinized Jessica with renewed interest, growing immediately more impressed by her steady, beautiful eyes and firm little mouth. He liked her. At last he said,

"Well, young lady, are you really prepared to act as my assistant? It will be hard work, you know. Lord Desmond may remain unconscious for a few days, and he will need lifting and fairly—er—intimate attentions as well as dressing the wound."

Jessica's smile was radiant in her pale face. "I accept gladly, Doctor—and Chalmers, who has looked after his lordship since childhood, will help me constantly. He will see to it that the proprieties are observed, I promise."

"You stayed with Desmond until I came—were you not afraid?"

"At first, yes indeed, but once I found the wound, I thought he would not die—although it was hateful foul play! I did not staunch the bleeding for the wound was in sore need of cleansing, and I felt it was better not to stem it. I think it may have been a rusty spike or nail at the end of Sir Walter's pole that struck him down."

143

"H'm. You certainly have your wits about you—and more intelligence than most young girls. Come with me."

Jessica followed willingly. She felt slightly in awe of this majestic man but determined to prove herself. She would be at Desmond's side, her deep love surrounding him and giving him strength to fight, while her hands performed their skills.

She never flinched while watching and helping Dr. Sandler at his task. First Chalmers was bidden to shave away the rich, chestnut hair around the wound, then it was Jessica's duty to have clean bowls ready to hold the swabs and warm water and towels for the surgeon to wash his hands. At last Desmond was bound up and seemed easier in his bed.

"You will do very well, my dear," Sandler bestowed a warm smile at last. "Now, we will leave our patient in the care of Chalmers while we see her ladyship. I shall leave a sedative for her to take tonight, and you must renew the dressing on that head at midnight precisely."

When Dr. Sandler left, promising to return at ten o'clock the next morning, Jessica went up to see that all was well before taking a swift, light supper with her ladyship.

Lady Shayne felt vastly relieved—and even smiled.

"Jessica, you are a treasure beyond price. I shall rest tonight, knowing my son is in your capable hands." Then she added, "And how just Almighty God has proved! For surely Lady Olivia has chosen exactly the husband she deserves!"

"Indeed, she has," Jessica agreed with her whole heart.

Then, having seen her ladyship to her room, Jessica returned to take up the first of her night-long vigils. Chalmers was to sleep in the dressing room next to Desmond's room, to be within call at all times.

As she drew a chair to the bedside, Jessica felt her heart would brim over with love. That it must break later she refused to contemplate. Desmond's recovery was her whole world.

Nine

On that first night when Jessica dressed Desmond's wound, her hand trembled slightly. She was not afraid for herself, but nervous of hurting him in any way; she was anxious, too, to please Dr. Sandler in the morning, otherwise he would send in a strange nurse. The wound itself, she thought, seemed less angry, although it was hard to be sure in the soft light of an oil lamp. Then with dexterity, she recleansed and dressed it. A faint sigh escaped Desmond's lips which startled her, but his eyelids did not even flicker. Perhaps he had simply an awareness, in the deep subconscious of his mind, that he was being cared for with tenderness.

When she had finished, it was half-past midnight. Chalmers had offered to wait up and assist her, but the elderly man was tired and strained, and Jessica insisted that he go to bed at ten.

"I promise to wake you if I need any help," she said firmly. "It has been a long, tiring day and you will have to keep vigil after Dr. Sandler has been in the morning, for then I shall sleep myself." Reluctantly, yet with relief, he went into the dressing room.

Now Jessica sat by the bed, the lamp lowered to a soft rosy glow. Surprisingly, she found she was not tired and fell to thinking. Surely Sir Walter had not made his lightning thrust with a deliberately rusted or otherwise contaminated spike? He was ruthless and cruel, yes, and determined to be the victor, but such an act might have resulted in a charge of murder had a less able physician been called. She shivered at the awful possibility. It was more likely that the spike had been implanted some days earlier and left—as Desmond's poles were—out in the stable yard where summer rain, dew, and early mists could have wrought the damage.

While her mind was so alert, she faced another hard task for it would surely lie with her to break the news of Lady Olivia's betrothal on that very day. But this, she decided, must rest on the way Lord Desmond put the question.

At two o'clock she ate two of the sandwiches wrapped in a clean, damp napkin and drank a glass of chilled orange juice. Then, in spite of herself, she dozed lightly in the chair, her hand in Desmond's so that the slightest movement would wake her.

Soon after dawn she renewed the dressing, then, when Chalmers came in looking mightily refreshed after a good night, she slipped away to her room to wash, take a light breakfast, and change into a morning gown.

Bella hovered anxiously. "How is His Lordship, Miss? We are all that worried in the servants hall—Cook, now, she's a born worrier and keeps remembering horrible stories of people dying in agony; I declare, we can scarce eat afterwards." Then she looked at her young mistress more keenly. "Some say as it was foul play, Miss—is that the fact?"

"No, Bella," Jessica lied firmly. "Lord Desmond's wound was an accident, and it is beginning to heal nicely. Such a story must *not* be put about. Do you understand?"

Bella blushed. "Never by me, Miss, by my troth— 'twould bring all Brighton buzzing around our ears! If you have everything you require, I will tell them what you say in the hall. They will be mightily relieved to hear that His Lordship is mending."

Jessica finished her coffee and prepared to return to the patient. But outside Lady Shayne's room she hesitated, then tapped lightly, not wishing to disturb a restful sleep. Her ladyship herself called: "Come in." And, when she saw Jessica, she held out her hands eagerly.

"How is he, my dear? I am about to visit him myself —for I insist on taking my share of the nursing. Indeed, I woke ashamed this morning to have laid such a heavy burden on your shoulders." Her voice was stronger, evidently Dr. Sandler's sedative had done its work well, but she was still a little shaky. Jessica smiled.

"Your son is progressing splendidly, my lady, and I swear I am not in the least weary. He will soon be back with us, filled with health and spirits, riding Hercules and coming home late for meals with such charming, lame excuses!"

Her ladyship gave a little quivering laugh. "Oh, that it may be so, Jessica. I declare I have never felt so alarmed since his father was brought home after that ridiculous duel so many years ago."

Jessica held out her hand. "Pray come and see him. He is not yet conscious but that is only concussion. There is no need for you to do any nursing. Chalmers is a staunch helper, and we are not in the least anxious." She paused, "I feel there is one important thing to be done— if you will pardon my presumption—but from something Bella told me, it seems the staff are too put about to be very discreet. They were so shocked by events yesterday —as we all were—that I fear they may have forgot the warning to say nothing and spread no rumors beyond this house."

Lady Shayne was instantly in control of herself. This was her task, and only she could wield the necessary authority.

"How wise of you to tell me, my child. I will just visit Desmond and then call all the servants to the main hall to remind and reassure them."

Jessica took her arm as they left for Desmond's room. "He is a better color this morning, my lady, and I

147

think Dr. Sandler will be pleased when he comes at ten. I fear, however, that you may be plagued with inquisitive callers this afternoon. I beg you to conserve your strength, for you will need all your consummate tact and charm to fend off the gossips!"

Lady Shayne brightened even more, "Jessica, you have pointed out my duty—the one way I can help Desmond beyond all others, for nothing has daunted my talent for turning away unwanted inquiries over the years, I assure you! They shall be sent away highly amused, chuckling over his slight concussion caused by his head hitting the ground. Besides they will be full of news of the famous betrothal yesterday."

Jessica gave a little laugh, "Is it not dreadful to feel so pleased about that ourselves? Oh, I know the news will distress his lordship at first, but I am sure he was aware of Lady Olivia's devious character and her unkindness; and he will soon recover from the blow, though his love went so deep it may take a year or so."

"Such a noble heart given to a preening, worthless—chit," sighed her ladyship. Then, straightening her shoulders, her expression calm, she preceded Jessica to her son's bedroom and took the chair respectfully vacated by Chalmers, while Jessica stood unobtrusively by the window.

For some minutes Lady Shayne gazed at her son's peaceful, unconscious face, only the forehead covered by bandages. Then, talking softly she murmured,

"Desmond, my darling, we shall soon have you well again; you are safe at home now, and in loving hands. I thank God you are in no pain; and when you wake, you will find dear, familiar faces around you. Fight quietly, my brave one, as your father fought back to health before you."

She fell silent and watched him for a short time longer. Then she rose.

"I must go and see the servants now, Jessica. Be sure to inform Dr. Sandler that I wish to see him, will you?"

"Of course, my lady."

She called Chalmers to help her straighten the bed. "We must not lift him, but he lies so quiet there is no need." They smoothed the top sheet, slightly disarranged by the necessary intimate offices carried out by Chalmers.

Promptly at ten o'clock Dr. Sandler was shown in, and Jessica sprang to her feet.

"There is no change, sir," she said, "But I think the wound is less inflamed." She was nervous now—afraid he might find fault with her dressings. Wasting no time he went to the bed, set down his bag, and took off the bandages. The silence stretched as he examined the wound. Jessica was aware of her heartbeats as she waited, tense. At last the doctor turned.

"You have done excellently, Miss Jessica, I could have trusted a no finer nurse, but . . . ." he paused, "I am not entirely happy with this deep scratch at one side, caused when the pointed object was removed so quickly. Look, I will show you."

Under his guidance, Jessica examined the small mark and saw that the edges had grown livid since her last dressing. She drew in her breath sharply.

"It still looked clean when I did the morning dressing. Now it seems infected."

"Precisely." The doctor removed his elegant coat, rolled up his sleeves and placed his bag on a nearby table. "I shall perform a small operation. Kindly have plenty of hot, boiled water brought up immediately, then lay out these small bowls and unroll my case of instruments. I shall need you to attend me. Will you flinch?"

"Certainly not, sir." Jessica's voice sounded firmer than she felt. A complication! But, to stem her dread, she quickly started performing her tasks while Dr. Sandler went to the bathroom next door to wash and put on his surgical gloves. Chalmers hurried to bring up the water, his face drawn.

It was only a small incision but unpleasant matter was released. Chalmers had returned promptly with two clean pitchers of hot, boiled water and Dr. Sandler cleansed the incision again and again until no more poison appeared. Then he said,

"Pass my small bottle of pure white alcohol from the left side of my bag." Jessica found it swiftly, unscrewed it and handed it to him. She winced inwardly as the doctor

149

applied it neat, on a swab, but Desmond remained still and quite unaware of the sharp sting. Then the wound was redressed and bandaged, the surgeon went to remove his gloves and wash before coming back, unrolling his sleeves and carefully adjusting the jewelled links and frilled cuffs. Then he turned to Jessica with the first warm smile she had received and which transformed his austere face,

"Let me look at you, my dear, for you have become my colleague and a perfect assistant." He studied her small, pale face and beautiful eyes, and his smile broadened. "What it is to be young and strong—and, no doubt, in love with our patient. Oh, pray do not blush at the truth—how could things be otherwise? Only a most devoted heart would willingly offer to perform such responsible services. If only more young women were like you, Miss Jessica, my duties would be halved! But alas, 'tis not so—when their menfolk fight senseless duels or come back wounded from some minor war, they have the vapors, swoon, behave like ninnies and become useless, demanding my services for their recovery as well. You are unique, young lady, and I salute you." He turned abruptly, shrugged on his embroidered dark coat, and snapped his bag shut, his professional manner returning. "You will now have a good sleep, for the bandages must not be touched until I return at five o'clock." He made for the door.

"Oh, Doctor—her ladyship asked you to call on her before you leave. Your sedative helped her a great deal, but she is extremely anxious."

He glanced at the gold half-hunter watch in his fob pocket, then said: "Indeed, I owe her five minutes reassurance. To bed with you!"

Jessica stood beside Desmond for a little while, gazing down at his inert form, her whole heart and mind concentrated on instilling her own strength and faith into him. "You *will* recover my dear, dear love. You must never be vanquished by a villain like Sir Walter! You will soon be mounted on Hercules, riding the countryside like the fine man you are."

Then, with strict instructions to Chalmers to wake her if there were the slightest change, she went to her room.

Bella came quickly, and, with the sense of a country-woman, did not speak. Deftly she helped her mistress to undress then brought in a soothing, warm tisane.

"You are to drink this, Miss Jessica—Dr. Sandler ordered it."

It was a comforting brew, Jessica thought as she sipped slowly, a little acrid but, as she neared the end, a pleasant drowsiness crept over her. She slid down between cool sheets and, within minutes, was peacefully asleep.

She was wakened, completely rested and refreshed, at three o'clock by the sound of voices below on the terrace. Surely it was far too early for conventional calls? The rules of the *ton* specified four o'clock. Then she recognized the younger voice and sprang out of bed, drawing on her robe and running to the window.

Grace Ashby stood below, in riding habit, making kind inquiries of the butler. Jessica leaned out of the window and yelled:

"Grace! Oh, it is wonderful to see you—pray come up to my room and I will ring for some tea." Hastily, Jessica brushed her short hair, sponged her face and put on a cool, summer dress. Bella showed Grace in; and, when Jessica ordered tea, she smiled.

"Faith, miss, you are to have more than that! Her ladyship has had a light luncheon prepared on a tray— we must keep up your strength." She turned to Grace. "Will you partake of a little cold chicken, Miss Ashby, if you have ridden far? Or shall I bring tea and fruit cake?" She beamed. " 'Twill do Miss Jessica a world of good to have young company, I declare."

Grace laughed, "I swear I have a true, Scots appetite. Besides, I have been riding since morning; if you are sure there is enough, I should enjoy sharing luncheon with Miss Jessica."

"Enough?" Bella laughed, too. "Cook is that anxious to keep up Miss Jessica's strength, she has prepared a whole chicken! And a sherry trifle with good cream." She departed to fetch the tray. The two girls settled on the window seat, for the afternoon was glorious.

"How is Lord Desmond?" asked Grace seriously. "You know you can trust me, on my oath."

Jessica hesitated only a moment. "Yes, you are a true friend and dislike gossip as I do. After all, since you know the truth of my heart already, I should like to tell you the rest. Desmond is very ill—though he will recover, I know. Sir Walter struck his head with some wicked instrument, and the wound is infected. But, oh Grace, I am so thankful that the small nursing skills taught by my mother are considered good by the Surgeon. I, and no stranger, care for my beloved—especially at night."

Grace's eyes misted with sympathy and she pressed Jessica's hand. "Thank you. I shall respect your confidence; and, by my prayers and visits, do all I can to help you."

"It is already a comfort to have one person I can talk with freely—for her ladyship must be shielded from bad news. She has suffered much shock and grown frail. Now tell me," her voice brightened, "what goes on in the season? Are you attending many balls and picnics?"

Her friend's color rose a little. "Not at present—oh, Jessica, it seems heartless to confide my good news, but I cannot keep it from you!"

"You have heard from your dear Robert!" exclaimed Jessica with sincere delight. "Pray tell me—tell me everything."

Grace warmed to her secret subject of joy. "I declare, he has tired of Mistress Jean. When he came to know her better he found her greedy for possessions, possessive, and wholly selfish. He is joining us here, at the Manor, on Monday next . . . . I dare to believe his visit can have only one purpose."

Jessica clapped her hands. "My dear, dear Grace—the story is to have a happy ending, I know it, and so well deserved by your faithful heart! Pray, pray bring him to see me, for I am sure he must be very fine."

"I will indeed. My dear wish is that you should become friends and that you will often visit us in Scotland." Then Grace remembered Desmond, "Surely, now, *your* story will end happily? For the hateful Lady Olivia must soon fade from his mind."

Jessica's face grew wistful. "Do not hope too much, Grace, his noble heart is as faithful as yours and mine.

152

He will accept defeat, yes, but recovery from her perfidy is another matter. I do not doubt that he may turn to me, but I love him too much to become a makeshift bride. I should be haunted by the knowledge that he would secretly be comparing my small assets to her brilliance and beauty."

Grace pondered this, then said slowly, "Yes—perhaps you are right. I know that I should not be receiving Robert so gladly had Mistress Jean cast him off for another."

At that moment Bella came in with a laden tray, setting it on a low table by the window. As well as the delicious food, she had brought a charming posy.

Jessica, admiringly, picked it up at once. "Bella, how perfectly you know my tastes. These flowers are exquisite."

Bella blushed with pleasure. "I know that you love flowers as I do, Miss, I dare to hope that you might carry a small vase of them to place by Lord Desmond's bedside. 'Twill strengthen you through the night."

Dr. Sandler was pleased at Desmond's condition when he arrived that evening promptly at five.

"The patient is doing well. There is nothing like loving care to strengthen an injured man; besides, I have much faith in his own youth and strength. He will survive, but do not hope for too quick a recovery of consciousness. 'Tis best he remains as he is until the immediate pain subsides."

Jessica gladly accepted his optimism, though she was to watch over her love for five more long nights before his senses returned.

On the sixth night she moved from his bedside to a chair by the open window after eating her sandwiches. The air was heavy with a threat of thunder. Indeed, there seemed scarce any air at all, and she knew that no breeze through the open window would chill him.

At three o'clock that morning the storm broke. The sky was rent by lightning followed by great roars of thunder and blessed cooling rain; she was forced to lower the window for the drops were heavy and splattered over the sill. Storms close to the sea were always spectacular and she had no fear of them. Slowly, the lightning flickered away over the horizon and the noise subsided into a mere echo in the distance.

Suddenly, a weak voice spoke from the bed and she started up.

"Jessica?" It was the first time he had used her given name and, although the syllables were a little blurred his eyes were open and focused. Lord Desmond was quite rational. She sank to her knees and took his hand.

"Hush, my dear, pray do not tax your strength by talking."

He turned to look at her and went on.

"I—think—you have been with me all the time. How long have I lain like this?" His hand tightened slightly on hers.

"Only a few days, my lord, and now you will soon be well." Then, quelling her ache to cry with thankfulness, she said, "Does your head hurt you? I will redress it if it does."

"No." His voice grew more positive. "He—Walter—he fouled me, I believe. We—we thrust at the body but something . . . yes, something sharp struck my head."

"Ssh! Don't try to talk yet or you will be tired."

His gray eyes, darkened by illness, were fixed on her face. "I—I heard her laughing as I went down . . . mocking laughter . . . I . . ." He seemed to fall asleep, and Jessica dared not move from her knees for fear of disturbing him. But a few minutes later his eyes opened again and he raised a hand to her face, caressing her cheek gently.

"How much I think I owe to you, Jessica—I know now, that you are mortal, beautiful and kind . . . not a sprite at all."

With a satisfied sigh, he shifted a little, then fell into the first deep, natural sleep that had come to him for a week. Jessica still knelt at his side, afraid to move lest she wake him, for such a sleep would bring more healing than all the ministrations to his wound.

Gradually, his hand slackened around hers as his sleep took firm hold, and she was able, very gently, to disengage her own. At first she was too cramped to move; then, with infinite care, she edged away, and, gripping the bedside table, stood up. A slight sound in the doorway made her glance up in surprise: Lady Shayne stood there in her dressing robe, shading a candle with her hand. She was smiling.

"I woke suddenly with a great sense of ease. Desmond is better, isn't he?" She came silently toward the bed and gazed down at his sleeping form.

After a little while, she beckoned Jessica back to the window where they conversed in whispers.

"What happened?"

"When the thunder stopped he called my name— my real name not 'Sprite.' He was very weak but quite rational, and he seems to remember the events of that dreadful day."

Her ladyship sighed with relief, "So, thank Heaven, the wicked blow has not deranged his senses?"

"Not in the least. I forbade him to speak very much, and, quite content, he fell asleep. Let me take you back to your room, for I swear he will not wake until morning."

"No, do not leave him, my dear. I feel your presence has sustained him all this time; the sixth sense that told me he was recovering has restored my strength, also. I need no supporting hand now." She left as quietly as she had come, her step firm and her head high.

Jessica drew the chair to the bedside and sat as she had done these many nights, only she felt no need to doze. Her heart was too full.

Dr. Sandler expressed great satisfaction both with his patient and his nurse.

"You have done splendidly, Miss Jessica. I see no need to call every day—unless you send for me, of course. Dress the wound night and morning, but you can safely leave him to sleep normally, while you take your own night's rest."

Jessica was glad, for she was tired and Desmond in a conscious state was far more difficult than when he was inert. He fretted constantly at the bandages.

"They are a pesky nuisance," he grumbled. "And who shaved my head? I declare, I shall be a laughing stock if I appear like this!"

Jessica was brisk. "How ungrateful you are, my lord! Everything has been done for your good, and your hair is starting to grow again already. Now, stop nagging while I apply a fresh dressing!" She could not resist smiling which quite took away her attempt at severity.

"You are a sterner gaoler than any nurse," he grumbled, but his eyes were laughing. "Very well, I submit gratefully."

She could not help but notice, to her dismay, that his hair that had been shaven was growing in again snow white—it would add a great distinction to his appearance, but she dreaded his reaction when he saw it.

She no longer had to be in constant attendance now, for he daily grew stronger, and, with Chalmers always at hand, Lady Shayne sat often by her son, reading to him in her quiet voice or bringing him amusing news from the world outside.

Olivia's name was never mentioned again.

One afternoon Jessica was sitting on the terrace when Grace Ashby was announced—a Grace transformed by love from prettiness to real beauty. With her came a tall, fair young man with eyes blue as the summer skies. A little shy, Grace said,

"Dearest Jessica—this is Robert, Laird of Glencross, and see—" she held out her left hand proudly on which a large diamond glinted in the sun, "we are betrothed."

Jessica sprang up and embraced her friend. "Oh Grace, I am so pleased—so *very* pleased for you!" She turned and held out her hand to Robert, liking him instantly. "I declare it is a great pleasure to meet you— and congratulate you with all my heart, for Grace is a rare being and a most true friend."

His smile was warm and his voice pleasantly deep, with a charming Scots burr to it.

"Faith, Mistress Jessica, do not think that I shall ever undervalue my enchanting jewel!"

Hearing young voices, Lady Shayne joined them, smiling.

"Oh, I declare it is a relief to hear happy young voices here in the afternoon! I have been plagued by bores, hoping for gossip and asking after Desmond. Fortunately they all accepted that he had slight concussion caused by his own fall. Besides, they could scarce contain themselves with excitement over what is proclaimed the *Wedding of the Year!* It seems the Prince Regent himself insists on giving Olivia Lufton away. Her poor father is forced to play second fiddle, but it is undoubtedly a great honor. Now, Grace I know, but pray introduce me to this gentleman."

Jessica proudly presented the laird and announced their betrothal. Lady Shayne clasped his hand, liking him from the first moment.

"How delightful to hear such news," she exclaimed. "I fear that Grace, like my dear Jessica, finds Brighton fops a little tedious. I believe her heart has always been in the highlands of her own country. Now, have you ordered tea, my child?" she asked Jessica.

"I confess I have been too carried away by Grace's splendid news, my lady," Jessica answered. "I will do so instantly."

On the tenth day Dr. Sandler pronounced Desmond well enough to get up and to need no more bandages. "The wound has healed well and is healthy. Much gratitude is owed to Miss Jessica for her tireless care, I must add. You may take luncheon downstairs, Lord Desmond, and sit or stroll gently in the garden. But no riding for a while yet, mind, or you will cause severe headaches."

Jessica was delighted, but, at the same time, her heart sank. Desmond would now have access to the mirror, would see the wing of white tendrils growing fast over the scar. She found them most becoming, enhancing his distinguished appearance. But how would he feel, at barely twenty-six, and, worse, how could he explain it? A simple concussion would cause no such change.

At first Desmond made no mention of the change. He came to luncheon with more than a trace of his former high spirits which delighted his mother who later confided to Jessica,

"He is, indeed, recovered by the grace of God—and the care of Dr. Sandler and you, dear child, who have been so devoted. Perhaps," she added hopefully, "the memories of that wicked day have been blotted from his mind."

Jessica knew better, but she said with a smile, "It is more than possible, my lady—and now you must rest, knowing that all anxiety has passed."

She prayed that it might prove so. Then, on the thirteenth night—a date Jessica had never feared until now, she went to his room to find Desmond sitting facing a mirror, his rapier and his dagger laid out on the chest before him. He was fingering his white locks.

"My lord, what are you doing with those weapons?"

His face was as she had never seen it before—cold and hard as stone, his gray eyes steely.

"Did you think, Jessica, that Walter's perfidy would go unpunished?"

Horrified, she cried, "You will not challenge him to a duel, my lord?"

"A *duel?*" His voice held bitter scorn. "That is a fair contest between honorable adversaries—or should be. There is no shred of honor in all Walter Cheston's being. He has proved it."

Her mind clouded with horror and nameless fears as he drew first one weapon then the other from its sheath. They gleamed wickedly in the evening light.

Terrified, Jessica cried, "Are you deranged, my lord? You cannot mean to *murder* him—to hang for such a worthless creature and bring your house into dishonor?"

There was a long pause, during which she held her breath. If he declared that to be his intention what should she do? He was so very strong, so obsessed by such an insane, yet understandable, desire for vengeance.

At last he turned to her with a wry smile.

"No, Jessica—oh, do not look so troubled, my dear! But, as I have lain here, my heart filled with hatred, I have found ease in daydreaming of his craven cowardice as I ran him through. This evening I have been exorcising that dream, I think, putting my choice of weapons in front of me to envisage, for the last time, what a petty triumph that would be."

Slowly, he resheathed the blades. Jessica dared not speak, for the weights were still evenly balanced. One wrong word might still swing them the disastrous way. He touched his white hair again, then turned back to her.

"By far the braver, the more noble thing must be to ignore his existence completely. Disdain is all he deserves, although he is so vain I swear he will not be aware of it. Besides, I intend never to see or speak to him again. I understand he is shortly to marry Olivia, with geat pomp?"

"Yes, my lord," Jessica answered in a low voice, then looked straight at him. "Does that cause you pain?"

His face was tired by the mental ordeal, but his tone convincing. "No, little one, I think they will slowly tear each other to pieces." His glance moved above her head, as if he were speaking his thoughts out loud. "Olivia is a veritable daughter of Satan, I believe, darkly blessed by that infinite beauty that enslaves men's hearts. She was an obsession with me, you know, a sickness of the spirit, a craving for possession of loveliness." He gave a small, bitter laugh. "Walter is too foolish to understand what a high price he will pay for that possession. It is Olivia herself who will mete out his punishment."

Then he collected himself, and his face softened as he rose and moved toward her, placing his hands on her shoulders.

"Jessica, my own dear true love, heart of my heart— can you forgive me for taking so long to understand what I have known, deep in my being, for so many months now? For it is *you* I love. You possess far more beauty, for not only your exquisite face, but your very soul shines clearly like a flame."

In agony, Jessica stood very still raising her great dark eyes to his. How she had ached to hear these very words, told herself they could never be. Yet now, at last, they brought only a searing pain, linked as they were to his open rejection of Olivia. For a moment, being intensely feminine, she exulted in the moment that would never come again and, sensing her surrender, Desmond bent his tall head and kissed her lips. The touch of his mouth was all she had dreamed of—so tender and with such gentle passion that, in spite of herself, she responded until his strong arms went around her and he kissed her with his whole heart.

At last, breathless, she released herself from the embrace.

Bewildered, he stared down at her.

"You cannot mistake me, my darling. This is no dishonorable advance, and surely I have not read your heart wrongly? I am asking—begging you—to be my wife."

She clenched her hands until the nails bit into her palms. How easy, oh, how blissful it would be to give in—to accept her own heart's desire while shutting her eyes to how closely her substitution was following his passion for Olivia.

At last she had her voice under control.

"You have not read my heart wrongly, Desmond, for I do love you with all my heart. But—I cannot accept you now, now while your own heart is filled with hatred for Olivia and Sir Walter. I—I feel somehow cheapened—a stop-gap to prevent your thoughts straying back to her beauty. For they will, you know, you have been obsessed by her a long time, and those feelings cannot be uprooted by events so recent."

"I do not understand, Jessica. I have just told you that my love for you has been growing steadily all the while. You cannot forsake me now!"

"I shall never forsake you, Desmond, but I must go away for at least a year. If you come to me again, after that time, I promise to consider things differently."

She held out her hand to him with the same formality as her words. They had cost her the last of her strength and she turned blindly to the door, her eyes filled with tears. Echoing in her ears came his last sentence: "You *must* not leave me Jessica . . . ."

Ten

Jessica half ran, half stumbled to her room, scarcely able to control her sobs. It was quite soon after dinner, and Bella would be having her own in the servant's hall, so she would not be disturbed.

But, this time, she could not fling herself down on the bed to cry her heart out, for she felt rigid with misery and shocked at her own words. So she stood, her head resting against the bedpost, her small hands over her face trying to check the tears as they began to trickle through her fingers. She must force herself to move, to go to the drawer and find a kerchief, but it still was not possible.

The door opened so quietly she did not hear it above the wild beating of her heart. Then strong, gentle arms enfolded her against Lady Shayne's breast. For some minutes her ladyship held her, caring nothing that the tears were marking her beautiful dinner gown; softly she began to speak as to a child:

"There, there, little Jessica, let us sit together on the bed. I have a nice, large kerchief here and I will dry your hands and face."

Obediently, grateful for the comfort of sympathy, Jessica found that now she could sit down. One by one, Lady Shayne drew her taut, cold hands from her face and wiped them on finest cambric. Then she tilted the small, ashen face in one hand and dried the cheeks. Jessica seemed to be all huge eyes, dark with sorrow, although the weeping had ceased.

"Now, my dearest daughter—for that you are, indeed —can you tell me what has distressed you so much? Or would you prefer to wait?"

"I cannot wait," murmured Jessica. "When Bella comes I must pack some essential things and then catch the early stage for London tomorrow."

"Is it your father? Have you had bad news?"

Jessica shook her head. "No, my lady, it concerns myself—and, perhaps, Desmond a little." She did not notice that she had not used his title; it seemed pointless now. Lady Shayne gave herself a few moments to collect herself for, under no circumstances, should she add to the girl's heavy burden.

At last she said calmly, "Have you had a quarrel? It is neither like you—nor my son."

"He declared that he loved me . . . I—most wickedly, I know, allowed him to kiss me and—and kissed him in return. Then he begged me to be his wife." She stopped, feeling the tender wonder of his lips, his arms around her just as she had often dreamed they might be, knowing the dream in vain.

Lady Shayne was bewildered. "But, my dear child, do you not, then, love him? I swear I have believed he had your heart for a long time past, and, for myself, to have you as my true daughter has been my own constant prayer."

Jessica struggled for the right words. "Oh, do you not see, my lady—it is far too soon? It is but two weeks since he rode out at the tourney determined to win the love of his heart—Olivia. I have, truly, loved him with all my heart and soul almost since I came to Shayne Park, but his feeling for her has possessed his whole being far longer."

Lady Shayne took her hands earnestly. "But I pray you to understand—you who are so deeply sensitive ... it was a passion, not *love*. Almost a childish longing to win the most beautiful, most desired creature in this country."

Jessica raised her eyes and spoke, "We both know she is an evil woman—but, to Desmond—whose heart is as honest and his feelings as true as your own, my lady —she was the love of his life." She went on with a touch of passion, "He believes he hates her now, but that will pass. I declare it will take many, many months, if not years, for such a love to fade."

Lady Shayne reluctantly knew that this was probably true.

"So—have you refused him?" She sounded very sad.

"Not outright, for my hopes will never quite die. But I have declared that I must go away for a year. Then, if he feels the same for me, he is to come and find me."

"A *year!* Away?" Her ladyship's face paled. "My dear, how shall we manage without you? Why, you are woven into our very lives here! Can you—can you not possibly change your mind?"

Sadly, Jessica shook her head again. "Even for you, my lady, whom I hold so dear, I cannot do that. Oh, do you not understand?" She cried: "If I accept him now there will be no joy, no certainty between us! Loving him as I do, each time he embraces me I shall wonder if he is aching inwardly for that tall, fair beauty! I *cannot* be a shadowy replacement bride to fill his empty arms!" She added softly, "He would despise me."

"I swear he would never do that! He holds you in very high esteem."

"Esteem is not enough," confessed Jessica sadly. "If I ever marry Desmond then I must know that he returns my love in full with no regrets, that Olivia's ghost no longer stands between us. Oh, my lady, I am truly sorry for it will break my heart to leave you."

"But—where will go?"

"To London. I hate it, I admit, but at least I shall have Papa, for this time I will not allow his new wife to

163

come between us. I have learnt much strength since I have lived here."

Her voice was positive, and Lady Shayne knew her words to be true, but her feelings were torn. She understood Jessica's reasoning and could scarce bear to part with a girl so dear, but there would be Desmond to help, too. Perhaps, in time, she could urge him to prove himself to Jessica, but not yet, not until Olivia was married and safely out of his way for some considerable time. Lady Shayne sighed,

"At least you must accept my carriage to take you to your father, my dear child."

Jessica gave a vestige of a smile. "It is a wonderful and most generous offer, but no, my lady. Can you imagine the furore caused by my stepmother and her daughters if I am borne back in a magnificent, crested carriage? Their chattering questions would torment me for days, for they are fearful snobs. Papa tells me in his letters that they are still pursuing noble husbands with no success. No, I must return as I came—by the stage, and in a simple gown and cloak."

"Then I insist that Bella accompanies you. Why, you may keep her with you if you wish. At least you could talk of Shayne together."

Jessica pressed the hands of her benefactress. "Again, thank you, my lady, but how could I subject that gentle child of the country to such a life? Bella is like the flowers she loves so much—she would slowly wilt and pine. No, I wondered—if it would not be an imposition—whether she might pack all my beautiful gowns in a trunk or boxes, then they can be stored in Brighton with Papa's books and his most valuable furniture. I will leave you the address."

"They will remain here," Lady Shayne retorted firmly. "For I shall never lose my faith that you will come back. Oh, Bella will tend them, washing and ironing as is needed and keeping the pomanders fresh in your wardrobe." She turned a tragic face to Jessica. "You will be always in my prayers, my daughter, for I *know* that you will one day take your rightful place as the young Mistress of Shayne Park."

This was too much for them both, and, weeping a

little, they embraced fondly without words—for now there were none.

At last Lady Shayne rose and went to the door. "I will send Bella up to help you pack whatever you need, and the carriage will take you to the stage. I believe it leaves Brighton at eight, but—I cannot allow you to travel alone and unchaperoned!"

"I shall wear the simple gray cloak and bonnet in which I came, my lady, no one will bother me I assure you." She smiled a little. "My love for Desmond is a more powerful chaperone than any lady could ever be!"

She saw Lady Shayne back to her own room, for they had agreed to say no more farewells.

The morning had a little chill with the first hint of early autumn, and a light drizzle fell, too. Jessica was glad. It would have been all too tempting to go back on her resolve if Shayne Park had been bathed in an amber haze promising sunshine.

Bella had wept copiously as she brought her early breakfast with a dew-fresh rose on the tray. Jessica admired the beautiful bloom, then handed it back. "Such freshness would not endure the dusty journey, Bella, pray keep it in here as a talisman that, one day, I may return."

At seven o'clock, she crept along the corridor, fearing to wake Desmond. But all was quiet. The carriage was at the door with her simple valise stowed, and, without wasting a moment, Jessica climbed in.

As the carriage drove away she sat dry-eyed, hands clenched as she stared straight ahead. She would not, dare not, look back. Then, as they reached the tall, main gates, the dreaded, familiar thunder of hooves drew close behind and the carriage slowed as Lord Desmond called out orders and rode up beside the window. Jessica pulled it open and looked out at the pale angry face of Lord Desmond on Hercules. Her first reaction was stupefied.

"Desmond! Dr. Sandler has forbidden you to ride for at least a week!"

"Doctor be hanged," he retorted vehemently, reaching for her hand. "You *must not go*, Jessica—you have had no time to think, to talk over what has happened. I beg you to alight and let us walk a little. I will go down on my knees, here on the grass, to entreat you if you wish. I swear that I love you—how can you run away without a word at dawn like this?"

Jessica's face looked stricken, but her resolve was firm.

"I *must* go, Desmond—but my offer remains: come to my father's house in one year if you still wish to wed me, and I shall receive you gladly."

He swore a great oath which startled the coachman. "London, of all places, which you hate so much! Oh, Jessica, my dearest love, can you not stay with your aunt if you must go? At least we could see each other."

The longing to step down, to succumb to his arms, made her feel quite faint but, with the last of her willpower, she released her hand and, in a small, steady voice she said,

"My decision is made, my dear one," and to the coachman she called: "Drive on, please, immediately or I shall be late."

She felt numb—*why* was she so sure that this was the right course? Desmond's face, pale and pleading, swam before her eyes.

For once, the stage to London was not crowded. Jessica had a corner seat by the window, so that she could see all her beloved countryside and the other four passengers paid no attention to the small figure so drably dressed. She turned her thoughts toward London. How would she explain her precipitate arrival without even a letter to warn her family?

Then she thought of her father—dear Papa, he would be so pleased to see her, and he never pried. Constance, Ophelia, and Juliet would chatter like magpies, agog for royal gossip and the latest modes from Brighton. How could they all have heads so empty? But here she held her imagination in check. She must not remember her old dislike of them all, for were not most women content to be so occupied?

In London the autumnal day seemed gloomy with gray skies and a light drizzle. The stage stopped at Charing Cross where travellers could take a cab if they wished. But Jessica, whose valise was not heavy, decided to walk the three or four miles to Pimlico despite the weather. Her legs felt cramped after the long drive and the air, though moist, was fresh.

As she had assured Lady Shayne, no one bothered to accost the small, gray-clad figure, walking briskly with her bonnet hiding her lovely little face. Then, as she approached the house her heart quickened with alarm—there was straw laid down in the street, a sure sign of grave illness since it deadened the sound of horses and carriages passing by. It could not—*must* not be Papa, but dread brought her to the door almost at a run. She tugged the bell.

An unfamiliar maid opened the door and said:

"No visitors are allowed, Miss—the Master is very ill."

Jessica pushed past her impatiently, loosening her bonnet strings with her free hand.

"I am his daughter, Miss Court," she said curtly. "Kindly let me go to his room without delay."

But Constance had heard voices and came out of the drawing room, her face drawn and a great deal older.

"Why, Jessica! We received no letter."

"I sent none," said Jessica. "I felt I was needed here and travelled at once. What ails my father?"

Constance wrung her hands; she was no longer the self-possessed woman who had descended on The Old Manor when Arthur Court was delicate and his daughter too young to manage properly. Jessica felt a small surge of pity for her.

"What does the doctor say?" she asked more gently.

Constance shook her head. "It is all so baffling, I declare. Your father collapsed two days ago, having shown no signs of illness beforehand. I called Dr. Henson immediately but he, too, can find no cause. He bled him and ordered straw laid down, but my poor, dear husband simply lies there and will say nothing—except that he is in no pain."

Jessica removed her cloak. "I will go to him, if you permit it, Constance."

"Oh, pray, pray do!" The older woman looked at

her curiously. "Upon my word, you have become a grown woman!"

"Yes." Jessica managed a faint smile. "I shall help all I can."

Then she sped up the stairs, fearful of what she might find. She opened her father's door quietly; the room was semi-dark since the blinds had been drawn, and the air felt stale. Arthur Court lay in his bed, eyes wide open. Jessica went straight to his side and knelt beside him, gathering his hands in hers.

"Papa! It is me, Jessica. Oh, but it is wonderful to see you again!" She kissed his pale cheek, and he turned his head toward her, his eyes showing some animation.

"Jessica! My dear little one—now, at last I can speak my heart. For I am *not* ill, only sick with worry—and the endless fussing of my wife and that fool, Dr. Henson, who still believes that leeches will cure anything! Why, your dear Mamma knew better years ago—but the doctor is very old."

Jessica felt tears of thankfulness rising, but she quelled them. She had a very real job to do, something to fill her mind and take all her care for many days. She rose, saying,

"Dearest Papa, you and I are country folk and I declare this room is stifling! I will pull up the blinds and open a window. The air is pleasantly cool but not cold and will revive you. Remember how you, Mamma, and I always loved early autumn?" She worked briskly as she spoke, and having made sure that no draft reached the bed, she returned to his side to find him smiling a little. She drew up a chair.

"Your coming is like a miracle, daughter," he said, his voice a little stronger. "I would not write and alarm you, for I wanted you to enjoy Brighton to the full."

"I did indeed, Papa—thanks to your great generosity. But that can wait until later. Do you wish to tell me of your anxiety now or would you prefer to sleep first?"

"No, no—sleep is filled with confused dreams and brings no rest; to talk freely, open my heart is what I crave—yet I fear my tidings may distress you, also."

168

"The only thing that can distress me now is ignorance, Papa, and for you to speak your worries is the sure cure—for you are not physically ill, praise Heaven."

"No—I fear my sudden collapse and malaise has resulted from cowardice, Jessica. I had worried alone for so long, yet, the last person I could confide in was Constance."

"Tell me."

"I think you know, as I do now, that she married me for my money. Oh, she brought tenderness, too," he added loyally, "and I cannot blame her, with two grown daughters of such stupidity! Good marriages were their only goal."

He paused and Jessica said softly, "And now your fortune has been spent. Dearest Papa, you must not fret, for it has all gone in kindness of heart and great generosity. Think how many men in your position squander their inheritance on gambling or drinking! You have only warmth for other, less fortunate beings to account for the loss. But do not despair. You still own The Old Manor. I know, for I have become friends with your summer tenants. Had you forgot?"

"Most certainly not! But I always intended that that dear house should be yours, Jessica, for I could not bear it to pass to strangers."

"Papa, my one desire is that you should recover, for that house is worth several hundreds of pounds, and I shall be well able to care for myself in future. Now, let us be practical. To ease your mind further, do you know a reputable, honest agent in Brighton who can handle the sale?"

"Alas, I do not, and that is what plagues me."

"But I think I can discover such an honest man. I have many dear friends in Brighton and, if you will leave it in my hands, I think I can guarantee an honorable agent to handle your affairs. I cannot produce an answer immediately—it may take two or three weeks of inquiry, but pray have a little patience, dear Papa. I am come in time to help you, and tonight you must sleep easily, for all will be solved."

"You will not tell Constance?" he pleaded, with a hint of fear.

"Not a word, Papa, I swear it."

"She might leave me else, and, although I have come to know her for what she is, she has been good to me, Jessica, and her companionship is comforting."

Jessica managed a warm smile. "I know, dearest Papa, and I will not hinder your relationship in any way. Now sleep, and do not be tortured by dreams, for a solution is at hand."

Jessica had meant to write only a brief note to Lady Shayne, thanking her for all her kindness and telling of her safe arrival in London. She felt ashamed to be forced to ask for still more assistance, but loyalty to her father must take precedence now.

Feeling depressed and not wishing to sound melancholy, she hesitated for a week before sending the letter.

Sad already in the knowledge that The Old Manor must be sold, when she went downstairs again from her father's room on that first day, she found a stiff, critical Constance waiting for her.

"Well, I declare, you've been up there far too long. No doubt you'll have worn out my patient completely. He is not fit to talk, but I suppose you have been tiring him with tales of your wild life in Brighton," she sniffed contemptuously.

Instantly, Jessica felt all the old animosity and drew herself up with equal stiffness. "Indeed, I have done no such thing—and I have had no wild life to regale him with. Papa was extremely pleased to see me, that's all, and I have been sitting with him quietly."

Constance sniffed again and marched out. As soon as she had left the room, Ophelia and Juliet set down their embroidery and surged on her eagerly.

"We know you could never tell Mamma about your adventures; if we had any we should not dare to tell her, either, she is so very proper!" Ophelia sighed, "But, alas, London has been plaguey dull, I declare!"

"Indeed yes," Juliet chimed in. "Mr. Court—your

Papa—has been most generous, and we have some modish gowns and fal-lals, but the men—" she cast up her eyes dramatically, just as her late father must have done when reading the tragedies of Shakespeare"—they are so *dull*— oh, they can dance quite well, but Ophelia swears they are too tightly corseted to feel the slightest passion." She giggled and blushed at her own daring.

Jessica knew it was going to be just as she had feared. The girls were just as vapid and no whit more attractive, indeed Ophelia was tending to plumpness, and Constance as resentful as ever. Although Jessica had matured enough to know that her attitude was caused not so much by un- kindness as jealously, this made it no easier to endure, however. And her heart ached to think that it was this woman and these girls through their mother's ambitions, who had reduced poor Papa to such a state of financial worry as to make him ill.

Ten minutes later Constance swept back into the room, her face black as thunder.

"Well, if your father dies of pneumonia don't blame me," she cried, angrily facing Jessica. "Opening a window wide like that! Let alone drawing-up the blinds so that the light should tire his eyes. I might have known that you would cause trouble the minute you walked in."

"Papa is used to country air," said Jessica as mildly as she could. " 'Twas he who suggested the room was very stuffy. Did you not always have windows open when the air was mild in Sussex?"

She knew quite well, without being told, that Con- stance was of the breed that dreaded even a thread of fresh air in the house so, without waiting for further wrath, she said, "I will take up my valise now and un- pack. I take it my room is still empty?"

"No," said Juliet happily, "it seemed a right shame for Ophelia and me to go on sharing when your room was empty, so Mama has put me in there. La, it will be fun to share with you, Jessica—we can talk half the night if we wish!"

Jessica's heart sank even further. So even privacy was to be denied in this house, the one thing she needed above all else if she were to survive her own heartache and unhappiness in London. But Juliet was gushing on as she ran to the door.

"I will come up with you now and help you unpack. I warrant you have bought some stylish gowns with you. We hear the season in Brighton is far more full of life and high society than it has been here."

Jessica followed the girl upstairs.

Naturally, Juliet had annexed the best bed, but her offer to exchange was so quick and generous that Jessica smiled.

"No, no," she protested, "this one will do me very well—if you will be so kind as to remove the gowns on it!"

Juliet blushed. "I am plaguey untidy, I fear; I will hang them up at once."

Indeed, she fussed around in such a flurry, clearing room for Jessica's things everywhere, that the younger girl began, reluctantly to like her. She was so very anxious to please, but her movements were a little clumsy, rather like a puppy ingratiating itself to a new mistress. When the bed was cleared, Jessica lifted up her valise and snapped it open, saying,

"Pray do not expect high fashion from me, Juliet. I do not think to join you and Ophelia in your social rounds in London. I have stored away my things in Brighton."

Juliet swung around from tidying the toilette, at present bestrewed with forbidden beauty aids such as a pot of rouge and a box of much spilled pink face powder. "You have been crossed in love, poor Jessica—I can tell," Juliet volunteered.

At this, Jessica laughed, "Far from it, I swear. I have had several suitors, yes, but none to my taste."

Juliet stared at her, the round blue eyes staring from her head in astonishment. "You mean—you *turned down* proposals? Why, we have had not one between us so far! Pray tell me, were any of them noblemen?"

"Yes, one or two—but for the most part they were extremely boring. You must not judge by a man's rank, Juliet," she went on more earnestly. "There are many good men who may have no title but could bring you great happiness."

Juliet's face fell. "Mamma will have none of it. I—I *have* taken a fancy to a fine young man, a Mr. Chater, and I—I know he likes me. But when he asked to call, Mamma was so short with him, he will never again have the courage. You see, his father is a draper—oh, a most respected one, there is even the royal coat of arms in the shop, meaning royal patronage."

"Poor Juliet. Perhaps, now I am here for a while, I can help you. I shall certainly try, although I fear your mother will not approve of my influence."

There never seemed to be any peace in the house. Jessica, who craved solitude from time to time, could find it only by taking long walks in the park as she had done before, and in her father's room, for his health was much improved since her offer to assist in selling The Old Manor. But it was six days before Constance announced, grudgingly, that "Dearest Arthur" was now out of danger, so she and the girls were to attend a *soirée* and small dance. She was glad that Jessica did not wish to accompany them, for her looks had improved to the point where even her stepmother had to admit she was a beauty. Of course, her gowns were plain and most disappointing, but her graceful figure and those enormous eyes might prove sad rivals to the attractions of Ophelia and Juliet.

Once they had gone, Jesssica settled thankfully in the drawing room to write to Lady Shayne. It was far from easy, and she tore up several efforts before she was satisfied. She wrote with gratitude and affection, then included a brief paragraph saying:

"I hate to be of trouble, but do you, by chance, know of an honorable agent in Brighton who might handle the sale of my father's house, The Old Manor? I fear he will never be strong enough to return, so regretfully, we have decided that to sell it is the wisest course. Pray do not put yourself out in any way, dearest lady, nor worry Lord Desmond for there is no urgency; but I fear I have a poor head for business and would feel happier if the

173

matter is handled by a professional man of good repute."

When it was finished, Jessica pulled on her gray cloak, covered her head with the drab bonnet, and went herself to the mailbox, knowing it would be collected for the stage next day.

Then she returned and went with a lighter heart to sit with her father. His worn face always lit up at her coming.

"Dear Jessica—how restful you are. Shall we read aloud a little as we used to do? I miss those times sorely."

"So do I, Papa. What shall it be? Oh, and your troubles will soon be over for I have enlisted the best adviser in Brighton that I know. We shall have an answer soon."

"How good you are. My heart will always ache that we have to part with your inheritance for all this—frippery."

"Come, Papa." She managed a radiant smile. "Times are changing, and, once you are recovered, I mean to seek employment."

"You have grown so beautiful—did you not have many suitors in Brighton?"

"La, yes! Two I liked immensely, but not enough to marry. And a third," she laughed, "shall I imitate his offer for you? It was truly absurd!"

He began to laugh, too. "You were always a wicked mimic, Jessica. How your dear Mamma and I used to chuckle. 'Twill do me more good than reading, I declare."

Jessica did a lively imitation of Lord Minden by the end of which Arthur Court was laughing heartily. Then suddenly, he changed and rested a hand on hers.

"Did you not meet one man worthy of your love? You have become so—different. Not only your beauty, but there is a new depth in you; and sometimes I fancy your eyes are sad when you sit quietly here beside me."

There was a long pause before Jessica answered, "Yes—I did indeed meet someone, Papa, someone most noble in character. But—I cannot speak of it at present; if I could it would be to you, believe me."

"Will you tell me just one thing, dear daughter—you were not jilted?"

174

Jessica stared at him, her color rising. "Far from it, Papa. It was entirely my decision to leave, I swear. Now, I will read to you." She sprang up and went to the three shelves which held all the books that Constance had allowed her husband to bring to London. "What would you prefer?" She was glad to be away from his searching gaze and deeply grateful when he took his tone from hers.

"Let us have a little of *Emma* by Miss Jane Austen. It was a sad loss to the world when she died scarce four years ago."

Jessica found the volume and returned to his bedside.

"Yes. But what riches she has left—literature that will live forever." She opened the book at his favorite passage and started reading in her sweet, low voice.

Within seven days Jessica received a charming letter from Lady Shayne. The embossed coronet on the flap of the envelope produced a flood of inquisitive questions around the breakfast table:

Constance began. "Pray read us your noble letter, Jessica. It is bound to be filled with gossip and news."

"No, it is from a very dear friend with whom I stayed."

Juliet could contain herself no longer, and babbled out a host of inaccuracies, punctuated by giggles. "I swear it is from one of her suitors, Mamma . . . did you know Jessica had many offers? La, dukes and earls were at her feet—mere lords were a sight too common for her, I declare. Oh tell, tell Jessica . . . is that letter not a *billet-doux?*"

Jessica, restraining herself, tucked the unopened letter beneath the edge of her plate. "It will contain no gossip, and my correspondence is private."

Constance's eyes snapped with annoyance. "You are a deal too young to receive private letters, Miss. I have a mind to demand that you hand it over."

Jessica rose quickly, the precious missive held against her breast. Her eyes flashed.

"You have no authority over *me*, Constance. I shall be out all morning."

Swiftly she fled from the room, three faces, vacant

175

with astonishment at such effrontery, staring after her.

Fearful that her stepmother might storm after her, Jessica waited not a moment. Still in her light, kid slippers she snatched the gray cloak from its peg in the hall, and without even pausing to adjust her bonnet, she left the hateful house.

It was a clear, September morning with a promise of sun later. At that hour the streets were almost deserted for the gentry were not yet astir. Only tradesmen, busy with hand-carts delivering freshly baked bread and fresh vegetables were about their business, young maids hurrying out on some urgent errand, or disdainful young footmen, compelled to walk a yapping pet dog up and down. No one paid Jessica any attention, assuming her to be one of them.

Reaching the park she found that, too, deserted but, much as she longed to open the letter, she walked some distance from the gates to a quiet, secluded bench.

There, with trembling fingers, she opened the envelope. Would there be news of Desmond—even some message, perhaps? But she was ashamed of her selfishness. Besides, after her very final farewell to him, she doubted if he would ever trouble his mind with her again. No, this letter must concern Papa's affairs, vital to his peace of mind, so she unfolded the sheets of thick notepaper.

Dearest Jessica,

I cannot tell you with what delight I received your letter. My only complaint is that you say too little about yourself, dear child, for you are most sorely missed by all of us at Shayne.

I was indeed sad to hear of your father's decision regarding The Old Manor, for I fear his new responsibilities must have cost him dear. However, I have excellent news already that I trust will cheer him. The most trustworthy man I know where property is concerned has already received a splendid offer which I hope your father may accept. It seems he has a client who has often ridden past the house and declared that it was exactly what he wanted. The buyer insists on remaining anonymous for the time being, for personal reasons of his own. I suspect he is buying it for his bride and wishes the surprise to be well kept. But I digress. You know how my romantic imagination runs away with me! In short, he is willing to pay ten thousand guineas for the freehold—a price, I think, that we could scare hope for if we were forced to sell Shayne Park! However, for such an offer he would like a reply as soon as possible.

Your friends, the Ashby family, returned to Scotland last week, for I understand that your friend, Grace, is to marry the charming young Laird she brought here, before Christmas.

Pray include more news of yourself, dear child, in your reply. Desmond sends his deepest regards.

Your devoted friend—

Her eyes momentarily misted with tears of love and gratitude, Jessica tucked the precious letter into the bosom of her gown. Then, on winged feet, caring not what time it might be, she sped back to the house in Pimlico.

Brushing past an astonished maid cleaning the stairs, she made straight for her father's room, forgetting in her excitement even to knock. Constance was at the bedside, talking in a low tone while her husband remained with his eyes obstinately closed. Now Constance rose like a wrathful Tigress.

"How dare you, Miss! Pray leave the room at once."

But Arthur Court, wide awake, sat up, looking past his wife to where his daughter stood, her eyes shining.

"Pray leave us, Constance!" His voice was commanding. "I wish to speak to Jessica alone."

With bad grace Constance went to the door, jostling the girl as she passed. Her eyes foretold a row ahead.

Jessica did not care, she ran to her father as soon as the door was closed.

"Oh, Papa, such news! I have heard from my most trusted friend, and an offer is made for The Old Manor of ten thousand guineas!"

"Ten thousand!" He sank back on the pillows, his eyes shining with pleasure. "Why—'tis a fortune . . . a miracle!"

"It is indeed Papa. May I accept? Only—I beg you not to tell your wife, or it will all go."

Her father gladly gave his permission and without further delay Jessica wrote to Lady Shayne accepting the offer.

Eleven

Christmas had come and gone. Arthur Court was much better although, as he admitted a little guiltily to Jessica,

"I keep to my room far more than is necessary, you know. It is a shameful luxury to enjoy the quietness, especially now that I have no financial worries and you, my dearest, bring me new books. But what of your own life, dear child? I declare you look a mite peaky these days, as if you were waiting for something that does not come."

"It is not yet time, Papa," she said, refusing to enlarge this statement. "But I am in excellent health. It is only the air and the constant bustle in London that I find tiring."

Indeed, Jessica had found a new friend, as far as this was possible with their different mental abilities, in Juliet.

One day before Christmas Jessica had asked permission from Constance to allow her daughter to escort her on a short shopping expedition. "I declare, I know none of the shops in London, and I wish to make a few purchases for Christmas. Will you allow Juliet to be my guide?"

Constance, instantly interested in the very word *shopping* since Arthur had not been quite so generous with funds of late, said,

"Should I not be a more suitable companion—especially if you wish to have new gowns made up?"

"La, no—though it is good of you to offer. I have no thought of gowns—only small gifts for the family. 'Twould be a shame to waste your time," and she gave a light laugh, knowing with inner delight that she was deliberately deceiving her stepmother. As soon as they had left the house Juliet asked,

"Where do you wish to go, Jessica?"

"Why, to Mr. Chater's famous establishment, of course. You tell me he has excellent merchandise."

Juliet blushed with pleasure and embarrassment. Indeed, she was so overcome with gratitude that her words came haltingly.

"Oh, Jessica—how, how good you are! Mamma—Mamma will not patronize Mr. Chater since his son asked to call. He—young Mr. Chater, I mean, is usually in charge there now."

"Then let us hope we shall see him." Jessica felt quite gay; it was sheer pleasure to be helping this hapless girl, caught up by her mother's social ambitions when she might have found her perfect level if left to her own choice.

Juliet's steps quickened eagerly. "It is not so very far," she cried. "I fear I have often walked by, although I—I have not dared to enter, since I am always escorted by Ophelia or a maid, and they would tell Mamma."

"Ophelia is quite caught up with that fat Baronet, is she not?" asked Jessica.

Juliet giggled, "Indeed she is! I declare he is horrible with his paunch and his dark red cheeks; but my sister does not care because he has a title, and she believes she will be a Lady."

"And will he offer for her?" Jessica felt a curious repugnance at this attitude to marriage.

"Oh, I am sure of it." Juliet had the grace to shudder.

"You are so wise, Jessica, not to attend Mamma's *at homes* on Thursdays. For he is there regularly and he sits down, with heavy breathing, and just devours my sister with his eyes. Why, he must be quite *old*. But she refuses to discuss the matter with me."

Jessica decided that Ophelia need not be her concern. She was her mother's daughter: insensitive, ambitious, caring nothing for the finer feelings so long as she achieved money and position. Juliet was cast in a rather different mold, not very clever, but romantic and seeking happiness above all else.

They arrived at Mr. Chater's establishment. The bow window display was most impressive and over the door hung the splendid sign of royal patronage. Juliet hung back, but Jessica said crisply,

"Come on, my dear, I am prepared to help you if I approve of your young man." She burst out laughing. "What a thing to say, when I am almost two years younger than you! Let us go in, my dear, and hope that he is there."

Charles Chater was there, indeed, and, at the sight of Juliet his face flushed as bright as hers as he hurried forward. "This is indeed an unexpected pleasure, Miss Browne, I had scarce hoped to see you again. Now, pray let me be of service. If you require any article that is not in stock, I will have it ordered immediately."

The two were so obviously entranced with each other that Jessica intervened: "I am the customer, not my stepsister, but I have not yet made up my mind on my purchases. May I look around quietly, while perhaps you will be good enough to entertain her?" Smiling to herself, Jessica betook herself to a distant counter and studied a display of handkerchiefs set out under glass. Charles Chater, she thought, was a most suitable, worthy husband for Juliet, and she was determined to help them further.

After quarter of an hour she dared tarry no longer or Constance might grow suspicious. She went over to the pair and said,

"I have made my selections, Mr. Chater. Do you manage this fine establishment all day, or do you have a little time to yourself?"

"Why, I—I only do the first part of the morning and again at four o'clock, so that my father can rest."

"I walk in the park nearby every morning between eleven o'clock and one, and of late I have managed to persuade Miss Browne to join me. I declare, we should be pleased to have your company on occasion, if you would care to come?"

It would have been most brazen had the invitation been for herself, but the pleasure in his face showed that he had not considered it in that light.

"Pray, tell me where I may meet you?" he asked eagerly.

Jessica described the secluded bench and the path to it in detail then, with a most touching gratitude, he attended to Jessica's purchases—six boxes of finest cambric handkerchiefs, a charming purse embroidered in petit point, two pairs of kid gloves, and a pomander set in porcelain.

When Mr. Chater had bowed them out of the door, his glance resting on Juliet, the ecstatic girl took Jessica's arm and insisted on carrying some of her packages.

"Oh, Jessica, how can I thank you? I swear, I had given up all hope of seeing him again, but I like him better than ever."

Jessica chuckled. "And his feelings for you are plain! I declare, I shall prove a splendid, conniving matchmaker. Mr. Shakespeare would be proud of me, I fancy! Your Charles Chater is a very pleasant young man indeed."

"But—if he does offer, whatever shall I say? Mamma will never agree."

"Leave that to me." Jessica was thoroughly enjoying herself. "Had you forgotten Papa? It is *he* who is your official guardian until you come of age, and he will be only too delighted to see you well suited; so wait until you wish to be betrothed, and I promise to enlist his help. Meantime, on our trips to the park, I shall go for one of my long walks once you are safe in Mr. Chater's keeping, for I swear he is a most honorable gentleman."

Thus, a month passed and spring was everywhere. As Jessica saw the first crocuses and snowdrops, then daffodils pushing up from their winter sleep in the well-kept beds, her heart began to blossom, too. It was not yet summer of course, but was it possible that Desmond was not counting the months? Could the miracle of his love have lasted such a long separation or not? Jessica was afraid to hope, yet unable to accept the desolation if he did not come at all. His face was in her mind constantly now—not the young face she had first met, but one more austere and gaunt after much suffering, distinguished by the white wing of hair over his wound. She prayed constantly, her prayers a confused pleading with both God and Desmond himself. Perhaps, she thought, it is a little blasphemous, but they are the only beings who can come to my aid.

Meantime, Mr. Chater had proposed to Juliet, and, radiant, she came to Jessica who led her up to Papa's room. If he were surprised he disguised this in delight at the visit. His vapid stepdaughters had appeared to care nothing for him, clinging to their worldly mother like limpets.

He laid down his book as Jessica sank on her knees beside his chair, her beautiful eyes laughing up at him.

"Oh, Papa, we have been extremely wicked, Juliet and I! Now we need your help, and I know that you will give it gladly. I have promised Juliet that you will." She launched into the story of Juliet's romance with Charles Chater, freely confessing her own connivance at which her father smiled. "And now it has all turned out so splendidly, Papa, and she needs your support. Juliet is not like Ophelia, craving a title at all costs. She has chosen a charming and prosperous Draper of whom I thoroughly approve. Constance will have none of him, for he is not a nobleman, but I have come to know him well, and Juliet will not only be happy and cared for but they will be divinely happy. Can any woman wish for more?"

Arthur Court smiled again and beckoned Juliet to come closer. Nervously she did so and he studied her joyous face, then he nodded. "I declare, I like your young man's father—not that I have been well enough to visit the establishment often, but I am convinced of his worthiness. So you wish to be betrothed, eh?"

"Yes, sir—Mr. Court—but I dare not tell Mamma."

Arthur Court burst out laughing: "My dear child, I think the whole arrangement is admirable—yes, admirable. Leave the rest to me."

Jessica embraced him warmly. "Papa, I *knew* we could rely on you! I fear Constance will be extremely irritated by my interference."

He patted her hand, and added, "Ask her to come up to my room, and you, Juliet, have no fear. I shall see to it that your young man is welcomed in my house."

Constance went upstairs promptly, and the two girls waited in the drawing room, trying to concentrate on embroidery; but soon Juliet put hers aside and turned to Jessica. "I cannot manage the stitches—I am so nervous."

Indeed, time passed slowly. Constance was with her husband for at least an hour. When she returned it was plain to see she had been weeping, also that she was out of temper.

"You, Miss," she turned on Jessica. "You have brought nothing but trouble to this house ever since you arrived. How dared you encourage my young daughter?"

"Because I am fond of her and wish her to be happy."

Constance shrugged and faced Juliet. "As for you— well, it is true that you have no prospects of bettering yourself and are nigh on twenty, so I suppose there is nothing but to allow this—this young draper to visit us."

Juliet was so overcome she ran forward and embraced her mother. "Oh, Mamma, he is so very charming and I— I am more happy than I ever hoped to be. You will like him, I swear it. When may he call?"

"Well," Constance said grudgingly, "Mr. Court seems to think he is wiser in this matter than your mother. He says the young man is to come tomorrow afternoon, and he will be down here to receive him."

That evening Jessica thanked her father, her eyes laughing. "La, but you have worked a miracle, dear Papa —and how good of you to say you will be there when Mr. Chater calls. It has set Juliet's mind quite at rest."

From then on affairs progressed rapidly until, by Easter, there was a splendid betrothal party at the Court house. The wedding would take place in June. Against her will, Constance had to confess that Charles Chater had

184

"some finer points," while Arthur Court was more direct. "Heaven be praised, one of the girls is settled—and settled well. The young couple are to be given a small house in Mayfair by Charles's father, and I shall see to her dowry."

Jessica was of course delighted, but she also felt very heart-sick on her own account. Would Desmond come before summer? She scarce dared to hope, and there had been no letter recently from Lady Shayne.

Just after Easter, Jessica set out alone for a long walk. Constance still made her feel unwanted, and Juliet was bubbling over with wedding plans, joy, and her new house. Jessica felt very lonely. Self-pity was not in her nature, but her longing for Desmond was sometimes almost too great to bear.

When she returned to the house that day she knew she was late for luncheon, but she no longer heard Constance's acid remarks.

Her surprise was overwhelming, when, on her arrival, the door was flung open by Constance herself and not the maid. Her face was wreathed in smiles and she drew Jessica inside with positive affection.

"My dear, you had a visitor this morning. By my troth he was as fine a man as I have ever seen, and an *earl*, no less. Why, his carriage was so elegant and the doors covered in armorial bearings! I declare, everyone in the street was staring out of their windows with curiosity!"

"Where is he?" asked Jessica, snatching off her hat and coat.

"Oh, he scarce stayed half-an-hour. He said he was returning instantly to Brighton, but he wished to see your father first."

"Did he leave no message for *me*—no word at all?"

At this moment Juliet surged out of the drawing room, her face alight with happiness. "Indeed he did, Jessica—a message so large I declare my arms will not hold it!"

Jessica ran past her into the drawing room, her feet on wings. There, in pride of place on the sofa, was a huge bouquet of exquisite hothouse flowers, their brilliant colors outshining the sun. There were long-stemmed roses of every hue, carnations, exotic orchids, her special, smaller

favorites the sweet-scented freesias and to a separate
bunch of lilies of the valley a long vellum envelope was tied
with gold ribbon.

For a few minutes Jessica stood paralyzed, staring in
disbelief that she was not dreaming—such a gift, and a
special drive to London to deliver it himself! Oh, if only
she had been here to welcome him instead of nearly giving
up hope in the park!

Carefully, she untied the envelope while three inquisitive pairs of round blue eyes were fixed on her face
from the doorway. She could not read Lord Desmond's
precious letter under such scrutiny. Carrying it carefully
for her legs felt quite weak, Jessica passed through them
and went up to the room she still shared with Juliet. She
locked the door behind her for she *must* be alone now.

Sitting on her bed she opened the big envelope with
care and, to her bewilderment, drew out a folded parchment document and only one sheet of Shayne Park note
paper.

*My eternally beloved Jessica—I can wait no longer
to deliver this into your hands. My love has not, as you
feared, grown dim or been forgotten; far from it. My impatience to be at your side has irked me sorely. You may
have found a new love in London by now, and I shall be
the last to blame you. But, if you have not, even if you will
not accept me as a husband, I have ensured that you have
your own, beautiful home, "The Old Manor," safely in your
possession for all time. At least we can be neighbors, and
my mother and I have restored all your father's treasures
and furnished it in a way that we feel will please you.*

*I need no thanks, for I remain the man whose heart is
utterly in your possession already. Desmond.*

She unfolded the parchment to find that it was true.
The document was in her name. The house was hers forever.

Jessica wept tears of utter thankfulness and humility.
This could only be the act of a man truly in love. Her heart
was overflowing with the desperate longing to be in his
arms—she would go tomorrow!

She ran to her father, throwing open the door without

even knocking. He was waiting for her in his chair, his face looking better and happier than she remembered it for many years. Speechless with tears again, she placed the document on his knee and sank down beside him.

Gently, he stroked her thick dark curls. "Oh, my dearest daughter—I, too, have wept a little for the happiness you so richly deserve. Lord Desmond is splendid—absolutely all I could have wished for you. I begged him to stay a little to see you," he chuckled softly, "but, I declare, he seemed *shy*—as if fearing a rebuff!"

"Oh, Papa, I have been eating my heart out these many months, just for a sight of him. But," a puzzled frown wrinkled her forehead, "when your check came, Lady Shayne declared the house was bought by an unknown purchaser, perhaps as a surprise for his bride. Desmond must have persuaded him to sell it again."

Her father's eyes were twinkling. "No, indeed. 'Twas he who bought it in the first place—for you, my dear; he swears that whether you will accept him or not, he wishes it to be your home."

Jessica went to the window and stared out, unseeingly. At last, in a low voice, she said, "And to think I doubted his love—insisted that he must wait a year to claim me because I could not believe it. Oh, Papa, I feel so shamed."

Arthur Court joined her and placed a comforting arm around her slim shoulders. "I think a delay for such a reason at your age is no bad thing. Why, you are still scarcely nineteen and he looks—older."

"That is because he suffered much. I have evaded your questions until now, but at last, Papa, I should like to tell you the whole story."

And so, through the long spring afternoon, Arthur Court listened quietly, amazed and proud at the spirit and staunch courage of his young daughter. No wonder she had captured such a noble heart! When she had finished there was a long silence, her mind still filled with all the momentous events at Shayne Park. At last she looked up, her eyes shining. "Oh, I can scarce *wait* to see him," she cried. "Will you come with me to Shore Vale tomorrow? Do you feel strong enough?"

"Nothing will stop me, Jessica. I declare I have not felt so well and full of heart for many years."

"And—do you realize, neither of us has taken luncheon?" Jessica sprang up, flushing. "How *could* I be so thoughtless—so selfish? Forgive me, and I will go straight to the kitchen and bring you something cold on a tray. For myself, I could eat nothing, but you have been ill . . . ."

There was a knock on the door and Juliet entered, bearing a laden tray, her face glowing.

"I—I feared to intrude before, although Mamma was pestering. But I have just had Cook make good chicken sandwiches and cut a fresh fruit cake; Bertha will be up directly with the tea. Oh, Jessica, I am so happy for you . . . I have put your lovely bouquet in a big bowl of water for I know you will want to arrange the flowers yourself."

"Come in and join us, Juliet. You will at least take some cake and a dish of tea?" Her stepfather had never sounded so full of life, so young.

"Of course you must," echoed Jessica, helping her to set down the heavy tray on a table. "We shall get little sleep tonight," she warned, laughing, "for now I declare I shall have wedding plans to discuss as well! You and Charles must come to Brighton for your honeymoon, for I hope you will act as my Maid of Honor?" Her beauty, so long dimmed by heartache, was dazzling and Juliet stared at the transformation, open-mouthed. Then she glanced past Jessica and exclaimed in dismay,

"Your father! Oh, Jessica—he is ill!"

It was true. The excitement and happiness of the day had brought on his old heart trouble, and, as both girls ran to his side, he lay back, gray and gasping in his chair.

"I must fetch Mamma," said Juliet quickly. "She has handled such attacks before, and I will send Bertha for the doctor." She hurried away. Jessica knelt holding his hand, her face white.

"Papa—Papa—it is all my fault. I did not understand . . . ."

Constance bustled in, taking charge at once.

"Be off with you, girl, you have done enough damage as it is." She sounded oddly triumphant.

Jessica was about to protest, but Constance pointed

to the door and Jessica went, reluctantly, not wishing to distress her father in any way.

It was not until two days later that Jessica felt able to leave the house and travel to Brighton. In spite of strong protests from Constance, her father insisted on seeing her alone for a few minutes.

When Jessica entered the room and went quickly to his bedside, he was propped up on pillows and looked a great deal better. He took her hands apologetically:

"Forgive me, Jessica—it was only a touch of tiredness, I swear, but I spoiled your plans. You *must* go to Lord Desmond immediately, I insist, and I am sad indeed not to be accompanying you. But do not fear, I am in no danger and I shall join you as soon as I can ... I can hardly wait to see our beloved old house again."

"Papa, I cannot leave you."

"Dearest child, listen to me. Do not think I do not know that the last two years have not been happy for you. Now you have the chance of a splendid husband and a radiant future—I shall be extremely ill through anxiety if you do not go."

All the same, Jessica insisted on seeing the doctor herself when he called that evening, in spite of Constance. He was a kindly man and already had a high regard for Arthur Court's daughter. When she posed her question frankly, he said,

"Most certainly you must go, my dear. You have my word on it that your father is in no danger. Besides, Brighton is but a few hours drive away should you be needed." He rested a hand on her shoulder. "And I will tell you this—if you tarry here on his account your father *will* have a relapse! We have talked much together, and your future happiness is his great concern; so go, Miss Court. Good news from you will be better than any of my physics, I swear."

So, with ill-concealed delight from Constance, Jessica left early on the following morning. Juliet insisted on escorting her to the coach, quite disregarding her mother.

"But Jessica," the girl protested when she picked up the light valise, "you have purchased no fine, new gowns!

Surely you will not go to such a suitor with only the quiet, modest ones you wear here."

Jessica laughed—her first joyous laugh since Papa was taken ill.

"Oh, Juliet, Desmond cares nothing for what I wear. Why, he has seen me clad as a stable lad when he was training for the tournament. And I will tell you a secret— I have a wardrobe filled with gowns such as you have never seen, carefully tended and hanging as I left them at Shayne Park. Lady Shayne has always been my dear friend, and she was so certain that I should return. Besides, I have planned our first meeting most carefully. Desmond first saw me in a simple gown, and I intend to return as I appeared then. If he proposes—and, oh Juliet, I pray that he will—then, that evening, I shall wear the gown that pleased him most of all."

Overawed by her small stepsister's brilliant success, Juliet walked beside her to the coach almost in silence.

Jessica had bid farewell to her father the night before, not wishing to disturb him at such an early hour, and had promised,

"Desmond and I will fetch you as soon as you are recovered, dearest Papa. He knows how much you care for The Old Manor and I am sure he has furnished it as much for your pleasure as mine. Has he not restored all your books?"

They kissed each other tenderly on both cheeks and, when she left the room, her father was smiling.

The stage coach was a little more crowded than when she had returned to London, and Jessica felt a small thrill go through her. Would they be attacked by highwaymen? And would Desmond on Hercules come galloping down on them as before? No, that was too childish. Indeed, she did not wish it so; above all she longed to surprise Desmond, to greet him on her own, for he would have been downcast at receiving no letter, no response to his magnificent gesture in driving to London bearing such a priceless gift.

But, as London was left behind, she grew more and more nervous. Did he *truly* want to marry her? Or was The Old Manor a hint that she should live there—at any rate for some time? Oh, he thought he loved her, yes, but suppose he found her changed and felt embarrassment at her presence when, perhaps, she should have simply written her thanks?

Then, as she stared out of the window, seeing nothing, her lips curved in a little smile. She would know at once. She knew his dear face so well, every expression, every look in his eyes, so to see him was the only way to be sure.

Next, she wondered if she was right to appear after so many months, in simple attire. She had had his praises and the compliments from his eyes only when she was wearing some beautiful ball gown or an afternoon one in the height of fashion.

Gradually her courage returned, allowing her heart to stop its wild beating and return to normal. She turned to more practical things. With a stop at an inn on the way, it would be about four o'clock when she alighted from the coach. She would walk straight across to the stables' entrance to Shayne Park, hiding her light valise in some bushes and, since the afternoon was pleasantly warm for early spring, she would leave her coat and bonnet there, too. She had resumed the hated bonnet in London. Her charming, chic hats would have drawn too much attention on her walks in the park alone.

Since he no longer met Lady Olivia, she prayed that he might have been riding all day and come back at about five o'clock, for Desmond always avoided his mother's callers who frequently came for tea.

The coachman was a little dubious about setting down such a young, pretty lass at a lonely spot, but he succumbed to her brilliant smile.

"La! Pray have no fears for me. My home lies scarce two miles across the fields." Her voice rang with a note of certainty that she was still far from feeling. "Everyone around here knows me and the worst I shall hear is greetings! It is much quicker from this place than if I go right into Shore Vale."

Still reluctant, he handed down her valise with a final: "Well, the Good Lord go with you, and be careful Miss."

"I will," she promised over her shoulder as, valise in hand, she went to the stile.

Her heart was fluttering again as she went into the stables. In spite of her doubts she looked enchanting in a plain, cream faille day dress, her dark curls shining—in fact she might have just come down from the park.

One glance told her that Hercules' stall was empty, the door set wide. Two grooms—one of them Brian—were polishing saddles and bridles, having drawn benches out into the sunlight.

Brian saw her first and stared, as if at a ghost.

"Why, Miss Jessica! Thought you was off in London town." The older man followed his gaze and gaped in astonishment.

Jessica smiled, a finger to her lips. "I have but just returned on the coach. Pray say not a word when Lord Desmond rides in . . . I—I do not wish him to see me immediately."

Brian grinned. "We'll be mum, Miss, never you fear. I swear your coming will cheer his lordship mightily. He has been low of spirits lately, and you could always manage him like no one else."

She had an ear alert for approaching hooves, but there was no sound yet. "Is he quite recovered in health?" she asked a trifle anxiously.

"Oh, aye, 'tis no physical ill that troubles him; 'tis more like some torment of his mind."

Jessica's spirits rose; he *had* been expecting her, or at least a letter. Desmond really had no patience, she thought tenderly.

Then she heard the sound—Hercules galloping home like one possessed, or driven on by one who could scarce wait to be home. With another warning gesture to the two men, she stepped into a patch of deep shadow close to the gates. Here, he would be past her before he looked up.

At sight of him again, her heart swelled with love. Oh, how she had missed him, ached for him; but concern welled up, too, for he looked older, more gaunt and there were fine lines of anxiety on his forehead which had not been there before. He rode straight to Hercules's stall and dismounted, the great stallion sweating from the hard ride back.

"I have ridden him too fast," he swiftly told the attentive grooms. "He will need a more thorough rubdown than usual, and be sure to add plenty of oats for him this evening."

The grooms said, "Aye, my lord," keeping serious faces, although they wanted to grin broadly, knowing of the surprise in store for their master. Tactfully, Brian led Hercules straight into his stall, leaving the stable yard empty.

Desmond hesitated, frowning—he had ridden hell for leather, remembering that the afternoon mail off the London coach would be due before long. But—suppose his hopes were again to be dashed? That the footman who met the coach and collected the mail, again shook his head? He doubted he could bear it.

Slowly, he moved toward the house. Her moment had come, and Jessica stepped silently out into the full sunlight. Very softly she called, "Desmond."

He swung around, unable to believe that the tiny, beloved figure was really there. Surely he was having an hallucination.

Then, with her loveliest smile, her great eyes brimming, Jessica took a few steps toward him, holding out her hands.

"Desmond, I am no dream. I am here indeed."

With a strangled cry, half ecstasy, half groan of longing, he was with her in two strides. Never taking his hungry eyes from her beautiful face, he came to her and, a second later she was close, close in his arms, her head on his breast at last.

Twelve

Half-an-hour later they were in the charming grove, where Desmond had first talked to Jessica and, later, Lord Minden had made his absurd proposal. Now Desmond sat her down, then,

"Now, my darling, I shall give you your due—something that ass, Minden, overlooked." Quickly he dropped on one knee, taking her hands. His face already looked years younger, and his eyes smiled into hers. "There is no homage that will ever do justice to your beauty, Jessica, but humbly dare I crave your hand in marriage? I am not worthy of you, but all my life I swear to cherish and adore you with my whole heart."

There were tears of joy in her eyes as she replied,

"I am honored, my lord. For I declare you will possess my heart forever." And gently she bent forward and kissed him.

He joined her now and for a while they looked into each other's eyes with such radiance that no words were needed. Then Jessica said,

"Now, my beloved, I must explain why my coming was delayed. Your magnificent gifts and your letter had me in such transports that Papa and I planned to catch the very next stage to Brighton—then, that night . . . ." and she told him all that had happened, ending, "I was quite beside myself at the delay, my darling, longing so desperately to hurry to your side. But his attack has passed now."

"And I was on the rack—suffering far more pain than after my wound, for I feared that you had—and rightly so, when I behaved so blindly while you were here—spurned me."

In reply Jessica melted into his arms, and they kissed long and tenderly, knowing that passion must be deferred, for a short time; but all life lay ahead, golden with promise, and each emotion would have its season.

At last Desmond drew her to her feet. "We must go to my mother, now. I swear her anxiety that you might not return has almost matched my own! You are already a daughter to her, Jessica."

"And I can scarce wait to greet her. Oh! I forgot—my valise, coat, and bonnet are still outside the further gate to the stables, I must fetch them."

His grip on her arm tightened. "I refuse to let you out of my sight, even for a few moments. Come, we shall send a servant to collect them."

Lady Shayne was on the terrace, watching for Desmond's return. He had been in such a melancholy state since his return from London. Suddenly she could scarce believe her eyes—coming toward her, arm in arm, their faces shining with happiness, were Desmond and *Jessica*. Her ladyship ran down the steps to meet them, her arms opened wide in welcome.

"Oh, my dear, dear children. I can guess your news and my heart is full!" She embraced them both, tears of thankfulness welling up in her. "How I have prayed for such a moment—and now it is here! But—how did you come, Jessica? I vow I heard no carriage."

"There was none, my dearest lady—I came by the stage, then walked across the fields, planning to surprise Desmond."

"Which she certainly did! For a moment I thought she must be a dream to haunt me."

They all went up into the house, Desmond with an arm around both of them.

Dinner at Shayne Park that night was a joyful celebration. Jessica wore her soft, jade green gown with the shawl Desmond had given her. Bella, overcome with pleasure at her dear young mistress' return, urged her to wear the grandest gown of all.

"See," she said with pride, "I have tended your gowns so carefully, they are all ready to wear. And—and a fresh posy has been placed on your toilette regularly, even in winter. We—we all knew you would come back."

Jessica hugged her in gratitude, reducing Bella to blushes of humility and pleasure.

"I confess, I lost hope on occasion, but it has been my dearest dream through all these weary months. And all my gowns are perfect, Bella, but—for sentimental reasons—I know that it must be the jade one tonight."

When she went downstairs, her beauty quite incandescent with happiness, Desmond was waiting for her in the hall.

"My dearest heart, you have read my thoughts! I see I shall have to guard them more carefully in the future or I shall never be able to surprise you!" he chuckled, taking her hand. "Yet, I think no thoughts of mine will ever be kept from you!"

He led her into the drawing room, ablaze with chandeliers, where a footman, all smiles, stood ready to serve champagne. Lady Shayne was not down yet. When he had pressed a glass into her hand, Desmond nodded dismissal to the footman.

"Now, my beloved, pray do not sneeze from the bubbles just yet! Let us first drink a toast to our love, then I must remove your glass for a moment." Lifting his glass, he said: "To my wonderful future wife."

Jessica, a little shy, for she had scarce dared to imagine the word before, replied, "And I drink to the man of my heart—my future . . . husband."

Having placed their glasses on the mantlepiece, Desmond drew a small, square leather case from his pocket and said,

"Pray close your eyes, Jessica."

Obediently she did so, feeling him lift up her left hand and sensing a smooth circlet gliding over a finger.

"Now you may look," he whispered, a trace of nervousness in his voice. "If you do not care for it it shall be changed tomorrow."

Jessica opened her eyes, then drew in her breath sharply. On her engagement finger he had placed the most magnificent solitary emerald she had ever seen. It glowed pure green fire under the lights, and she could hardly speak. At last she looked up at him.

"Desmond, this must be the most perfect jewel in the world. I do not know how to thank you except to say it shall never leave my hand again!"

"It must, indeed, on our wedding day to make room for that band."

"Then I shall wear it around my neck on a gold chain during the ceremony. Oh, my darling, I know you can perform miracles—like buying this shawl on the very day —but I only came back at five o'clock today!"

Desmond flushed a little. "I must confess, I was so deeply in love with you after you left, that I ordered it to be made many weeks ago, feeling, I think, that the strength of my love must draw you back."

At this point Lady Shayne entered, wearing silver gray chiffon which emphasized her beauty and soft, silver hair.

From then on, through a very special dinner, they fell to discussing wedding plans. Desmond was all fevered impatience.

"Why not next month?" he demanded. "It matters not what gowns she wears, Jessica always looks so beautiful. A trousseau and endless fal-lals cannot be necessary."

Jessica held her peace for fear of seeming forward. She, too, longed for the wedding but she also wanted new gowns to please him. Lady Shayne was firm.

"I know you have both waited a long time, but this will be the most fashionable wedding of the year in Sussex," she declared. "I think all can be prepared by the end of June but not one moment before."

"Mother," Desmond protested, "we only need a simple affair—the village church in Shore Vale, perhaps, and a few close friends here afterward." He turned to Jessica, "Or would that deprive you of your great day, my love?"

Jessica was torn, loving both mother and son. She wholly agreed with Desmond, but she felt that Lady Shayne wished it to be a grand affair for her only son. She remained silent.

Her ladyship smiled. "How tactful you are, my dear. I confess, I can guess your own preference, but I swear every member of the *ton* throughout the county will be agog when your betrothal is announced tomorrow. You have so many friends and well-wishers, you know."

"Indeed, I know, my lady." Jessica laid her hand on her future mother-in-law's. "We shall do whatever pleases you most."

"Besides, I have the Dower House to prepare for myself," Lady Shayne went on. "It is in excellent repair but I have many arrangements to make."

"Oh! Surely, surely you will remain here, my lady? It is your home." Jessica was so sincere it touched the older woman's heart.

"Dearest child, I know you would always welcome me, but 'tis better for you to start freely on your own. Every young couple enjoys privacy. Besides, you will have many people of your own age to entertain—perhaps wish to give balls and masques, too. I dearly long to see young life returning to the park. I have my own friends who prefer quieter pleasures! The Dower House is in the grounds, you know; and I shall always be most ready to give you advice or assistance whenever you ask."

"Always considerate, Mother—", Desmond smiled gratefully, "though I echo Jessica's feelings. You will be our most welcomed visitor at any time."

Jessica now asked the question that had been pushed to the back of her mind in all the excitement: "Pray, when may I see The Old Manor? I declare your generosity is endless! Oh, I was so overcome with gratitude when I learned that you had not only purchased it, but furnished it for me! Would—would it be more correct if I stayed there until the wedding?"

"Gracious, no, Jessica!" exclaimed Lady Shayne. "All your gowns and trousseau will be stitched here, and you and I must discuss furnishings for, I vow, you may change anything you wish."

"There is nothing I would change," Jessica assured her quickly, "except to make sure you will have all your personal, treasured things around you at the Dower House."

"So that's settled," said Desmond, with a touch of relief. "I suggest that we all drive over to The Old Manor in the morning. Mother, you must come too, for you had as much a hand in it as I did."

Jessica slept little that night, for she had no need of sleep. Instead, she lay in a blissful, restful state, the emerald still on her finger. When moonbeams stole through the open curtains (for she refused to have them closed), she held up her hand until the great stone flashed silver green fire. Desmond's ring! Her joy and thankfulness were so great she scarce dared believe it.

In the morning she asked Bella to lay out her smartest day gown—pale turquoise with a close-fitting jacket edged with sable.

"La, all my gowns must be out of date by now," she said, looking at herself in the mirror.

"Don't you go frettin' over that, Miss. You always look lovely, and there'll be your fine trousseau being made by next week! 'Twill be the proudest moment of my life when I help dress you for your wedding."

"No one else shall help me but you, Bella, I promise," laughed Jessica as she adjusted her little hat and took up her gloves.

Desmond was waiting in the hall ready to embrace her since they were alone.

"By my troth, June seems a lifetime away!" he exclaimed. "I scarce dared to wake this morning in case you had vanished!"

"I shall never vanish, Desmond—unless you banish me!"

They were laughing when Lady Shayne came down, and, since Desmond's carriage was waiting, they set off for The Old Manor. As they approached her beloved home, Jessica felt a wave of emotion. If only Mamma were here to share this happy spring and summer, to advise her on the many personal questions that were in her mind, she thought.

"Would you prefer to go in alone at first?" asked Desmond, thoughtful as ever.

"Oh, *no*—you and Lady Shayne will have done everything to make it perfect—please come and share my delight!"

Indeed, The Old Manor was not only perfect but, in her father's library, she turned to Lady Shayne in amazement.

"My lady—how did you guess? I declare, it is the self-same room where Papa taught me to read, and he and Mamma and I shared so many happy evenings!"

Lady Shayne smiled. "I did not have to guess, my dear—on my rare visits, your mother usually received me here plus I have a good memory."

After touring the whole house they were in the hall, Jessica speechless in her gratitude so that all she could do was to embrace them both warmly. At last she said:

"It nearly breaks my heart to think that no one will live here after all!"

"I wondered," said her ladyship tentatively, "whether perhaps your father might treat it as a refuge from London now and then? He will have you and his sister close by, so that if he should feel sick, help will always be at hand."

Jessica clasped her hands. "Oh, but that is a splendid idea! I swear he hates London as much as I, and—and he and my stepmother have never been really close." She made a small grimace. "In fact since her elder daughter has failed to marry so far, and Papa can no longer be quite so generous, I fancy she would welcome the idea as much as he will. I shall write to him at once."

Time sped by. Jessica and Desmond became society's darlings once the betrothal was announced, which was gratifying but not exactly pleasing to them as, if they ac-

cepted all the pressing invitations, they should have scarce
any time alone or for their shared passion for riding.

"I have quite decided that I shall bear you off for a
long, peaceful honeymoon in France, my darling," Des
mond announced when a footman brought the silver salve
almost overflowing with requests for their company. "We
shall stay away until the season is over."

"Desmond! I declare I have never travelled, yet I have
longed to do so! And, with you as a guide, France sound
like a paradise!"

But first there was to be a grand betrothal party and
then the five hundred wedding invitations to be sent out
Between these and endless fittings for her trousseau, Jes
sica was forced to tell Desmond that he must ride out more
and more by himself.

"It is only six weeks, now," she cried, holding him
close. "Believe me, I deplore every moment not spent with
you—but soon, so soon we shall be free of it all and on
our way to France."

"If only Mother had agreed to a quiet wedding," he
said testily. It had never occurred to him that he could be
lonely when riding Hercules over the countryside, but Jes
sica was such a perfect companion, responding to every
mood, to each beautiful view that came in sight, he missed
her sorely.

On one of these solitary rides he saw an all too familiar rider waiting for him in a quiet spot, her habit as
impeccable as ever, her fair hair coiled close in a net beneath her silk hat.

Olivia!

He had not seen her since the tournament; now she
trotted toward him with her beguiling smile, her manner
as charming, if a little harder than a year ago.

"Desmond! This is a delightful surprise, I declare."
She rested a hand on his as they drew level, and she pouted
a little. "You did not come to my wedding."

Desmond looked at her coldly, seeing clearly at last
how easily she had entrapped him in the past.

"Surely you did not expect me to, Olivia? Did you
not hear that I was extremely ill after the treachery
planned between you and Sir Walter worked so well?"

Her blue eyes widened in reproach.

"Desmond! You cannot think that *I* intended you harm?"

His eyes turned to chill steel and he made no reply apart from raising a cynical eyebrow. This unnerved Olivia as he had never seen her before.

"I—I soon discovered that I had made a sad mistake! Walter is a brute—a beast. I swear he does not understand the word 'love' at all." Her mouth trembled.

"And do you?" asked Desmond quietly. "I think not, Olivia."

Wheeling Hercules around he cantered back toward Shayne Park. Olivia watched him go, her face now a mask of fury—so confident had she been that she could win him back if she just lifted her little finger. The knowledge that he was going to marry the whey-faced child, Jessica Court, incensed her. How could he when he loved her, Olivia, so deeply? The imperious beauty still wanted all the adoration and power she had enjoyed before marriage—and Walter, too, of course, for some of his brutish ways, excited her deeply.

As Desmond rode into the stables, he was laughing, and, when he found Jessica in the morning room addressing invitations, his face was still amused.

"Oh, my darling. How are the mighty fallen!" he cried, swinging her around in his arms.

"Desmond—what has happened to put you in this mood?"

"Olivia," he chuckled. "The grand Lady Olivia was waiting to waylay me! What a treacherous, shallow fool she is! I truly believe she thought to win me back to her side as an obedient slave. Dearest heart, how can I have been so bamboozled—so blind—for so long?" He suddenly looked down at her anxiously. "Do you not despise me for such stupidity?"

"No, my darling. I have never seen such a beautiful woman but, but I am *glad* you have seen her again."

He stared down at her in astonishment. "You never dreamed that Olivia could come between us, surely? That *I* should be such a fool?"

Jessica slowly shook her head and gave him a tender,

impish smile. "I only know that if I ever lost you, I would stop at nothing to try and win you back."

At last it was June and the wedding scarce ten days away. Jessica thought she had never been so happy in her life. Juliet and her husband, Charles Chater, had driven Papa down to The Old Manor where, it seemed, his last traces of ill-health disappeared in his pleasure at being home again. Grace Ashby and her very new husband, Robert, were to reach Brighton from Scotland in three days time, and Grace had promised to act as the second maid of honor to her friend.

The trousseau was almost complete, and only the diaphanous wedding gown required a few, final touches. It was designed and made by the finest dress designer in Brighton of yards and yards of sheer white chiffon embroidered with tiny jewels. The bodice was simply cut to emphasize the bride's small waist, the low, square-cut neckline edged with pearls and diamonds. From there the skirt swirled out gently as she moved. Jessica was speechless when she saw her reflection, rewarding the designer with her heightened color, most brilliant smile and the fervent clasp of her small hands. The veil would set a new fashion, coming scarce to her shoulders and held in place by the famous Shayne coronet of finest diamonds, set high on her dark hair. Juliet and Grace were to wear gowns of deep blue silk with garlands of fresh flowers in their hair. Both were delighted for the color emphasized their fair hair and blue eyes.

On the morning of the wedding day Lady Shayne was shocked when Jessica and Desmond went out riding.

"It simply is not done, my dear," she protested. "On this, the most important day of her life, a bride should lie late in bed then partake of a light breakfast and give herself to the ministrations of her maid. To go out riding with the bridegroom is unheard of, I swear."

Desmond entered in time to hear the last few sentences.

"Dearest Mother," he teased her, smiling, "you cannot deny us the only peaceful time that Jessica and I will have together on this day? A girl of her spirit could never lie languishing in bed! No, she shall be delivered to your care by eleven o'clock, which will give you and her attendants at least three hours to make her thoroughly nervous!" And, stretching out his hand, he led his radiant bride to the stables.

The grooms, not to be outdone, each wore a flower in his cap and had decked both Flame and Hercules with garlands. They would all be in the church, of course, but there would be no further chance to pay tribute to their new countess.

Desmond shook every hand, and Jessica, thanking the men for their kindness, said,

"Within six weeks, Lord Desmond and I will have returned from France and resume our riding. Meantime, the horses could not have better guardians."

For half-an-hour they rode side by side, feeling no need of words. Then, as if by mutual consent, they reined in in a charming dell they had often visited before. There, Desmond lifted Jessica to the ground, and they stood, his arms encircling her waist.

"My most beloved, it is here, in this quiet place that I would pledge you my vows. The formal ceremony, watched by so many eyes, will give a blessing on our union, but the words are too few and oft-used to convey my dedication. Here, I offer you my heart and soul, swearing to hold you in love and protection all the days of our lives."

She lifted her face to his, her lovely eyes clear and shining in the early sunlight.

"And I, Desmond, vow to cherish you as my beloved husband as long as I shall live. I—I pray that God will grant us children and that I may bring you joy and also support in the difficult times that must come to all people."

Solemnly they kissed—a reverential kiss to seal their bond. Then laughing happily, their private ceremony over, Desmond lifted her to her saddle and, hand in hand they cantered back.

"Now," he said triumphantly, "let the women do their worst to make you nervous, my love! In our own hearts we are joined already. A trembling bride is considered *comme il faut,* remember, and I shall know that inwardly you have no tremors at all!"

Indeed, the rest of the morning proved a sore trial on her nerves. Had Jessica not held the glorious moment in the dell closely in her mind she might have come near swooning with the fussing and warnings offered to her by such loving hands.

Lady Shayne proved to be the worst.

"Dear child—you have no mother and I should have given you wise advice about what will be expected of you!"

"Do not be anxious I pray, my lady—with Desmond at my side, I shall have no qualms, I swear."

Then came Juliet and Grace, filled with new knowledge of the married state.

"I fear the first night of a honeymoon can be a mite bewildering, but if you love your husband, 'twill all come right," offered Juliet.

Grace, however, was aglow and, with her Scots honesty, she added, "Marriage is ten times more wonderful than I ever dreamed." She blushed a little. "And Robert and I are doubly blessed now. I expect our first child at Christmas!"

Jessica embraced her warmly. "Grace, I declare you are like a breath of cool, sweet air from your Scottish mountains."

And Grace replied, "Remember, now—you and Desmond must visit us directly after your honeymoon. You can ride to your heart's content for Robert keeps a fine stable."

At last Lady Shayne shooed them both out as she and Bella set about dressing the bride. Not until Lady Shayne had personally placed the famous Shayne coronet on her head did Jessica dare to look at the final effect.

Bella was weeping sentimental tears of admiration by then, and Lady Shayne herself was misty eyed.

"You will prove the most exquisite Shayne bride in the family portrait gallery—for you must be painted just like that on your return. Oh, I am so proud and thankful to welcome you as my daughter!"

Then her ladyship went to don her hat and Bella

brought in the finishing touch, the wedding bouquet sent by Desmond.

"Oh," murmured Jessica softly, for it was not the flamboyant sheaf carried by most brides, but a delicate posy of gardenias and rosebuds with charming streamers of single blooms threaded on silver ribbon that fell to her feet.

The butler himself knocked on the door to inform her,

"Mr. Arthur Court is waiting below, Miss Jessica, and your carriage will leave for the church in ten minutes."

Jessica sped downstairs, glad—much as she loved them all—to be free from feminine emotion for these last few minutes.

Her father watched her come, his own heart too full for words. He held himself erect, an elegant figure in dark blue velvet with a silver-topped ebony cane in his right hand.

"My very dear child, what a proud day this is," he said steadily. "You must not be nervous for, I swear, had I travelled the world I could have found no worthier husband for you than Lord Desmond. You will be the happiest of couples, I know."

"I know it, too, Papa," she replied. "Only it is alarming to have to walk up the aisle between so many people! Oh, I know they are all friends and well-wishers, but members of the *ton* do stare so!"

He laughed and drawing her hand through his arm he patted it soothingly. "You must forgive them on this occasion, for they will never have seen a bride as beautiful as you!" He bent and kissed her forehead.

It was but a short drive to the church, where Grace and Juliet were waiting for her in the porch. As Jessica alighted, they arranged her skirt carefully, then the organ began the Voluntary, stilling the hundreds of whispering voices.

Proudly, on her father's arm, Jessica copied his measured steps, her small head held high in spite of her inner tremors. Desmond and his Best Man seemed a mile away, waiting at the altar. Then Desmond turned to welcome her, his loving smile filled with admiration and assurance.

After that all the people in the church faded away as Jessica moved smiling toward him, her nerves quite forgotten. She was scarce aware when Papa moved aside, leaving her to kneel by her bridegroom.

They took ship from Folkestone for France, the boat setting sail at midnight. Until it was under weigh, they stood alone in the prow, his arm around her waist as they watched the moon rise higher, spreading a silver path across the calm, dark sea.

At last Desmond turned her toward him.

"My darling, I can wait no longer to possess you," and his mouth met hers with all the passion he had suppressed for so long. Gladly she responded with all her being then, hand in hand, he led her to their state room . . . .